Tossing his pen aside, the senator got to his feet and stretched to his full height— all long legs and broad shoulders and sexier than the star point guard in a NBA locker room

Liza's heart screeched to a halt and her mouth went dry with unadulterated lust.

He moved closer, his ruthless gaze skimming her from top to bottom as he approached, pausing as he made his way down her hips and legs, missing nothing and savoring everything.

He wasn't the presidential candidate. Not now.

This was a man who desperately wanted her and wasn't afraid to show it. A man who would, with very little provocation, slide his hands up her bare thighs and under her skirt, slip her panties down and lift her so that she could wrap her legs tight around his waist.

And she, with very little provocation, would welcome him.

Books by Ann Christopher

Kimani Romance

Just About Sex
Sweeter Than Revenge
Tender Secrets
Road to Seduction
Campaign for Seduction

ANN CHRISTOPHER

is a full-time chauffeur for her two overscheduled children. She is also a wife, former lawyer, and decent cook. In between trips to various sporting practices and games, Target and the grocery store, she likes to write the occasional romance novel featuring a devastatingly handsome alpha male. She lives in Cincinnati and spends her time with her family, which includes two spoiled rescue cats, Sadie and Savannah.

If you'd like to recommend a great book, share a recipe for homemade cake of any kind, or have a tip for getting your children to do what you say the *first* time you say it, Ann would love to hear from you through her Web site, www.annchristopher.com.

CAMPAIGN
FOR
SEDUCTION

ANN CHRISTOPHER

KIMANI™
ROMANCE

To Richard

KIMANI PRESS™

Recycling programs for this product may not exist in your area.

ISBN-13: 978-0-373-86130-9

CAMPAIGN FOR SEDUCTION

www.kimanipress.com

Printed in U.S.A.

Dear Reader,

Senator Jonathan Warner (cousin of Andrew and Eric) is an extremely busy and ambitious man. The gentleman from Ohio is running for president and his campaign is on the ropes—circling the drain, really—but he's determined not to go down in flames. The last thing he needs at this crucial juncture of his life is the distraction of falling in lust with a journalist in his press corps.

Senior Washington correspondent Liza Wilson has her eyes on a big prize: the anchor chair for the evening news. A scandal is out of the question. So is a love affair, a dalliance or anything else that might jeopardize her chances of grabbing the brass ring.

These two people, in short, are *not* supposed to fall in love.

Unfortunately, a late-night interlude alone in the senator's private cabin on his campaign jet will change everything for both of them....

I hope you enjoy their story!

Happy reading,

Ann

ACKNOWLEDGMENTS

Special thanks to Jonathan Freed, Sheila Gray and Rob Williams for sharing their journalistic expertise and answering my endless questions. Any mistakes are my own.

Hugs and gratitude to Lori Devoti and Caroline Linden for brainstorming help. Caroline, this is two in a row. Next time, can you just do the whole book for me…?

A special thank-you to my editor, Kelli Martin, who has a knack for getting me to write a better book.

Chapter 1

"Senator! Can I ask a follow-up?"

"What about tomorrow's speech, Senator?"

"Senator, will you be commenting on any personal romantic relationship developing between you and Francesca Waverly? One of the tabloids has allegedly received some pictures—"

As usual, the barrage of shouted questions followed Senator Jonathan Warner up the aisle toward the restricted section of his Boeing 757. He calculated the number of steps between him and a chance to relax—less than ten, he thought—and wondered how soon he could get to the other side of that precious divide.

A smarter man would've kept his butt up there in the front of the plane, where it was safe, rather than come back here and spend a few minutes with the press corps, but he'd been riding the high after the campaign rally in Detroit and wanted to see what kind of feedback he'd get from the press.

But then one answered question had turned to five, and now it was after midnight and he hadn't begun to prepare for tomorrow's events, much less sleep. Sleep. *Ha.* He remembered it well. Something about getting in a bed, putting your head down on a pillow and closing your eyes.

Unfortunately, he'd given up the idea of sleep for the duration, and so had his cohorts here. Everyone on the jet was bleary-eyed and exhausted, and since the primary season was just getting under way, the widespread sleep deprivation would get a whole lot worse before it got better.

Pausing, he glanced back over his shoulder into the bright lights of various camcorders, pushed his rolled shirtsleeve past his watch to check the time—12:39 a.m. now, *wonderful*—and considered which, if any, of the additional questions he should answer.

The pause, naturally, gave the reporters the chance to shout more questions in a never-ending cycle. If he stood right here and had the pilot circle Detroit until they ran out of fuel, the reporters would still be shouting questions at him as long as the coffee ran hot and strong.

The life of a presidential candidate. Nothing but glamour.

She hadn't asked him a question.

Darn woman.

The object of his unwilling and unrelenting fascination was Liza Wilson, the newest addition to his traveling family of fun, who sat in the back and attracted his attention the way a mirrored ball attracts disco fans. Thirty-seven and divorced, she was the popular senior Washington correspondent for one of the big three networks.

As if that didn't keep her busy enough, she also worked on that network's cable news affiliate as an analyst and was reputedly in negotiations for the evening news anchor position. If she got the job—and she had the chops for it, no question, having covered both political and military wars—she'd be both the youngest and the first African American anchor, ever.

She had a reputation for brashness, and the word was that her executive producers had their hands full managing her. He could believe it. A Chicagoan born and bred, she'd graduated from Northwestern and had a Georgetown MBA in journalism. Brilliant, ambitious and hardworking, tough but fair in her coverage, which was always scrupulously ethical, she'd won a handful of

Emmy Awards and a Peabody or two, and he supposed she ~~~~~~~~~
to win another handful of awards for primary coverage now that
she was embedded with him.

Embedded. In bed with.

Something deep in his gut awakened and sizzled with awareness. That thing, whatever it was, fixated on Liza Wilson with unnerving focus even though he had zero time, opportunity or desire
for romance here in the fishbowl. If he did have time, though, she
would be the first and only name on his list of potential lovers.

Unfortunately, it was a moot point.

His life was about one thing only: winning the nomination and
then the presidency.

Period. End of story.

So, look away from the pretty woman, Warner.

Yeeeeeaaaaah… No.

Point-three seconds was all he could manage before his gaze was
drawn right back to where she sat in her remote corner of the plane.

What was it about that woman? Why couldn't he ever
remember that she irritated him like a pebble in his shoe or an un-
scratchable itch between his shoulder blades? Why weren't his
overactive hormones getting the message?

Liza Wilson.

Liiiiiiza Wilson.

Yeah, he didn't like her. It was the arrogant tilt of her chin that
did it, her thin veil of contempt, the way she gave the clear impression that she was deigning to acknowledge his bothersome
presence whenever she asked a question in that husky-sexy voice.
As if his existence was an annoyance to her even though she
made her livelihood off him and his activities.

But…she was, as the Commodores would say, a brick house.

He'd noticed over the years, sure. The problem was, seeing her
on TV and seeing her in person were two very different things.

Seeing her on TV was pleasant. Seeing her in person was…
startling.

If he could've put together a Perfect Body Wish List—breasts,
butt, legs, hips, in that order—Liza Wilson would have been the
spectacular result. And yet that didn't fully account for her
appeal; last week, during one of his fundraising stops in L.A.,

...been propositioned by three—no, four—mouth-watering starlets, but starlets didn't interest him. Liza Wilson did, for elusive, intangible reasons that seemed to have nothing to do with her body.

Partially because of her wide brown eyes, which were tilted at the edges like a cat's and mocked him every time she spoke to him. Partially because of the velvety warmth of her brown skin as it disappeared beneath the neckline of whatever she was wearing on any given day, revealing a hint—always just a *hint*—of breasts that would overflow his hands. Partially because of the way her tender lips curved and her sleek black hair, which was short and angled on one side, always slipped over the corner of one eye like she was giving him a come-hither look—*yeah, right, Warner, you wish*—or had a delicious secret to tell.

His gut tightened with unrequited lust.

As a candidate who had the misfortune of being both widowed for the last ten years and the focal point of enough media and print reporters to fill a football stadium, he was doomed to celibacy until at least the first Wednesday in November, if then, unless he was prepared to jeopardize the campaign by turning it into a tabloid circus focused on his private life, which he wasn't.

Votes were too hard to come by without risking them for something as ultimately meaningless as sex. Why take the chance? It wasn't like he was in the market for a wife.

Attractive women everywhere, therefore, were an annoyance to him, and this one was no different. There was, in other words, nothing special about Liza Wilson.

So...if he didn't like her and wasn't going to seduce her, why couldn't he just ignore her? Why did he always feel this gnawing compulsion to engage her?

The reporters had quieted down a little, and he spoke into the dull roar.

"What was that, Liza?" he asked on impulse. "I didn't hear you."

Five rows back, Liza started with surprise and looked up from her notes.

Even though John knew damn well she'd been the only journalist on the plane who hadn't asked him a question, he cupped a hand to his ear, cocked his head and waited for her reaction. No journalist worth her salt would pass up the chance to ask the candidate a question, Liza least of all.

All the other reporters shut up and looked back over their seats at Liza, craning their necks to keep her in sight. John felt a moment's guilty pleasure at catching her unawares and forcing her to acknowledge his existence in one fell swoop.

Guilty pleasure and the slow burn of excitement. Mostly the latter.

But then she gave him a shrewd smile, studied him with those cool, disdainful eyes and asked a question on the one lousy topic that had been simmering along without erupting into the full rolling boil he'd hoped to avoid.

"I was just asking—" she lied smoothly in that smoky voice that was like the stroke of her fingers low across his belly "—whether your spending time here with us at the back of the plane is part of a new policy for you?"

John schooled his features, refusing to wince.

"A new policy?" he echoed, stalling for time.

"A new policy of greater press access." Those arched eyebrows inched higher, making her look wide-eyed and earnest and not at all like the circling shark that she was. "Because it's been three days since you answered any questions at length, and when you do talk to us here on the plane, you almost always insist on things being off the record. Meanwhile, Senator Fitzgerald gives her press corps twenty minutes every day…."

Liza let the delicate innuendo hang. *Senator Warner hides from the press while his opponent, Senator Fitzgerald, gives her correspondents free access.*

The moment stretched, but John refused to squirm even though he saw a clear *gotcha* in Liza's bright eyes. Even if no one else could see it, he could. As he scrambled to frame an answer that wouldn't land his butt in the frying pan with the heat on high, only one thing was on his mind, and it wasn't the press and its level of access to him, free or otherwise, and it wasn't his opponent or the primary season.

Shit.

Why didn't he know by now not to mess with Liza Wilson?

*** *

Don't blink, Liza. Don't. Blink.

She met Senator Warner's irritated gaze and kept her chin up, acutely aware of her skittering nerves, the rolling cameras and the digital voice recorders picking up every inflection of both her voice and his.

This was the ultra-civil Gentleman from Ohio? Ha. A primitive light shone pretty bright in his eyes right now, and he'd probably be happier to share his plane with his opponent—or even several thousand poisonous snakes—than Liza. The brilliant senator from Cleveland, he of the reputation for honesty and fair dealing, wanted her out and would no doubt be thrilled to personally do the ejecting. If they happened to be at thirty thousand feet at the time, so much the better.

It was amazing the way his blazing dislike for her radiated out from his piercing dark gaze, bypassed all the other journalists, traveled back to her row and tightened around her throat like flexing fingers. That animosity followed her to rallies and campaign stops, trailed her when they were all on the campaign bus and pretty much enveloped her whenever they occupied the same zip code.

Lucky her.

What the heck had she ever done to him? She searched her memory banks for the billionth time and came up blank. Again.

She hadn't spent fifteen years as a journalist and gotten to her position—senior Washington correspondent at a major network, thank you very much—without stepping on a few toes and making a few enemies. Fine. No problem. Sometimes people were wounded or irritated by her coverage. Again—no problem.

But what was up with Warner? Why did his hostility feel so intense and personal even though they'd never exchanged more than a few public words? Her reportage of him had been no worse than her colleagues', so what was the deal?

Oh, and add one more item to the list of things she didn't understand: her powerful reaction to him.

Well…yeah, she did understand it. It was just that she didn't like it.

To her everlasting dismay, she reacted to him the same way

women all across the globe reacted, which was pretty much an *Oh, my God.*

Forget attractive. Forget handsome. He was way past all that. The senator was, in fact, breathtaking. At forty-four, he had severe dark looks, intense eyes, heavy brows, a long straight nose and granite-sharp cheekbones.

A few lines at the corners of his eyes and bracketing his mouth made him all the more intriguing. Ruthlessly athletic, he played soccer and had the kind of muscular, broad-shouldered body that practically made a woman come just by looking at him.

More than that, he was tall, imposing, fierce and presidential. Other than an early loss when he ran for the House of Representatives, he'd been a power broker all his adult life, a winner. He walked in the room and brought an aura of prestige, brilliance and sophistication with him. People instinctively knew that if the North Koreans launched a missile at some unsuspecting target, Senator Warner was the man they'd want in charge.

And God help them all whenever he switched gears and made a joke or teased a reporter. Suddenly those harsh cheeks turned dimpled and boyish, and his flashing white smile reduced all nearby women—Liza included—to quivering masses of hormones laced with desire wrapped in want.

He was that political rarity, a man who was charming and natural rather than charming and smarmy, and it drove Liza crazy because she couldn't write him off as another soulless politician.

Charisma was one thing, but they weren't dealing with charisma here.

What Senator Warner had was charisma to the millionth power. A pheromone that got women hot, bothered and squirmy with no conscious effort on his part. A lethal weapon that would lay waste to mountains and dry up rivers if he ever fully unleashed it.

And Liza was supposed to ignore all that.

As a TV news correspondent, it was her job to ask the tough questions and hold the man's feet to the fire. No one had ever said it would be easy to overlook his sexual appeal, and it wasn't. Still, Liza tried. Every single day she did her best to ignore her thrumming pulse, fluttering belly and hot, thick blood. She worked hard to focus on her questions and listen to his answers without wondering how his mouth tasted.

Like right now.

"Did you hear me this time, Senator?" Liza kept her shoulders squared and her voice cool.

Senator Warner's eyes glinted with just a hint of the anger she knew he was trying to control. "I'll have to see what I can do about giving the press more access, Liza." That famous grin started at one corner of his mouth and his dimples deepened. "Maybe I can work out a deal with you folks—I'll give you more time, and you can give me better coverage. How'd that be?"

This little joke, naturally, broke everyone up. If there was a single person in the cabin, from the most battle-scarred war correspondent to the greenest intern, who didn't laugh, Liza couldn't see who it was. She glanced around, disgusted, because they were all giggling like a bunch of teenage girls. Again.

Why didn't they all just start wearing I Heart Senator Warner buttons along with their press badges and be done with it? Even the groupies for the Rolling Stones were more dignified than *this*.

"Your coverage has been pretty good, Senator," someone called.

Warner shook his head, looking wry. "That's a matter of perspective." He flashed the whole smile this time as he edged toward the front of the plane. With a wave, he turned to slip through the doorway to the private area. "Y'all get some sleep now."

Liza's irritation grew. He was so shrewd that she just couldn't win a point with him; he played the press like B. B. King played Lucille. There he went again with the winning folksy charm, the magical stuff that made people forget that: a) he was a Yale-educated lawyer from a wealthy family who'd been born with a platinum spoon in his mouth; and b) he hadn't answered her question.

Really, he should bottle it and make more millions.

Pursing her lips, she seethed and watched him go, but then something strange happened.

He glanced over his shoulder at her, and their gazes locked for one beat…two beats…three…and a charge went through Liza the same as if she'd reached out and grabbed a lightning bolt. In his unreadable expression she saw hints of many unwelcome emotions. Whatever he felt when he looked at her so intently was dark, turbulent and primitive, and he clearly didn't like it—or her—at all.

Brilliant, Liza.

She'd just set the world speed record for pissing him off. Though she'd only been doing her job, she almost wanted to kick her own butt for blowing this journalistic opportunity, as she surely had.

Judging from that sharp-dagger glare he had just given her, he was planning to boot her off his plane at the next stop.

Chapter 2

John wrenched his gaze away from Liza, walked into the campaign staffers' cabin and worked on getting his heart rate back to normal. No dice. There was something about that one annoying woman that vacuumed out his brain, got rid of all his concerns about the campaign and his policies and left only *her*.

Her looks and what they meant, *her* smiles, *her* voice. And, worst of all, his desire for her, which grew by the day. Damn woman, taking his mind off his campaign. What the devil was wrong with him? He never lost focus.

"You've got a serious problem here, John," said a voice.

John, who'd been yanking at his tie, which now felt like a noose, glanced around and experienced a moment's surprise to see Adena Brown, his senior adviser, talking to him. The engineer of all his political success since he first ran for the Senate years ago and an attractive woman even though she'd never tied his guts in knots like Liza did, Adena watched him expectantly. So did several other members of his staff, all of whom hunched over their various computers and looked as bleary as he felt, their cups of coffee clutched tight in their hands.

They really should buy stock in Starbucks. It fueled his campaign.

Coffee aside, he tried not to look guilty or conspicuous. Was he that obvious? Had all the major networks just taped him making eyes at Liza Wilson? Good thought. He could see the caption already, along with the video over at the YouTube website: Senator Warner Sniffs After Liza Wilson. He could also see the headlines in the major papers the next day: Senator Warner Thinks with His Private Parts, Poll Numbers Plunge. Wouldn't that be great going into Super Tuesday?

Keeping his expression bland, he decided to play dumb. "What problem?"

Adena, who was sunk deep into her seat with an elbow propped on the armrest, ran a hand through her long black hair. "I'm talking about press access—"

Whew.

"—and this perception that you're hiding while Senator Fitzgerald answers questions any old time. We need to get out in front of that issue."

"Why?"

John couldn't keep the bark out of his voice, namely because his traveling press corps was a major pain in his ass that he tolerated because he had to. No one who was serious about public office could do otherwise, and he'd made his peace with that reality long ago.

But that didn't mean he enjoyed dealing with journalists and his staff's relentless focus on winning every news cycle. It felt like the press covered every waking moment of his life and probably knew what brand of toilet paper he used. What could he do about it? A big fat nothing. Privacy was, unfortunately, a thing of his distant past.

Cry me a river, Warner.

True, the press gave him good coverage more often than not, and for that he was profoundly grateful. But he already gave several, if not dozens, of interviews to the local press at all his campaign stops every day, not to mention his biweekly chats with the anchors on the network morning shows and whatever other interviews were needed as a result of breaking events.

Now he was supposed to hold the hands of his whining traveling press corps? How many hours was he supposed to squeeze out of his overscheduled day? When was he supposed to focus on shaping policy? Did anyone care about that?

"Just because one reporter wants more access?" John continued, leaning against the nearest seat as he stared down at Adena. "I've already given—"

"It's not just one reporter," Adena said darkly, and the heads of Jay Hunter, the campaign's communications director, and Linda Canning, the press secretary, nodded their somber agreement. "A couple of the blogs picked up this access thing today, and if we don't do something the networks will start a drumbeat about it. We don't want that to become an issue going into Nevada and South Carolina."

John cursed and checked his watch, irritated by the flare of this new fire to put out, as if he didn't have enough fires already. 12:45 a.m. now. The night was ticking away and he had briefs to read and a major policy speech about health care to edit. Anything more than an hour or two of sleep seemed to be off the table, and that woman was partially to blame.

Thank you, Liza Wilson.

Thinking hard, adrenalin pumping, he ran through his options. He was, luckily, a stellar problem solver, which was one of the reasons he'd be a good commander in chief. With any luck he could put this issue to bed—again with the bed references, Warner; you really need to knock it off—and move on to the next crisis du jour.

What was the best choice here?

Well, he could ignore the press access issue. Bad idea. Things like this never went away by themselves. They were much more likely to fester and grow. On the other hand, he could deny it. Another bad idea. All the pundits over at, say, the MSNBC news channel and even the faux-news anchors at the Comedy Central channel would trot out statistics on how often both he and Senator Fitzgerald spoke to the press, and he'd look like either a liar or an idiot because he knew good and well that his opponent granted her corps more time.

Or…a new idea flickered, faded and then flickered again, brighter this time.

What if…what if he granted one media outlet "exclusive access" to the inner workings of the campaign for a while? It'd been done before, of course; President Clinton had had that whole *War Room* documentary back in 1993. John could do it, too: let a correspondent and cameraperson into his situation room— "Sitchroo," as they affectionately referred to it here—and let them film some of the meetings where the decisions were made.

That could work, couldn't it? They could do it for, say, a month or so, and then they'd go back to the status quo. By then, hopefully, the allegations that he avoided the press would have passed, the media would be onto some other hot topic and he'd come up smelling like a rose.

The more he thought about the idea, the more he liked it.

All the actual strategic decisions concerning his campaign would still be made behind closed doors, of course. John was no dummy, and he wasn't about to give away the battle plan to his opponent, who was already running him ragged and forcing him to earn every single vote. Only a fool would reveal the true inner workings of a campaign on national TV *before* the election.

But…he could grant enough additional access to make it look good.

"Here's what we'll do," he told Adena. "We're going to let one media outlet behind the scenes for, say, a month or so. Grant them access to Sitchroo. That should stop the wagons from circling for a while."

Adena narrowed her eyes. "I don't know about that. Could be much more trouble than it's worth." She paused. "On the other hand, voters are dying for more information about you. You'd have to be personally available, though. People don't want to see a lot of nonsense about your chief of staff deciding who to hire and fire."

John hadn't thought about that, but he supposed it was true. "Fine."

"Who do we want for the job?" Adena asked.

"Liza Wilson."

The name was up and out of John's mouth before he could think twice about it, and once it was said, he didn't want to take it back. Nor did he want to think about why he'd chosen Liza or, come to think of it, whether he'd dreamt up the idea as a way to get to know Liza better. All he knew was that he liked the plan—liked it a lot, actually—and wanted to go through with it.

Adena, however, looked horrified. Her cheeks flooded with color, leaving pink behind and heading for purple. Scooting to her feet, she glanced around at their avid audience, all of whom were watching the conversation with wide eyes, took John by the arm and steered him into the next cabin, which was a small conference room with a couple of tables.

Behind closed doors now, Adena let him have it. It was amazing the way this one tiny woman could resemble a snarling wolverine when she wanted to.

"What the hell are you doing?"

John settled one hip against the edge of a table and felt his hackles rise. He was way too tired for this, and Adena's questions always cut too close to the bone because she knew him so well.

"I'm addressing the issue you raised. The press wants more access. I'm giving them more access. What's the problem?"

"Liza Wilson's the problem. She won her last Emmy slicing Senator Gregory to shreds, in case you've forgotten."

"Senator Gregory had a serious drug habit." John kept his voice low and calm. "He had a good slicing coming."

Adena rolled her eyes, the picture of outraged reproach. "Let's not play games here, John. It's just you and me. And I've seen the way you look at her. I've been around the block long enough to know when a man's thinking with his southern hemisphere."

This was hardly a surprise. Adena's sharp gaze didn't miss much, and, bulldog that she was, she hadn't gotten to be the top campaign strategist in the country by being blind or having poor instincts. John was lucky to have her on his team, and he knew it.

On the other hand, he was a grown man and, the last time he checked, it was his campaign. If he couldn't control his interest in this one woman, he'd make a pretty sorry president, and he had no intentions of being a sorry president.

Still, he didn't want to alienate Adena unless he had to. They'd been a winning professional combination for too many years to rock the boat now, and he knew that cinching the nomination without her on the team would be a Herculean task.

"I've got it under control, and there's nothing to worry about anyway," John said. "Thanks for your concern."

Adena didn't look remotely convinced. If anything, the worried grooves running across her forehead deepened. "I've got three words for you, John—Helen of Troy."

John choked back a snort of laughter even though the image of Liza as a woman whose beauty could drive sensible men insane with lust and spark a war didn't seem that far-fetched at the moment.

A lot was at stake here, and John was excruciatingly aware of that fact every moment of every day. He was behind in the polls and, by many accounts, a snowball had a better chance spending the summer in hell than he did winning the nomination.

Getting involved with a journalist covering his campaign fell firmly into the stupid category; he knew that. The tabloid and mainstream presses would both have a field day, and his credibility as a serious candidate would be forever ruined. He'd never been stupid and didn't plan to start now. Even though lust for Liza was, admittedly, scrambling his circuits.

Luckily, he was all about focus and had no intentions of getting involved with Liza, no matter how tempting the idea might seem. Maybe spending time with the woman who slid under his skin so easily wasn't the brightest idea he'd ever had, but neither would it ruin his campaign. He wouldn't let it.

"Like I said," he told Adena. *"I've got it under control."*

"John, she's brash and hardheaded. There's no controlling her. She's going to be a constant thorn in our sides, and meanwhile her viewership will go up because the public loves her. She'll be getting ratings for making us look bad."

Straightening, John patted Adena on the back to soften his words. "When it's your name on the side of the plane, you can make the decisions—"

Adena glowered.

"—but until then, I want you to call Liza's executive producers and get this thing arranged."

Grumbling, Adena turned toward the staffer's cabin. John let her get almost through the doorway before he lost the silent battle he'd been waging with himself.

He wanted to see Liza again tonight. He shouldn't want to, but he did.

Anyway—what could it hurt? It was already late and he was only going to get a little sleep anyway. He might as well get a little less. And his nagging curiosity about Liza wouldn't let him go unless he did something to satisfy it.

Satisfaction. What a lovely—and ultimately hopeless—idea.

Since sexual gratification was thin on the ground these days, he may as well indulge in a little intellectual stimulation. He wanted to have sex with Liza but, failing that, he could spend a few minutes finding out more about her. He'd take his pitiful pleasure wherever he could find it and, more than likely, within thirty seconds she'd irritate him enough to destroy his weird fixation on her anyway.

"Adena," he said.

Poor Adena's footsteps slowed and her shoulders drooped, as though she knew what was coming. Turning back around, she faced John like a dog expecting a kick.

John didn't care. "Send Liza and her producer back," he said, anticipation already heating his blood and clearing out the last of his exhaustion. "You can talk to the producer, and I want to tell Liza she's going to be spending a lot more time with...us."

The word *us* was a last-minute substitution. With *me,* John thought with fierce satisfaction. She's going to be spending a lot more time with *me.*

Chapter 3

"These red-eyes are killing me." Takashi Nakamura, Liza's longtime producer and friend, hung up his air phone and collapsed back in the seat next to Liza. "It'll be damn near 3:00 a.m. before we get to the hotel. That's not even worth getting into bed for."

Liza, who'd just finished her own phone call, grunted. Then she arranged her neck roll, lowered the satin blindfold over her bleary eyes and pulled her small fleece blanket over her shoulders in what was sure to be a futile attempt to get a quick catnap. Man, was she beat.

Also hungry, frustrated and agitated.

It was going to be a truly awful night. Having forgotten to charge her iPod, she couldn't listen to music to drown out the loud hum of the jet's engine or the ongoing dull chatter of the cabin's other occupants.

She was definitely going to be cranky tomorrow.

Beside her, Takashi reclined his seat and heaved a harsh sigh. "We're too old for this nonsense."

"I'd noticed." Liza's thirty-seven-year-old body didn't adjust to the constant travel and time changes like it used to; lately it didn't seem to adjust at all. The trip last month to Beijing with the president had nearly done her in, and her poor internal clock still didn't know what time it was.

"We also don't get paid enough for this nonsense."

"Amen to that," Liza said.

This wasn't exactly true. She made a huge salary even if she never had the time, energy or inclination to enjoy it. Still, a great salary did not equal a great life. Divorced years ago from Kent, a cheating rat bastard who'd taken most of Liza's travel assignments as opportunities to screw other women, Liza didn't do relationships because there was no percentage in them. Nor did she do anything other than work and charity work for an Alzheimer's foundation.

Her Georgetown brownstone sat empty most of the time, even when she was home, because she was always on the trail of a story. She could only vaguely remember her last official vacation, which was two or three years ago.

With no children, no significant other and no hobbies, Liza was hardly the picture of Zen-like balance or happiness, not that she had the time to address this problem. Why bother anyway? Life was pleasant enough, and her career was certainly exciting even when it threatened to kill her with exhaustion.

Maybe she'd never have children, but she was slowly coming to terms with that aching emptiness. Wasn't a thrilling career a fair trade for her lack of family?

"Was that your agent on the phone?" Takashi asked. "What're they quoting you now?"

"Twelve."

Takashi snorted. "I thought they were serious."

"Not yet," Liza muttered. "They're getting there."

They lapsed into a moment's silence, during which Liza wondered what her father, a retired army colonel, would say if he knew she was talking about a twelve million dollar a year offer to host the nightly news as though it was chump change. Then she thought of what he'd say if he knew she was holding out for more money—and shuddered.

You always screw things up, girl. That's what he would say.

It wasn't that she didn't want the job. She just didn't want it as much as she'd thought she would during all those years when she was clawing her way up the ladder.

That was probably her exhaustion talking, though, because the travel was really getting to her.

The chance she'd been working for—the highest aspiration of any TV journalist—was finally hers, and she didn't plan to waste it. Nor would she let the network have her services for cheap, especially since the travel and pace would be nearly as excruciating as they were now.

Her body of work spoke for itself, and she'd subbed in the anchor's chair dozens of times. Though she was not the most senior correspondent, she was one of the most popular, and the ratings soared every time she filled in.

The bottom line was that she had the chops for the job and fully intended to have it soon now that the current anchor, who'd been in the chair since Moses floated down the Nile in a basket, had announced his upcoming retirement.

In the meantime, while her agent worked on the negotiations, this gig on the candidate's plane was the final stepping-stone to the professional glory that would soon be hers.

She tried to relax a little, but the tension through her shoulders and the cramped leg space made that difficult at best. Worse, the lingering adrenalin surge from her encounter with the senator still had her blood pumping. Just as she started to scrunch her shoulders up and down in one of those on-plane relaxation exercises that never relaxed anyone, her air phone rang.

Great. And here she'd thought she was lucky to be working on a tricked-out plane with all the finest communications upgrades that allowed her to get calls at her seat. Riiiight.

"Liza Wilson."

"Is that you, girl?" her father barked by way of greeting.

Liza stifled her groan. "Hello, Colonel." She'd always called him Colonel because his stern face and gruff demeanor made diminutives like *Daddy* and *Pops* unthinkable. "How are you? Why aren't you in bed?"

"When are you coming to take me home, girl?"

Liza's heart sank. He was having one of his bad days, which were becoming the rule rather than the exception. She should've known; an after-midnight call from an eighty-year-old was probably never, as a rule, a good thing.

"You are home. Remember?" Liza cringed as soon as the R-word was out of her mouth. Saying things like *don't you remember?* to an Alzheimer's patient wasn't a great idea. "You live at the Regency now, Colonel. That's home."

Silence.

She waited, feeling the wheels turn in his mind, the old memories rising to the top to confuse him and the recent ones sinking to the bottom, useless and forgotten. "I live on Crooked Oak Lane," he finally said, referencing a house he and Mama had lived in forty-odd years ago. "I don't live in this three-room dump."

Lord, give me the strength to deal with this man tonight. Amen.

That three-room dump, as he so lovingly called it, was one of Washington's best and most expensive assisted-living facilities, most of which she'd visited and researched before placing him late last year. It had a clean record, a beautiful building and caring people to look after him.

It was not, by any stretch of the imagination, a *dump.*

"You do live there, Colonel. You've got all your favorite things there with you. Are you in the bedroom? Look at the comforter. That's the one I picked out for you. And see the—"

"You picked out that ugly comforter?" The Colonel's disdain came through the phone loud and clear, so noxious she could practically smell fumes. "Better get your eyes checked, girl. You always screw things up, don't you?"

Remembering that the Colonel wasn't in his right mind never quite did the trick during these conversations. She rolled her eyes at Takashi, looking for a little commiseration, but he was busy reviewing his e-mail and couldn't hear the Colonel's side of the conversation anyway.

Liza told herself she was being stupid. You'd think she'd be used to this kind of thing by now—this generalized grouchiness and dissatisfaction from her father—but no. It was no good telling herself that he didn't know what he was saying, that he had dementia or that he really appreciated her deep down. Those things worked only when the behavior was a recent change, the result of the disease. The Colonel had never thought she was much good at anything and most likely never would.

But…he was her father and only living relative.

Determined to take the high road, she changed the subject and tried again, her hopes low. "Did you see my report on the news earlier, Colonel? About Senator Warner and his campaign?"

"Yeah, I saw it," he snapped. "I had to hang my head in shame over in the activity room tonight. Daughter of mine giving a black candidate a hard time. What're you thinking, girl?"

Just like that he was clear and focused again, centered on the present and Liza's most recent failings. She supposed she should be glad for these fleeting moments of lucidity, but it was hard when he used them to attack her professionalism, which was somehow worse than his personal attacks.

"I'm thinking about giving objective coverage—"

"There wasn't anything objective about your coverage," he muttered. "Black reporter criticizing a black candidate—"

Okay. Enough was enough. She'd really tried, but now her blood pressure was in the red and she could hear her pulse pounding in her ears. Time to cut her losses before this man sent her into stroke territory up here at thirty thousand feet, where decent medical help was unavailable.

"Uh-oh, Colonel," she interrupted. "The captain just told us to stop using the air phones. I'll see you this weekend, okay?"

"When are you going to take me home, girl?" he spluttered.

"Bye."

She hung up. There was a moment's silence, and then Takashi spoke.

"Daddy Dearest?"

Liza snorted. "I like to think of him as Ward Cleaver."

The last thing she saw before she lowered her blindfold was Takashi's sympathetic smile. Because she didn't do emotions of any kind, especially pity, she flashed him a warning look that only earned her a soft chuckle in return.

Men. They were so aggravating.

If only she could wave a magic wand and rid the earth of them. It would be a much better place.

After thirty seconds of blessed silence, an annoying new sound hit her ears: the unmistakable crinkle of a food wrapper. Feeling grouchier by the second, Liza slid the blindfold up to her forehead and cracked open her left eye to watch Takashi rip into a bag of— she squinted—dried apple crisps.

"Yuck." What a disgusting waste of calories. "Why can't you ever eat any decent junk food?"

Takashi winked one heavily lashed dark eye at her and flashed the dimpled white grin that turned women far and wide to jelly. "Want one?" Crunching loudly, he tipped the bag in her direction.

She snorted before collapsing back against her seat and re-arranging the neck roll. "Why would I eat that? Wake me up when you break out some Cheetos."

"No Cheetos. I've got soy nuts, dried apricots, and...*uh-oh.*"

"Hmm?" she said sleepily.

"Wake up, Za-Za," Takashi hissed. His sharp nudge to her ribs jarred Liza fully awake and she yelped. "The Princess of Darkness at twelve o'clock, and she's looking right this w—. What's up, Adena?"

Liza snatched the blindfold off and looked up to see a new visitor to row twenty back here in the tail end of the plane.

Adena Brown—Senator Warner's senior adviser, gatekeeper and consigliere, a couture-clad political marvel so shrewd, disciplined and fierce in her protection of her candidate that the press universally hated her—stood in the aisle next to Takashi.

Liza snapped to attention and sat up straight.

Adena looked annoyed, as usual, but made a token attempt at politeness. She stretched her perfectly lined lips past her teeth in the grimace that was the closest she ever got to a smile, tossed her hair over her shoulder and spoke to both of them even though the worst of her narrow-eyed glare was reserved for Liza.

"Got a minute?" she asked.

"Of course." Liza tossed her blanket aside and scooted to the edge of her seat.

"The senator would, ah—" Adena's feeble attempt at pleasantries slipped away and she heaved a long-suffering sigh "—like to see you, Liza. And I need to talk to you, Takashi."

Liza blinked. Senator Warner wanted to see *them?* As the

Scooby-Doo cartoon character liked to say, *Ruh-roh*. Yeah, this was it. She'd known she was getting tossed.

Exchanging a discreet sidelong glance with Takashi, who looked as puzzled as she felt, she tried to act as if being summoned to talk with the candidate in the middle of the night was an everyday occurrence.

"Ah," she said, "is everything okay?"

"Peachy." Adena checked her watch. "Coming?"

Liza stood and exchanged a *Help me!* look with Takashi as she edged past him and into the aisle. Takashi merely shrugged and stood aside for her.

They fell in behind Adena and marched toward the front of the plane. A few of her cohorts gave them curious looks as they passed their rows, but for the most part the cabin was quiet and people were trying to get a little shut-eye.

They passed through the adjacent cabin, which was filled with drowsy campaign staffers—they all looked like they were twelve or younger, anxiously awaiting that first growth of facial hair so they could run out and buy a razor—stretched out in their seats.

Liza looked around for the senator, but he wasn't there. The three of them kept moving into the next cabin, which held a conference room.

Here, Adena stopped and put her hand on Takashi's arm. "Wait here. Liza, the senator's in here." She pointed to the next cabin. "Follow me."

Liza, who thrived on adventure and was in her element whenever she put a politician in the hot seat, gulped. With the random and, she hoped, ridiculous thought that she may never see Takashi again, she slipped into the senator's private digs.

Wow.

Must be nice to have the money to outfit the plane like a smaller version of *Air Force One*.

This cozy little cabin had six or eight large leather seats, the kind that were plush, comfortable and totally unlike the torture devices the press was consigned to in the back.

The lighting was mellow and intimate. So was the music—that anthem of longing and need and one of her own personal favorites: Patti LaBelle's "If Only You Knew"—which was piped in from invisible speakers.

Liza's thoughts shifted automatically to lovers, bedrooms and feverish kisses in the dark. Remembering a piece of candidate trivia that every person aboard knew, namely that Senator Warner liked to unwind to Motown music and soulful '70s soul jams did nothing to dispel her first, overwhelming thought:

What a seductive little hideaway.

Adena stepped aside and there he was, Senator Warner, the presidential candidate and the sexiest man Liza had ever seen.

Especially now, when he seemed like any other man.

A more imposing man than most others, true, but still just a man who was human, vulnerable, and…touchable.

He sat at a table poring over his paperwork, his shirtsleeves rolled up, his tie now gone, his brow furrowed with concentration and his face weighed down with fatigue.

But he glanced up when they came in and looked straight at Liza.

Liza's feet slowed and stopped, leaving her frozen and exposed. As a television journalist she was used to bright lights and people staring at her, but the senator's intense interest was somehow different.

Standing quickly, he came around the table, and Liza's skittering heart went into overdrive. Thankfully he kept his distance and stopped when he got within three feet of her.

Making no effort to hide what he was doing, he stared at her with shrewd eyes, studying and assessing. Liza kept her chin up and submitted to this appraisal, somehow holding his unfathomable gaze even though it was too bright, too powerful and too curious.

Liza forced a breath into her straining lungs and waited for him to speak. He didn't. Adena, apparently growing impatient with all this silence, cleared her throat. This, finally, spurred Senator Warner to action.

"Thanks, Adena." His deep voice, which was commanding and impressive at rallies and on the Senate floor, was now low, husky and as enticing as the stroke of velvet across Liza's skin. "I can take it from here."

"But—" Adena began.

"I'll catch up with you in the conference room."

There was no arguing with the senator when he spoke in that tone, and Adena seemed to know it even if she didn't like it. Her expression dour, she crept toward the door at a glacial pace, showing every sign of not wanting to leave the two of them alone together.

Liza wondered whether the two were lovers. They'd worked together for years and spent every waking moment together on campaign business, so they definitely had the opportunity—

Wait a minute. Wait, wait, WAIT. What the hell was she doing?

Liza shook her head to get rid of the weird thoughts and remembered two things.

First, from all reports, the senator was leading the celibate life of a priest.

Second, Adena was married.

Not that it would ever be Liza's business anyway.

Period. End of story. Over and out.

And then, even though Liza was nowhere near ready, Adena left, leaving Liza alone with John Warner.

Chapter 4

Liza had never been this close to the senator before, and being the focal point of his attention was an intoxicating experience, especially because he seemed too interested in studying her to interrupt his perusal with, say, blinking.

The air between them shifted until it crackled with its own energy, a living thing with a power Liza didn't understand and couldn't control.

Realizing she could no longer hold his piercing gaze any more than she could stand on the equator at noon and stare at the sun, she looked away on the pretext of checking out this unfamiliar part of the plane.

A lame conversation starter popped into her head at last, but she had to clear her voice twice before it worked. "Nice cabin. The other peasants and I don't have this much space in back."

He laughed.

Shoring up her courage, Liza risked a glance at him and had that same old predictable reaction: *Oh, my God.* He was so unbelievably sexy. Though his laugh was guarded, it was still dimpled, thrilling and enough to squeeze the breath right out of her lungs.

She looked away again before he damaged her retinas.

"Don't complain," he told her. "Senator Fitzgerald only has a 737."

This time Liza laughed. "I'm not complaining."

His smile slipped away, bit by bit, and he stared for another beat or two while Liza tried not to fidget with nerves. Did she have leftover dinner lettuce wedged between her front teeth? Was that it?

God, she was antsy. When would he get to the point?

With rising desperation, she glanced around and wished there was something—*anything*—for her to feign interest in, but the space was austere and unhelpful. Seat...another seat...whoops, another seat with his soccer ball in it...table...paperwork...dark windows through which she could see nothing.

That was about it.

A troublesome new thought came: why hadn't she worn something other than the cornflower-blue suit her network-provided stylist had picked out for her? She supposed it was pretty enough, but—

Wait a minute. Thinking about changing clothes to impress a man, Liza? Hang your head in shame, girl. Obviously she was not in her right mind. Time to speed things along and get out of here.

"So," she said. "Was there something you needed from me?"

Nothing about her word choice was particularly amusing as far as she could tell, but his eyes crinkled at the corners anyway, and she had the distinct feeling she was missing a crucial detail about something.

"You could say that. I hope Adena didn't wake you up."

"Don't worry." She studied the tips of her pointy-toed black heels and tried to brace herself lest he grin again. "I don't think anyone on the plane is going to sleep until November 5th, anyway. Do you?"

Another rumbling laugh, every bit as exciting as the first. "I was just thinking the same thing a few minutes ago."

"So...I'm assuming you're going to ask the network to replace me?..."

"What makes you say that?" he asked.

"I don't seem to be your favorite person."

"What makes you say that?"

The words were the same, but his inflection was a little sharper the second time around. Looking up, she discovered that his gaze had become narrowed and speculative.

"I think it was the way you glared at me earlier, Senator. That was a clue."

A slow grin crept across his face. "And here I thought I'd been so subtle."

"*That* was subtle?" She widened her eyes in mock alarm. "I'd hate to see direct."

"Well…your coverage hasn't been that easy on me, has it?"

"You didn't expect me to go easy on you, did you?"

"Liza," he told her, "I wouldn't expect anything about you to be easy."

There was a husky new note in his voice that made her wonder if the topic had changed without her knowledge, but nothing in his bland expression or relaxed posture gave him away.

And yet she still felt pleasantly agitated, her skin a degree or two warmer than it had been a second ago. "I give you the same unbiased professionalism that I give all the politicians I cover. That's fair, isn't it?"

"I'm not sure former senator Gregory would think it was fair."

Liza scowled. Naturally the role she'd played in the downfall of one of his colleagues would be a sore subject for Senator Warner, but that didn't mean she was an unethical reporter. She wasn't. She was a shining example of journalistic integrity, and everyone knew it.

"Senator Gregory shouldn't have had his aides buying drugs for him to support his coke habit." Liza tried to keep the huffiness out of her voice, but that was a lost cause. "He contributed to his own downfall. In fact, I'd say he hand-picked the most spectacular downfall he could find and then enthusiastically worked for it like it was his lifelong goal. I just broke the story." She shrugged. "And anyway, any other reporter would have done the same. Like the CNN news reporter who broke the story of the governor's affair a while back. It's news."

Liza froze.

What? *What* had she just said? Had she just mentioned Beau

Taylor, the governor of Virginia, who was married to the senator's sister, Jillian?

Smooth move, girl. Way to move the conversation along.

Liza wanted to glue her big fat mouth shut, but the senator merely grimaced and ignored the subject of his wayward brother-in-law.

"I…see." Leaning a hip against the side of the nearest seat, he crossed his muscled forearms over his chest and flashed a wry smile. "So as long as I don't do something that stupid, I have nothing to fear from you?"

"Have you done something that stupid?" Now that Liza knew her brashness hadn't derailed the conversation, her journalist's keen instincts sniffed the air, on the scent of a potential story. "You could give me an exclusive. Just in case you feel the sudden urge to confess to anything."

"No. But I will keep you in mind in case I have any sudden…urges."

"Please do," she said, distracted by his gaze, which flickered to her lips and then returned, brighter than before, to her eyes.

"I do have you in mind for something special, Liza."

Liza blinked and tried not to wonder too hard about why he'd been looking at her mouth. "What's that?"

"There may have been something to what you said earlier about me granting the press more access. And that's where you come in."

"*Me?*"

"Yeah, you. Congratulations. You've just been granted exclusive access to Sitchroo for the next month or so. You get to hang around, see the decision-making process and generally make a nuisance of yourself. I'm going to instruct my staff to answer all your questions. I'm sure I'll live to regret it, but…there you go. Adena's talking to Takashi right now to get things formally arranged."

A wild rush of triumph ran through her body, getting all of her professional juices flowing. Could she be this lucky? Complete access to Sitchroo? What a coup! As soon as all her cohorts in the back of the plane heard, they'd be Grinch-green with jealousy.

Ha! What a way to go out before she took the anchor chair!

While she resisted the urge to clap her hands and jump with glee, she couldn't quite stifle her Cheshire-cat grin. Senator

Warner smiled back, and the atmosphere shifted into territory that was sensual and exhilarating, as though he'd trailed one long finger up her spine. Renewed awareness of him as a man skittered over her skin, and her breath caught.

As though he sensed some of her turmoil, he stopped grinning. Oh, no. Did he know how attracted she was to him?

Maybe that was what was going on here. Maybe he'd detected her soft spot for him and intended to use it to his advantage. Yeah, that was probably it; he was known as a brilliant strategist, after all.

If the press was clamoring for more of his time, he was probably thinking, why not grant more time—to the female journalist who had the hardest time controlling her hormonal surge? Why not count on foolish, horny Liza to soft-pedal the coverage?

Or…maybe something else was going on.

She was the most senior black correspondent on the plane, so maybe he hoped—just like her father did—that she'd give him more favorable coverage on the basis of the race connection. Maybe the good senator figured a black correspondent wouldn't give a black candidate a hard time. He should know better than that.

Frowning and suspicious now, she snapped at him. "Why me?"

This seemed to catch him by surprise. Quickly turning his head, he pushed away from the seat, walked back to his table and looked down at his paperwork. "It's never a good idea to look a gift horse in the mouth. Unless you think you're not ready for the assignment?…"

This subtle dig raised all of Liza's hackles, as he'd surely known it would. "Of course I'm ready. I just want to make sure that you don't have any unrealistic expectations about working with me."

Though the lighting in the cabin wasn't the greatest, she saw a dull flush rise up and over his sharp cheekbones. For a minute he sifted through the papers, looking for something, and then he looked up with an inscrutable expression.

"*Unrealistic expectations?*"

"Maybe you think a black journalist—"

His eyes widened with sudden comprehension—he almost looked relieved—and a bemused smile inched across his face. "I wouldn't expect any special treatment from you, Liza—"

"Because I'm not going to pull any punches—"

"When have you ever pulled any punches?"

"—and if you're granting me access, I want access. None of this off-the-record business when I ask tough questions. No closed doors when the real decisions are being made. If that's what you have in mind, then I'm not the right woman for you."

"You're the right woman."

Liza paused.

Suddenly she wasn't quite certain what she was fighting for or even if there was a disagreement. Some combination of the lateness of the hour, her sleep deprivation and, probably, wishful thinking, made her mind play tricks on her. She could almost believe that she heard longing in his husky voice, saw smoldering want in his intense gaze.

If this was a sign of things to come, then she was in deep trouble.

The senator's charisma was part of his immense appeal. She knew that. He was one of those rare people—like, say, JFK, Bill Clinton or Sting—who had the knack for looking at a person—especially a woman—and making him or her feel like the only other person in the world. It was one of the keys to his success, this ability to create the feeling of intimacy where there was none, to make a meaningless person feel important.

Liza understood this in the rational part of her brain. The problem was that the rational part of her brain went AWOL whenever she was in the room with him.

She blinked, wondering what, if anything, had been resolved.

"So…we're agreed?"

"Agreed."

A faint smile floated across his face as he sank into his chair and looked back at his paperwork. Normally she would have shaken hands to seal a deal, but the last thing she needed—ever—was to touch this man.

He picked up his pen.

Time to go, Liza. Return to the back, where you belong.

Right now.

Let's go.

Liza didn't move. Her feet ignored the command because she didn't want to go and he didn't kick her out. In fact, although he didn't look at her again, he didn't seem particularly interested in whatever was spread out on the table in front of him and gave no sign that she'd worn out her welcome.

With no clear instructions, she stayed put, paralyzed with indecision.

For the first time in a while, she became aware of the music. Earth, Wind & Fire's "Reasons" was now coming through the speakers, ratcheting up her loneliness. The generic longing she'd felt for years, ever since her divorce, was more acute tonight, probably because she was sleepy and her defenses were down.

She sighed.

Her wayward imagination began to wander. Before she knew it, she'd superimposed Senator Warner's face onto the body of the nameless man she periodically wished she had in her life.

She wanted—

"Something on your mind, Liza?"

His low voice, husky now, caught her off guard.

"I—" She blinked and stammered. "I'll just let you get back to work."

His dark eyes gave nothing away, but his jaw tightened. Nodding sharply, once, he lowered his head, silently granting permission.

Everything within her body—each bit of subatomic particles—seemed to protest, to deflate. So that was it. Their interlude was over and she was now consigned to the back of the plane, far away from him, its heart and center.

Turning, she trudged toward the door to the conference room with slow and resistant feet. A burning patch between her shoulders felt like his lingering gaze, but of course that was only her runaway imagination wreaking havoc again.

Delusional or not, she just couldn't go. Not yet.

Hesitating on the threshold, she looked back to discover that he *was* looking at her, his expression troubled, his paperwork forgotten.

"Can I ask you a question?" she said on impulse. "Off the record?"

It took him a long time to answer. "You can ask me anything."

"You seem so sane. Why do you want to be president?"

The corners of his eyes crinkled. "Only a wacko would want the job, you mean?"

"Exactly."

"Maybe I'm a wacko."

"No, you're not."

He stared at her, no doubt seeing too much, and embarrassment rose up in her cheeks, hot and uncomfortable. She hadn't meant to disagree so vehemently, but, really, everything she'd ever seen or read about this man—everything her gut screamed at her right now—told her that, despite his wealth and privilege, he was a true public servant. A man of the people who wanted the best for all Americans.

He was not, and never had been, a wacko.

"Why?" she asked again.

"Do you want the sound bite answer, or—"

"I always want the real answer, Senator."

"You'll laugh."

"No, I won't."

Something in his expression softened, swirling into a mesmerizing image she could study for hours if not days. Nerve endings prickled to life low in her belly and in her breasts, and that was before he raised a hand to beckon her and spoke in that black velvet voice.

"Sit down with me, Liza."

Drawn into his orbit, a poor circling planet seeking the sun's warmth, she sat in the seat across the desk from his and held her breath, waiting for him to confide something clearly private and meaningful.

"My mother died when I was in grade school. Brain tumor."

Liza blinked. Whatever she'd expected, it wasn't this. She'd known they had this shared tragedy in common, but there was something unbearably intimate and raw about discussing it with him now.

"I know." She hesitated. "My mother died when I was ten. A...stroke."

Their sad gazes locked in mutual understanding—their mothers both died when they were young and no more needed to be said about it—and the invisible connection between them tightened as though someone had bound them together with black crepe.

"My father was a real piece of work," he told her. "If he could have slept with all his millions under his pillow at night, he would have. I never understood him, and he sure as hell never understood me."

His late father, Matheson Warner, had been a giant in the publishing world, having started a magazine in the sixties and growing it into an empire that eventually included newspapers and TV stations before it was sold upon his death—what was it?—twenty years ago. She'd also known that Matheson, along with his older brother, Reynolds Warner, who'd built his own clothing empire, WarnerBrands International, was a cutthroat businessman.

What she hadn't known was that his son was anything other than proud of him and the family name.

"Oh," she said.

"You probably have a great father. Wasn't he in the army?"

Startled as she was that he knew this detail about her private life, her stubborn streak would not let her sit by while someone used the word *great* in the same sentence with her father.

"My father has Alzheimer's—"

His face fell. "I'm sorry. My uncle Reynolds had Alzheimer's."

"—and before that he was an army colonel who never had a conversation with me without trying to make me feel bad because I wasn't the boy he wanted. His expectations of me are exceptionally high. To the best of my knowledge, I've never met one of them."

He looked as if he wanted to say something sympathetic—they did have a lot in common, didn't they?—but sentimentality wasn't her thing.

"Are you trying to dodge my question, Senator? What have difficult fathers got to do with the presidency?"

He paused and she had the feeling he was marking her confession, cataloging it for later review and analysis. "My father thought he was entitled. That the rich should get richer and the poor should sit down and shut up. That if you worked full-time but still couldn't afford college for your kids or health insurance it was because you were too stupid to get a better job or too lazy to get a second job." He shrugged. "It pissed me off. Why shouldn't everyone have the same opportunities I had? Why couldn't the gardener's son, who was my best friend growing up, by the way, afford to go to Yale when he got in just like I did? What sense did that make?"

"You want social justice?"

He grinned. "Let's just say I'm a big fan of Robin Hood."

"Lots of people admire Robin Hood, Senator, and they don't subject themselves to Washington politics."

The grin widened. "Did I mention I like the behind-the-scenes deals and the strategizing? I like engineering solutions to complicated problems. And I'm good at it."

"And modest."

The grin turned wicked and so hot that she could feel its effects in her flushed skin and the deep ache between her thighs. "If you show me a politician with a small ego, Liza, I'll show you a person who doesn't have the juice to be elected dogcatcher."

They laughed together, and it was so deliciously wonderful and perfect that Liza's breath caught and held in her throat. The pull she felt toward this man was so strong it thrilled and scared her. She shot to her feet with all the grace of a beached walrus.

"I should go. You're busy."

His face darkened with what looked like disagreement, but he nodded anyway and rifled his paperwork. "Yeah. Great."

"Great." She headed toward the door as fast as she could.

"Did I hear that you're in negotiations for the anchor's chair?"

She froze and cursed under her breath because how could she leave when the conversation turned to her favorite topic—herself? Glancing over her shoulder, she smiled.

"I'm afraid you don't have the clearance for that information, Senator."

The senator, who was on the influential Foreign Relations Committee and therefore had a clearance level that made him privy to state secrets that would probably uncurl her hair, thought this was pretty funny.

"I'll take that as a *yes*. For the record—I think you deserve the job."

"For the record—you're darn right I do."

Another delicious moment followed, one with smiles and the glorious warmth of his amusement and approval on her face.

"What's that I smell? A big ego?"

Liza shrugged. "Big egos have their place, don't they?"

"Darn right they do," he told her. "You're not as prickly as I thought you were, Liza."

"Don't fool yourself, Senator."

Staring at him, wanting him, it was a physical effort to keep her feet where they were, to stay on her side of the cabin when she wanted to be in his lap, straddling him. The ache between her legs was now a wet throb and would soon be a torment.

Time to go. Past time.

"Good night."

She was determined to escape this time, because it was becoming harder to convince herself that this was a business meeting and they weren't flirting with each other.

"I'll answer one last question if you want," he told her. "For the road."

Curses. The offer to answer questions was like crack to a journalist—irresistible. Fortunately, she had one ready.

"What's all this like?"

"This?"

"Being the candidate. The media attention and lack of privacy. The security." She hesitated, trying to find a word big enough to encompass all the sacrifices he'd made to get to this point in his life. *"Everything.* What's it like?"

He shrugged. "This is what I signed up for. I knew it wasn't day camp."

"Yeah, but it can't be easy. What do you most miss about your old life?"

"What do I most miss?"

Uh-oh. Why was he looking at her as if she'd developed green-and-white stripes across her face? Mortified, Liza clamped her jaw tight shut, but the horse was already out of the stupid barn and galloping away.

"Sorry," she said.

Why didn't she know when to keep quiet? It'd seemed like a reasonable thing to ask, but now she felt D-U-M-B, especially with him giving her that furrowed-brow look. Poor man. He was probably regretting his decision to work with her and worried she'd next ask about his favorite color.

"Dumb question." She edged toward the door. "I'll get out of your hair—"

"*Wait.*"

Something in his expression had changed, grown dark and hot. When their gazes connected, she felt that lightning bolt sensation again, as though a powerful charge of electricity had shot between them and then radiated out to illuminate the cabin.

This wasn't flirting. Flirting could be innocent.

This, whatever it was, wasn't.

It felt so strong that she wondered if the force of it would interfere with the plane's systems and knock it out of the sky.

Tossing his pen aside, the senator got to his feet and stretched to his full height—all long legs and broad shoulders and sexier than players in an NBA locker room.

Liza's heart screeched to a halt, and her mouth went dry with unadulterated lust as she waited to see what he would do.

Chapter 5

He came closer, his ruthless gaze skimming her from top to bottom as he approached, pausing on her breasts, hips and legs, missing nothing and savoring everything.

Oh, God. He wasn't the presidential candidate. Not now.

This was a man who desperately wanted her and wasn't afraid to show it, a man who would, with very little provocation, slide his hands up her bare thighs and under her skirt, slip her panties down and off, plant his palms on the cheeks of her butt, and lift her so that she could wrap her legs around his waist.

He would unzip his pants, free himself and plunge deep inside her body. He would press her against the cabin wall and pump his hips back and forth—endlessly, expertly—until she passed out from pleasure with tears in her eyes and his name on her lips.

And she, with very little provocation, would welcome him.

He came right up to her, breaching the divide between them until she had to crane her neck to look up into his glittering eyes and the flaming warmth from his body burned her. Until the faint but addicting scent of his musky cologne invaded her senses, fogged her brain and clouded her judgment.

"In my old life," he told her, "If I thought a woman was the most beautiful thing I'd ever seen, I'd say so."

"Oh," she said, stunned.

He drifted closer and his hoarse voice dropped until it was a mesmerizing whisper that she felt inside her body rather than heard with her ears. The secrets poured out of his mouth, and she greedily absorbed them, knowing, but not caring, that each word complicated her life and inched her closer to the kind of trouble that ruined careers and lives.

"If I thought of a woman all the time, even when I was supposed to be doing my work, I would tell her. And I would ask if she ever thought of me."

Liza, hearing the question buried in his words, couldn't deny him even though a smarter woman would. One corner of her mouth turned up in a tiny smile, a *yes, I think of you, too,* and she did nothing to stop it.

A tremor went through him and his breath hissed softly. Raising one hand, as though he wanted to cup her face, he let it hover inches from her overheated cheek without ever making contact, killing her with her own longing and need.

His gaze lingered on her lips. "If a woman had a beautiful mouth, I would kiss it. If her hair looked like silk, I would run my fingers through it. And I'd—"

He would what? *What?*

Liza waited and hoped but…nothing. For several long seconds he tortured her by not answering and letting the delicious images writhe through her brain without giving them complete focus.

And yet it was all there in the depths of his gleaming dark eyes: him slipping inside her body…the two of them flowing together…the friction and slide of their damp skin…the excruciating thrill of his absolute possession.

The need to make this scene a reality was too great to stay quietly inside Liza's body and she gasped. Was this really happening? Could the sexiest man in the world really be attracted to *her?*

Searching his intent face for answers, she found one: he knew the risks and was as troubled by their chemistry as she was. This was not the gambit of a player who tried it on every woman he met, just for kicks, nor was it the habitual practice of a man who stood beneath a tree weighted down with ripe peaches, shook a branch and caught the easy fruit in his waiting hands.

He wanted her despite all his best intentions, and he didn't like it one bit.

Dropping his lids to cover his fever-bright eyes, he took a harsh breath. When he met her gaze again, the heat had disappeared. The man was gone and the candidate was back, erecting such a solid wall against her that she could almost see each brick.

Though he wanted her, he wanted to be president more, and that was that.

"But I'm a candidate and I can't do those things." He used his speech-making voice now, the one that did the voice-overs on all his commercials—*I'm Senator Warner and I approved this message*—rather than the husky voice of a man who wanted. "Can I?"

"No," she agreed.

That would have been the end of the conversation except that something came over her. Part need, part temporary insanity and part the kind of irresistible impulsivity that made kids dart into the street to capture runaway balls. Whatever it was, she couldn't ignore it or let this moment pass without touching him—just this once.

What could it hurt? Who would know?

"You can't do things like that now, Senator." She paused. "But I can."

He stilled.

With the sound of his labored breath, her own thundering pulse and Teddy Pendergrass's "Love T.K.O." filling her ears, Liza reached out. She didn't know what made her do it—only that she had to. Cupping his strong jaw in her palm, absorbing his surprised gasp into her body, she ran her thumb along his lush bottom lip and the heat surged between them

One touch wasn't enough. She'd been a fool to think it would be.

She had to taste those lips.

Standing on her tiptoes, exerting slight pressure to bring his face lower, she tipped her chin up and brushed her mouth over his.

Mmm.

He was perfection. Pleasure fanned out from that point of contact and filled her until she mewled with the sensation.

The tiny sound sent a shudder rippling through him.

Not pausing to think, she ran her tongue across his tender lips and tasted mints and something so primal and delicious that she wanted to gorge on it until it killed her.

He shifted closer.

Yesss.

When she felt the vibrating energy of his growing lust beneath her fingertips and the insistent clenching between her thighs, reality intruded.

Stop, Liza. You have to *stop*.

With all the reluctance in the world, she pulled back and let him go.

He'd just started to reach for her, but now he dropped his hands and stared at her with glazed eyes. They watched each other for a minute, both sets of lungs pumping as if they'd just sprinted a hundred meters, and Liza's face and scalp prickled with the new heat of embarrassment.

But she wasn't sorry. If she'd just committed career suicide, that kiss was a fine consolation that would keep her warm for many nights to come.

"I don't—I don't know what made me do that."

Lame, yeah, but the best excuse she could offer for her behavior.

"I think you probably do."

The magnitude of her recklessness began to sink into her lust-fogged brain, and she wanted to throw herself out of the nearest emergency exit. In addition to making a move on a man, something she'd never done in her life, she'd just broken more ethical rules than she could count with the person who might one day be her president.

If he wanted to, he could make one phone call and get her fired. On the other hand, if she wanted to, she could tell her story to a tabloid and start a feeding frenzy that would damage his chances of winning the nomination.

Where did that leave them? Nowhere good for either of them.

Her hand, moving on its own again, went to her mouth. Whether it was to hold his kiss there or wipe it away, she didn't know.

"It won't happen again."

One of his eyebrows rose, making him seem vaguely irritated and, if she wasn't mistaken, amused by her naiveté. That riveting black gaze sent goose bumps racing over her skin.

"You crossed a line I wouldn't have crossed, Liza."

"Forgive me, Senator."

What else could she say? Ducking her head and giving herself a swift mental kick in the butt for her unspeakable impulsivity, she hurried out before the mortification sent her entire face up in flames.

There she was.

John saw Liza Wilson the millisecond he walked through the double glass doors of the conference room at his Cleveland headquarters and all but cartwheeled with excitement.

It was still dark outside and ungodly early—five-thirty in the morning. They'd all been up for hours because John had gone with his staffers and the whole entourage for an early-morning swim at his club, and yet she looked fresh and beautiful in her green dress and black boots, her head bent low over her clipboard as she murmured with Takashi and their cameraman over in the far corner near the sideboard. They'd begin filming soon, so her heavy on-camera makeup was in place, but John found himself wondering how she'd look without so much paint. After a minute he came to the unwelcome conclusion that she'd be more beautiful rather than less.

Damn woman.

Two long days had passed since The Kiss because she'd been recalled to Washington to confer with her executive producers about the logistics of her new assignment with him and Sitchroo. But she was back now, and the sight of her made all his body's systems—pulse, temperature, breath—go haywire, just like always.

Edging past the bleary-eyed but cheerful staffers already assembled at the massive table, calling good morning as he went, John could acknowledge the magnitude of his mistake in spending time alone with her. What had he thought? That Liza would irritate him? Had he actually been that stupid?

Yeah, Warner. You were *that* stupid.

She'd been so irritating he'd almost swallowed her whole.

What else had she been?

Unexpectedly sweet. Charming and funny, but also fierce and strong.

Sexy enough that his blood still ran hot every time he thought of her. Really hot. So hot he was in danger of melting the clothes off his own body.

And her smell…some sophisticated combination of a spring garden with a healthy dose of sultry siren thrown in. The kind of scent that made a man's knees weak, his mouth water and his eyes cross.

Liza, Liza, Liza.

The woman demolished his reserve, destroyed his focus and made him think crazy thoughts, like the following:

Campaign? What campaign?

Or: *what harm could there be in kissing her?*

Or this little gem: *I wonder if I can lock this cabin door, throw her across my table and make love to her until the plane lands. Would anyone really notice if we were in here alone together the whole night? It could work, right?*

That's right. He, Jonathan Matheson Warner, who had never in his life done anything impulsive, had been millimeters away from grabbing that woman and taking her any way she wanted it. Hard and fast? No problem. Soft and easy? No problem. Well…no problem after the first hard-and-fast time. Upside-down while hanging off the plane's wing? Whatever Liza wanted, he was there. Who cared about a presidential campaign when there was a woman like that in the world?

John shuddered. Five minutes alone with Liza Warner and he was now wallowing in self-destructive behavior. Could playing Russian roulette be far behind?

He already had a paparazzi fire to put out at this morning's Sitchroo meeting because a tabloid was running pictures of an airheaded celebutante kissing him at a Hollywood fundraiser last week. His poll numbers had already taken a hit because of it—a small hit, but still a hit—and he didn't have any more numbers to lose.

The last thing he needed was another fire about his personal life, and he wasn't fool enough to think he could have an affair with Liza—even a discreet affair—and keep it secret for very long. No matter how much he wanted to.

Luckily he had the gift of focus. Without too much trouble he could usually hone in on the real issue in any given situation, the one that needed addressing. That focus would help make him an exceptional president if given the chance.

Normally focusing on his work was no big deal; it was how he'd become this successful in his career and managed to control the three-ring circus that was a presidential campaign.

On the other hand, normally he wasn't obsessed with Liza Wilson.

Concentrating on his work had gotten him through the last couple of days without seeing her, but it was easy to resist temptation when temptation wasn't there. Temptation was back now, and his work didn't seem to mean jack or shit when she was this close.

Determined not to stare at Liza, John sat at the head of the table, ready to get this party started. *Forget Liza Wilson,* he told himself. *Forget her.* And he started to. For nearly half a second he did. But then the insidious thoughts started working on him and he glanced her way again, hoping for some flicker of acknowledgement in her eye, a half smile, a blush, a look…something…anything…but she kept her head low, and there was nothing for him to cling to except the powerful memory of her sweet lips on his.

Adena, meanwhile, was staring across the table at him with a knowing and irritated look in her eyes. "John." The warning in her voice couldn't have been louder or clearer if she'd used a megaphone. "Should we get started with the—"

Screw that.

John held up a hand to silence and dismiss Adena and, with her, John's doubts. He could make time to say hello to Liza; it was only polite. And anyway—what could happen in a room full of people?

"Give me three minutes." He stood again. "I need some coffee. Talk amongst yourselves till I get back."

The staffers resumed their chatter, and John left the table with Adena's glower skewering him through the shoulder blades. He shrugged it off, his mind on Liza with a single-minded focus that was so absolute he was barely aware of the other people in the room.

"Takashi." He held out a hand. "The Pats lost last night. That's another large you owe me."

Takashi, who had the unfortunate habit of betting on every losing team in the NFL, NBA, or any other sports league with three letters, looked around with a sheepish grin and they shook. No money would ever change hands between them and they both knew it, but it was always fun to rub Takashi's face in another loss.

"The Celtics are still in play, though, Senator. Should we make it double or nothing?"

"No. I want to leave you some cash for your retirement years."

Maybe Takashi said something else, but John's entire existence was now centered on Liza and he didn't hear it. She'd glanced up from her clipboard long enough to give him a tiny smile that made him unreasonably happy.

"And how are you this morning, Liza?" John took excruciating care to keep his expression friendly but not intimate and his voice exactly the same as it'd been when he'd greeted Takashi.

Her color heightened as she looked up with a wry twist of her lips. "Not as good as I'd be if you started your day at a decent hour."

Staring at her, smelling the flowers on her skin, wanting her, John felt the first cracks in his discipline and hated her for it.

Why, at this critical moment in his life and the country's future, had this woman arrived to torment him? If he couldn't have her, he shouldn't want her. Not this damn much.

"Takashi." God, he couldn't take his eyes off her for a second, even when he was talking to someone else. How crazy was that? "Give us a minute."

Takashi hesitated, as though he knew that what was on John's mind was nothing innocent, but then he walked off. Right about then, an unwelcome thought crept up on John, screwed with his mind and gave him another reason to be angry with this woman who jammed his circuits at every opportunity:

Was something going on with her and Takashi?

None of his business, but tell that to his knotted gut.

He stared at Helen of Troy and tried not to think about how much he wanted her sweaty, moaning and naked in his arms. That was hard enough. Not thinking about how much he wanted to spend time alone with her and learn everything about her life was impossible.

"You shouldn't have kissed me," he told her.

Chapter 6

Reaching for a coffee mug, John tried to keep his voice even and his hands steady.

Liza, unfortunately, didn't cooperate and had the nerve to sound huffy. "I already apologized, Senator—"

"The damage is done." He put sugar in his coffee and stirred it roughly until it sloshed over the sides. Cursing, he reached for a napkin. "I'm having a little trouble getting the genie back in the bottle. What do you propose we do about that?"

"Nothing."

"Nothing?"

She looked up at him with those wide eyes, the model of innocent bewilderment, as though she couldn't understand what the big deal was and why he insisted on yammering about it.

"It was one small kiss that'll never happen again. Why should we get all worked up about it? We're both profession-als, aren't we?"

Choked with sudden anger, John gaped at her. Nothing she could have possibly said would have goaded him more. *One small kiss?* Was that what she was calling the job she'd done on him with her lips the other night? When she'd given him a small taste of heaven and then snatched heaven away?

Because it sure as hell hadn't been *one small kiss* to him. It'd been the unwelcome explosion of something huge, the insertion of a Liza chip into his brain that sent him off on endless fantasies of Liza naked in his bed when he should be thinking about health care and Social Security.

Seething, he fired the words out like bullets. *"One small kiss?"*

Hitching up her arrogant chin, she shrugged and gave him a cool, distant smile designed for the sole purpose of telegraphing how meaningless he was in her life, how forgettable.

"I can be professional, Senator. Can't you?"

She was good. He'd give her that. If not for the telltale patches of color high over her cheeks, he'd want to strangle her for her indifference when he was panting after her like a dog with his first bitch in heat.

A beat or two passed during which she stared at John without blinking. He got her silent message loud and clear. Whatever attraction she may have felt for him came a distant second behind her career and always would—end of story.

John understood. This was right and appropriate.

Period. Whew. Bullet dodged.

And still he felt the overwhelming need to rise to her challenge. To demonstrate in explicit detail that she couldn't just kiss him senseless and then pretend it meant nothing. To explore the budding attraction between them and see where it led. To claim both prizes he wanted: the presidency *and* Liza Wilson.

The Sitchroo meeting began a few minutes later, after the senator formally welcomed Liza and Takashi to the group.

The two of them occupied one corner of the conference room and tried to be quieter than church mice at St. Peter's Cathedral while they observed the proceedings. The senator's staffers, twenty or so of them, all juggled laptops, cell phones and coffee, and all looked bright-eyed and eager to conquer the world.

The plan, which had been finalized after much negotiation between the senator's people and the network, was the following: in addition to trailing the senator all day, which Liza was doing anyway, he'd answer a few of her questions at the beginning and end of every day.

These segments would air on the network's morning and evening news shows, and Liza would continue to provide analysis several nights a week on the network's cable affiliate. She'd also use all the behind-the-scenes footage for a one-hour special, *Inside Sitchroo,* to air either after the primary season ended or, if the senator won the nomination, after the general election in November.

Liza and Takashi's instructions for today and every day were therefore the same: shut up, observe and shoot. After the meeting ended in a little while, Liza would have five minutes to question the senator about whatever she wanted; then she'd do the morning show, and then they'd all traipse off for another full day of campaign activities.

Simple, right?

Not even close.

The trying to be quiet and observe part was generally no problem for Liza. Trying to banish the senator's taste from her mouth, well, that was impossible.

He still wanted her. The heat in his eyes had been banked since the other night, yeah, but it was still heat and still there. It was real, this attraction between them. Powerful, real and dangerous.

She'd almost convinced herself that she'd imagined the whole interlude with him the other night, but seeing him again proved that the worst-case scenario was not a figment of her imagination. He was as violently attracted to her as she was to him, and every endless day on this campaign was going to be a tormenting exercise in futile longing and unfulfilled desire.

Spending time alone with him had only thrown gasoline and kindling on her fire. He was genuine, to her everlasting dismay, and she liked him. He was also shrewd, funny and nice. What you saw with him was what you got, and she couldn't be more furious about it. What was he trying to do to her by being likable? Why couldn't he be a jackass like everyone else?

And *why,* Liza thought as she irritably uncrossed and recrossed her legs in this uncomfortable chair, was she evaluating him as though he were relationship material?

Feeling glum about her apparent lapse in sanity, Liza watched and tried not to doze while a couple of staffers debated the latest poll numbers. Had she thought covering Sitchroo meetings would be exciting? *Ha.* So far this morning it'd been a yawn fest. The only good thing about it was the opportunity to stare at the senator, and since her breasts always swelled and ached at the sight of him, that wasn't really a good thing, now, was it?

He wore today's dark power suit, white shirt and yellow tie and looked as though he'd been sent over from central casting to play the president in some blockbuster action-adventure movie. Everything about him aroused her, including his hands, which were the current objects of her obsession.

Those long fingers with their neat nails were now wrapped around his omnipresent soccer ball, the one he allegedly couldn't think without, as he strode around the room listening to various reports from assorted people. That was another bit of trivia about the senator: his relentless energy rarely let him sit still for long and he did his best thinking, or so he said, while holding his soccer ball and pacing.

When Adena changed the topic to the tabloid photos of Francesca Waverly, which had just hit the stands, Liza stopped daydreaming and started paying attention. Waverly was a size-two Hollywood airhead with no talent and a bikini collection vast enough to outfit every woman in America. What had the senator been doing with *her?* The question suddenly had a whole new relevance.

Takashi passed Liza a copy of the magazine, which was flipped open to the right page, and Liza studied the picture with a bitter taste in her mouth and a concrete ball in her gut that felt a lot like…jealousy.

Under the caption Business and Pleasure? was a close-cropped photo of the good senator smiling down at the starlet—she of the big eyes, thirty pounds of hair and teeny-tiny dress—while holding her in his arms at a fundraiser in L.A. just before Liza came aboard the campaign.

The article had the usual speculation about whether the two were involved in a "secret relationship" because they'd "seemed so much in love," according to "sources close to the campaign."

Liza snorted and tossed the rag to the floor with a loud flap of paper.

The senator's sharp gaze swung around to her and he paused, the soccer ball pressed between his palms. "What's that, Liza?"

Liza gave him her sweetest smile around gritted teeth. "Nothing, Senator."

He studied her with narrowed eyes before turning back to Adena. "What were you saying?"

Adena shot Liza a glare—Liza wasn't being quiet enough, obviously—before answering. "We've released the full video and posted it on the YouTube Web page."

The senator nodded with grim satisfaction. "Good. I don't have time for any Francesca Waverly nonsense. What's next?"

Full video? What full video? Liza, who hated being in the dark on anything, looked around at Takashi. He was already tapping on his laptop. Without a word, he turned the screen to Liza and hit Play.

The two watched a ten-second clip without sound that showed the senator working a receiving line with dozens of people. He got to the eye candy, smiled and extended his hand. Ignoring this gesture, the starlet threw herself into his arms and gave him a hug. The senator looked startled but laughed, extricated himself and moved on to the next person in line without looking back.

That was it.

That was it?

Of course that was it. The senator had already issued a statement saying he didn't have the time or inclination for dating. This only proved it. He'd had that woman in his arms only while on the *receiving line.*

Feeling suddenly light and airy, Liza couldn't suppress a satisfied grin—until she looked up and caught the senator staring right at her with an I-told-you-so look on his face.

Liza wiped her face clean.

He held her gaze for a beat or two and then turned away.

Liza fidgeted. *Get a grip, girl,* she told herself, disgusted.

The senator resumed the conversation he'd begun while Liza was watching the video. "But you still haven't told me anything *specific.*" He strode back and forth in front of the windows, through which yellow streaks of the coming dawn were finally visible. "Why should we get excited about nonspecific threats?"

"The field office doesn't have anything specific," said Barbara Klein, one of his top advisers, a note of frustration growing in her voice. "The two things they keep pointing to are the Internet chatter from those same supremacist groups, which seems to be getting more vocal as your coverage increases, and the interest surrounding your upcoming Midwest visit."

Coming up to speed, Liza realized the new topic at hand was the senator's stubborn and continued refusal to use the secret service protection he was entitled to as a presidential candidate. *Idiot.*

"That's it?" he asked.

"That's it," Barbara said. "But we have to be aware that some supremacist yahoo may try to make a big name for himself by taking a shot at you."

Thank you, Liza thought. Finally—the voice of reason.

The senator, however, did not seem convinced. He frowned, collapsed in his chair, stacked his wing-tipped feet on the table, leaned back and stared out the window. No one said a word. Then he stretched out one long arm—his gold cuff link winked from the snowy sleeve of his shirt—and bounced the soccer ball on the desk.

"Roy?" he asked, still staring at the sunrise.

Roy Martin was the cocky liaison from the private security firm that provided protection for the senator on the senator's own dime. Liza, who had a violent allergy to smarm and arrogance, had never liked him one bit, and she wasn't starting today.

The SOB shrugged as though having to explain the security procedures in place to ensure someone's safety was an annoyance. "You know the drill, Senator. We work with the local police at each venue. We've got the electronic equipment we need and the visible manpower. Everything is covered—"

"Except for the countersnipers and helicopters," Liza murmured, unable to stop herself because her head might explode if no one pointed out the obvious. "Those are appropriate measures the secret service could provide to manage the kinds of crowds the senator has been drawing."

There was an audible gasp from somewhere. Every head turned

in Liza's direction, and every mouth gaped. The senator dropped his soccer ball, and it rolled across the floor. Adena looked angry enough to throw Liza out of the conference room by her scruff. Takashi, sitting next to Liza, emitted a quiet groan, probably because he knew about her generally well-managed but sometimes uncontrollable streaks of hotheadedness and impulsivity.

Oops.

Had she said that aloud when she was supposed to be a quiet little church mouse? Well, so what? Someone in the room needed to outline the flaws in this little plan, and she'd sat quietly with her blood boiling for long enough. The senator's life was on the line here, and everyone was acting way too casually about it for her taste.

The senator sat up, dropped his feet to the floor and shot her the kind of withering look designed to make her shrink into a chastened pile of nothingness where she sat.

"Liza," he drawled, his heavy brows slashing over his eyes, "when did we put you on the payroll?"

Liza hated being silenced, especially when she was making an important point. Still, she was, first and foremost, an unbiased journalist who kept her opinions to herself. Speaking out was inappropriate and unprofessional and she needed to shut up.

"Sorry." The word tasted bitter on her tongue. "Please continue."

"Oh, good, everyone," the senator said. "We have Liza's permission to continue our meeting." Mollified but still irritated, he shot her another dark glance before turning back to Roy. "You were saying?"

"Between our resources and the local police," Roy said, "Things are—"

"You don't have bomb-sniffing dogs, either," Liza interjected, her bullshit tolerance factor now well into the negative digits.

"Damn, Liza." Takashi shook his head at her.

There was dead silence after that. Liza kept her chin high and held the senator's furious gaze while she waited for her punishment, which was swift.

He unfolded his big body from the chair and stood up, a towering wall of bad attitude. "Barbara," he said, addressing his senior adviser but never looking away from Liza, "we're done here. We're going to keep security the same, for now, and we're not going to comment publicly about it. We'll talk about it again tomorrow, and you'll let me know the second the FBI gives you word of a specific and credible threat. Roy—"

Roy snapped to attention.

"—I expect you and your company to keep me alive to campaign another day—"

"This is not a *joke*," Liza muttered, disbelieving.

"—and Ms. Wilson, I need to speak with you." The senator's nostrils flared. *"Right. Now."*

"Game over," Takashi whispered.

Like she couldn't see that for herself.

Recovering quickly, Liza barked out an order, which always made her feel better. "Get the shot set up over there, Brad." Gesturing to their camera man, who'd been hovering in the background this whole time, Liza pointed to a couple of chairs facing each other near a potted palm tree in the corner. "I'll have my morning questions for the good senator in a minute."

The senator held his arm wide to direct her down the hall and into a smaller conference room. Whatever. She squared her shoulders, marched inside and pivoted to face him with her arms folded across her chest.

He followed, slamming the door behind them.

"What the hell do you think you're doing?"

"I was pointing out a few obvious things that no one else in the room seemed to think were worth mentioning even though your life is at issue."

He seemed as determined to control his anger and remain professional as she was; only his flashing eyes told her how furious he was.

"You are an invited guest here," he reminded her. "And if you can't remember that, I will get on the phone with your executive producer right now and get you out of here. I knew you had a reputation for being brash, but I thought you could control yourself."

Arrogant jackass. It'd serve him right if some sniper nailed him right in the middle of his oversized head. "A thousand pardons, Senator." She smiled pleasantly. "Please forgive me. Can I ask my questions now? I need to get ready to go live."

Without waiting for any answer—maybe he wasn't done with

her, but she didn't give a damn—she wheeled around and stalked out, leaving him gaping behind her.

"Let's go," she snapped to Takashi when she got back to the main conference room.

"What the hell was that?" he asked her.

Liza glowered. One of the benefits of being the news division's brightest star was that she could occasionally throw her weight around and get away with it. "Don't lecture me, okay? I spoke up in the meeting, I shouldn't have and now we're moving on."

Takashi didn't look as if he was moving on, so she squared her shoulders and put her hands on her hips.

Takashi blinked first.

Score one for Liza.

"What're your plans?" Scowling, Takashi flipped through his clipboard. "You're asking him about the secret service issue and the Francesca Waverly thing, right, and the—"

Liza, who'd pulled out a compact and begun dabbing powder on her face, froze and frowned. "I'm not asking him about that Waverly thing."

Takashi glanced up. "Why not?"

The real answer was, *Because I don't want him to think I'm jealous and/or care about his personal life,* but Liza wasn't about to say that. Instead she shrugged, put the makeup down and inserted her earpiece. "It's a little beneath us, don't you think?"

"No, I don't think," Takashi said, looking at her as though she'd started clucking like a chicken.

"Why not let the tabloids hash it out?"

"Because his poll numbers have taken a hit and it's a real issue, not to mention the fact that every other network is going to be covering it. What's gotten into you, Liza?"

Good question—one she'd been asking herself. But the senator appeared at that moment and saved her from having to answer.

Within five minutes Liza and Senator Warner were seated facing each other under the lights, boom and umbrella, Brad was filming and Adena, Takashi and other staffers were watching.

Though she was still fuming—*what kind of macho idiot refused to ask for the secret service protection that was his due?*—Liza put her game face on for the camera and dove into the questions.

"Senator, other news outlets and bloggers have repeatedly commented on your lack of secret service protection."

An infinitesimal tightening of his jaw told her he didn't appreciate her broaching a topic he'd said the campaign wouldn't discuss. "Mmm."

Liza kept her expression polite and curious as she framed her question so no one would ever know that she thought the senator was making foolish choices. "The FBI has reported a steady stream of Internet chatter against you and the kinds of racist threats that Senator Fitzgerald doesn't receive. As a presidential candidate, you're eligible for Secret Service protection. Why are you refusing to ask for it?"

Whoa. He looked as if he wanted to lunge for her throat.

"I don't see the need for it at this point, Liza." The senator shrugged, recapturing his bland expression. "I'm very well protected. My security team has been with me for years, and they continue to work with local authorities on all our campaign stops. I'm fortunate enough to have the resources to pay for it myself, so why burden the taxpayers with the $45,000 per day expense?"

"The taxpayers may be grateful, Senator, but your supporters are concerned. You've heard the protesters and seen the signs at some of the rallies. Some of this stuff is very nasty and very threatening. Why not take the secret service protection if it's available?"

"Well, again, Liza, I have my security team—"

"A team that isn't in the business of protecting a presidential candidate or managing the sorts of crowds you've been drawing, Senator."

"Listen, Liza—" his pleasant smile never wavered although she saw the hard glint of anger deep in his dark eyes "—no one's more interested in keeping me alive than I am. I'm very well protected, and my team is the best in the world. Down the road we may revisit the issue, but for now I'm satisfied."

"Ask him about the Waverly issue," Takashi hissed in her earpiece. "See if he'll say anything else about his personal life."

Liza pulled her earpiece out and left it dangling on her

shoulder, effectively hanging up on her producer. Takashi would throw a temper tantrum later, but she didn't care. There was no way she could be detached and professional while asking the senator about his personal life on camera. Sorry.

She wrapped up the interview by asking him about the latest economic news, and then her time was up. The second they finished, they stood, dropped the fake smiles and stalked away from each other as fast as they could.

Just as the senator's staff began to buzz among themselves again after being quiet while the camera was rolling, Takashi marched up, looking furious.

"What the hell was that?" He took off the headset through which he'd been speaking to Liza while she was on air. "Why didn't you ask him about Waverly?"

"I was wondering the same thing," said the senator, who'd silently reappeared at her shoulder. Liza winced and hoped she could get away without another confrontation, but no dice. "Can I borrow Liza for a minute, Takashi?"

"Keep her." With a last, withering look, Takashi walked off.

Her heart sinking, Liza braced herself and faced the senator. If only Adena or someone would rush over and demand some of his time, but no, everyone was busy for the moment, scurrying around like busy little bees determined to produce a gallon of honey each before noon, and Liza was on her own.

"Why didn't you ask me about that actress, Liza?"

Uh-oh. The predatory glint in his eye set Liza's nerves on edge and didn't match his benign voice. She tossed her head in what she hoped was an offhand gesture that discouraged further questions. "It would be tacky."

His lip curled without amusement. "Tacky? Really? It wasn't because you were jealous and didn't trust yourself with the topic?"

Chapter 7

The moment stretched until the silence became awkward and, finally, painful. It was hard to laugh gaily when what Liza really wanted to do was scratch his eyes out, but she tried.

"I don't do jealousy, Senator. And I need to get back—"

"Because," he said, plowing resolutely ahead, "I'm not seeing anyone."

He wasn't? *Really?* She worked to keep her expression blank and disinterested.

"How sad for you, Senator."

He ignored this. "Are you? Seeing anyone?"

Luckily, she had a standard answer for this question. "I don't do relationships."

The predatory light in his eyes intensified. So did an unmistakable look of satisfaction.

"You'd do the right relationship."

Just like that he made her hot and bothered again, with flushed skin and squirmy belly. More disgusted with herself than she was with him, she gave him a pitying look and a condescending pat on the arm.

"*The right relationship?* Do you believe in Santa, too, Senator?"

An irritated red flush crept over his face.

"If there's nothing else…"

"There is one more thing, Liza." A muscle ticked in his hard jaw. "Don't they teach you something about being impartial in journalism school? Or am I mistaken?"

Was this about the whole secret service issue? Good. Maybe he could be blasé about his safety but she couldn't, and she had a few more words to say on the topic.

She'd been to the rallies, she'd seen the hatemongers, she'd heard the jeers and the slogans. There were people in this country who wanted the senator dead because he was a black man who had the temerity to campaign for the presidency. She'd stood yards away from people who, for all she knew, were capable of taking a rifle, aiming it at the senator's broad chest and pulling the trigger.

The thought of Senator Warner being hurt, killed…

Ignoring the dread trickling down her spine, she gave him a cool smile.

"So sorry, Senator. I just thought the public needed to know that the man they're thinking of voting into the highest office in the land is too stubborn, arrogant and, frankly, *stupid* to take the most basic steps for his own protection." She waved. "Have a nice day."

As she swept off, she got a satisfying glimpse of his face turning to stone, but then Adena materialized at her side, teeth all but bared, her resemblance to a rabid pit bull a fearsome sight.

"Does it not occur to you, *Liza,*" she snarled, "that maybe it's not a good idea to announce to the world that the senator doesn't have secret service protection?"

"*Announce?*" What? Was Adena for real? "I didn't *announce* it. Everyone already knows."

Adena didn't back down one inch. "You claim you're concerned, and then you harp on it in front of millions of people to boost your ratings—"

Liza opened her mouth to defend herself, but the senator's quiet voice interrupted.

"That's enough, Adena."

"It's *not* enough, John, and I—"

"I said," he repeated with the kind of quiet but vibrating anger that stopped people—even zealots on a righteous mission like Adena—cold in their tracks, "that's *enough*. If you have a problem with Liza, you'll discuss it with me. Understand?"

Choked, her face now a vivid purple, Adena glared at the senator, then Liza. She looked as if she wanted to say something else—Lord help them all if she did—but she seemed to become aware of their audience of staffers, most of whom were now listening openly while pretending to go about their business.

Swallowing hard, struggling for control, Adena hitched her lips into a grimacing, one-sided smile and turned back to the senator. "Oh, I understand." She wheeled toward the door. "Much more than you think."

"Sorry." The senator turned back to Liza, looking embarrassed. "Adena gets a little overprotective at times."

Liza was so astonished to have the senator ride to her defense that she couldn't manage a response, but it didn't matter anyway because he clapped his hands once and spoke to the room at large.

"Let's saddle up, people," he said. "We've got a nomination to win."

Next on the senator's agenda: a pancake breakfast.

After Liza's live appearance on the network's morning show, during which she'd introduced the taped interview, commented on the senator's schedule for the day and answered the anchor's questions about life on the campaign trail, they'd all headed to a fundraiser at a tiny Cleveland diner whose booths were so over-crowded that Liza expected a visit from the fire marshal.

The senator wore one of those heavy white aprons, rolled up his shirtsleeves and went to work behind the grill, connecting with the hardworking voters who formed his base. Then he sat at one of the red vinyl booths, listening intently to the concerns of a steady stream of working-class people.

Liza and Takashi observed it all and Brad duly taped everything for the nightly news segment, and nothing remotely interesting happened until the end, when Liza was searching for her coat.

A wall of bodyguards blocked her from reaching the coatrack. Peering over the nearest burly shoulder to see what was going

Ann Christopher

on—it was almost time to get back on the press bus, and Lord knew they'd leave without her if she was late—she saw Senator Warner pull back from hugging a woman in her forties with sporty auburn hair and vivid blue eyes that were currently wet with unshed tears.

Fascinated, her impatience forgotten, Liza watched the senator's Adam's apple bob as he handed the woman a handkerchief from his back pocket and held her at arm's length.

The woman dabbed her eyes and murmured to him, oblivious to their rapt audience. "—and we didn't understand it. He never smoked a day. He was only thirty-eight."

The senator shook his head, his expression somber. "Way too young. Like Camille. She never smoked, either."

His wife.

Liza's ears pricked because he never talked about his wife or her early death from lung cancer. The dull roar of the crowd over her shoulder was a huge annoyance, and she wished she could yell for everyone to shut up. Edging closer, she strained to hear.

"I never thought he would die," the woman continued. "Right up until the end, I just thought that God wouldn't let anything like that happen. Not to such a good man. Not when we had young children who needed him."

"I understand," the senator said. "You just don't think—"

He broke off, obviously too moved to continue. Watching him, seeing his sadness, Liza felt her heart break a million times.

The woman clutched his forearms tighter and spoke with increased urgency. "You've got to increase funding for *research*. Health insurance for everyone is important, yeah, but so is *research*. I don't want lung cancer to get one more person. Not *one more*."

"I'm going to do everything I can," he told her. "Everything I can."

This was the point in these types of conversations where Liza normally had to fight the urge to gag. Political promises. Yeah, sure, whatever. The candidate was going to try to make the world a better place, with *better place* being subjective and open to interpretation. To the oilmen it meant drilling in the wildlife refuges, and to the environmentalists it meant protecting the wildlife refuges.

For any particular speech it all depended on the makeup of the audience. Blah, blah, blah…sound and fury, signifying nothing, as worthless as leprechaun's gold.

But watching the senator with this widow, knowing he'd lost his beautiful young wife to lung cancer, having read about his incredible philanthropic donations for research over the years and seeing the ferocity in his eyes right now, somehow Liza believed it all: The senator didn't make empty promises; he would do everything possible to increase funding for cancer research, even if he had to personally walk from coast to coast, knocking on doors and asking for donations as he went; and his word—on this and everything else—was good.

Liza didn't want to respect him more, didn't want to believe, but she did.

So did the woman. Reassured, she smiled and wiped her eyes again. "I know you'll do what you can. That's why I came. To meet you and say thanks."

Adena, who was lingering at the senator's elbow, as usual, discreetly cleared her throat and tapped her watch. "John."

The senator nodded and refocused on the woman. "Thanks for coming."

"Oh, you're welcome." The widow waved a hand as though it was nothing to brave sleet to show up at an ungodly prework hour, fight hundreds of people to meet a presidential candidate and eat cold pancakes. "I'm getting remarried, by the way. I never thought I would, but I am. In the spring."

The senator gave her a grin so ecstatic that Liza wondered for a minute if he was going to ask if he could give away the bride. "Congratulations. That's wonderful."

"You should find someone, too," the woman said. "You're still a young man."

"Well." The senator, looking bashful now, hung his head and his ears glowed bright. "I can't exactly register for some online dating service, can I?"

"Don't laugh," the woman said, although she did just that as she smacked his forearm. "There's someone special out there for you. You just need to find her."

"I think I need to focus on one thing at a time," he told the woman. "But I will keep your advice in mind."

They said their goodbyes and the woman was besieged by reporters trying to get her name and interview her about her moment with the senator. Liza could see the headlines now: Widow Shares Tears with Warner, Gives Dating Advice. Then the senator allowed his handlers to steer him toward the door.

Liza backed up to give the entourage space because it was either that or risk being flattened by the nearest giant, but the senator glanced at her and raised his voice to be heard over the general roar.

"How'd you like my pancakes, Liza?" he called.

What? He knew she was right there in this roomful of people?

If only he'd stop catching her off guard. If only he'd stop affecting her so much and worming his way under her skin. It irritated the hell out of her.

Pursing her lips, determined not to simper or possibly faint like a rabid fan at a rap concert, Liza remembered her duties.

She was a journalist doing her job. Period. There was no room for anything else.

"Your pancakes were too pale, Senator. Brown them more the next time."

Throwing back his head, he laughed and lingered when the flunkeys would have shuttled him through the vestibule and into the gleaming black SUV idling at the curb.

"There you go being prickly again, Liza. Or is it just me?"

What was it about the way he said her name? It threw her off every time. A husky note was there, a slight deepening of his voice and something indefinable that made her name a little more special when *he* said it.

And she was absolutely losing her ever-loving mind if she imagined undying lust in every syllable the poor man uttered to her.

Liza shot him a cool smile, the one she gave the paparazzi whenever they surprised her on the street, and hoped she looked bored rather than bewildered by her sudden longing for things she shouldn't want.

"Prickly?" She raised her eyebrows. "I've been taking it easy on you, Senator."

He laughed again and that beautiful, good-natured sound echoed right through her. Turning quickly away, she wished she could clap her hands over her ears and block it out.

* * *

This was one of the best parts of the job, no question.

Elementary school visits, where he got to wear khakis and a shirt rather than those stupid suits and ties. Mrs. Barnes's first-grade classroom. Colorful pictures of Thomas Jefferson and Lewis and Clark on the walls, along with the alphabet in cursive and an enormous world map. A papier mâché model of the solar system, including a huge orange-and-yellow sun, hanging from clear strings overhead. The smell of chalk, crayons and questionable lunch items wafting from the cafeteria. What could be better?

John sat cross-legged on the floor with a cute little future diva with a thousand beaded braids plunked in his lap. She'd commandeered this place of honor early on and showed no signs of ever getting up. All around him in a semicircle were adorable bright faces with gap-toothed smiles and the occasional milk mustache. On the floor beside him sat Dr. Seuss's *One Fish, Two Fish*, which the little monsters had thoroughly enjoyed listening to him mangle.

A few members of his staff and the press, including Liza, to whom he'd tried to give a wide berth in the last several days, lined the perimeter of the classroom and watched and filmed the proceedings. Mrs. Barnes hovered, making sure her little charges didn't say or do anything too outrageous or embarrassing. The poor woman was so flustered and nervous by this circus descending on her classroom that John could almost laugh. He wanted to take her aside and tell her not to worry, that he loved children in all their unpredictability, but he was afraid it would send her into cardiac arrest.

"One more question," John said, pointing to a blond boy on the end. "You've had a hand up for a while. What's your name?"

The boy lowered his hand and sat up straighter, grinning so hard he was in danger of splitting his cheeks. "John."

"*John.* Good name." Everyone tittered and Mrs. Barnes looked pleased. "What's your question for me?"

"I wanted a Pop-Tart for breakfast, but my mom made me eat oatmeal." John scrunched his face, leaving no doubt about his opinion on oatmeal. "I don't think that's fair. Can you write her a note and tell her it's okay for me to eat Pop-Tarts?"

"Wow, John." John tried not to laugh. Clearly this was a serious issue in this young man's life. "I'm not sure I have any power over moms and breakfast items. Have you tried any honey or brown sugar on your oatmeal? That might help."

"Nothing helps," the boy said flatly.

"Tell you what," John said. "Why don't you offer your mom a compromise to see if you can both be happy? You tell her that on school days you'll eat your oatmeal—*without complaining*—"

John groaned.

"—if she'll let you eat Pop-Tarts on the weekends. Could that work?"

John brightened. "I'll try it. Thanks, John."

This was too much for Mrs. Barnes, who turned a thousand shades of purple and leaned in to bark at the boy in a stage whisper.

"*John.* Please call him Senator Warner. Where are your manners?"

"It's okay, Mrs. Barnes." Scooting the little diva off his lap and standing at last—man, his creaky knees were getting too old for this floor sitting—he smiled and caught his soccer ball when Adena tossed it to him. "We're all friends here. Who wants to play a quick game of soccer with me before I have to go?"

A joyous cheer rose up from the kids, and there was a crazy scramble to get lined up at the door. This gave John the cover he needed to check on one little girl in the corner. He'd been worried about her the whole time he was there.

She was glum. Despite her cute little blue dress and tights, which he knew should cheer up any young girl, she'd hardly smiled at all, and even her sandy shoulder-length curls seemed to droop. John edged around the general chaos and gave her a grave look.

"Hi," he said.

"Hi." She dimpled but didn't give him the full smile.

"What's your name?"

"Maggie."

"Tough day, Maggie?"

"Yeah." She drew out the word, making it at least three syllables.

"What's up?"

She handed him a picture and swiped at her enormous blue eyes, which were now sparkling with tears. "It's Sampson."

John studied the shot, which was of a clear glass tank. Inside was a green frog with bulging red eyes surrounded by all kinds of rocks and plants.

"Sampson?"

"He's dead."

"Oh, no."

"When I went to feed him this morning, he was all shriveled and...dead."

"I'm so sorry," John told her. "Will you have a funeral?"

"After school."

They stared at each other, and John wished he could ease the weight of the world off her tiny shoulders. Yeah, he'd like to solve the Social Security problem, but this was a real issue, too.

"Should we say a prayer?"

Maggie sniffled. "Okay."

They joined hands and bowed their heads. "God, please look after Sampson, who was a good and loving frog. Please welcome him into heaven and give him a nice pond to swim in, giant lily pads to jump on and, ah, lots of juicy flies to eat."

John cracked one eye open and checked with Maggie. "Anything else?"

"And a nice log to hide in."

"And a nice log to hide in," he added. "Amen."

"Amen."

John tried to give her back the picture, but she didn't want it.

"You keep it," she told him. "So you'll never forget Sampson."

What a sweet child. He'd sure love two or three like this one someday. John pressed the picture to his heart and smiled at her. "Thank you, Maggie."

Beaming, she bounced off to join her comrades in line just as Adena materialized at his elbow.

"How long do we have for soccer?" he asked her. "I was hoping—what the hell are they doing?"

Adena looked around in surprise. "Huh?"

He waved at Liza, Takashi and Brad, who were standing a few feet away, watching him rather than packing their stuff up and getting ready to go like everyone else. John stared at them with dawning irritation.

Had they just filmed that whole thing with him and Maggie? Probably. Brad's camera was out.

Incensed, John stalked over to confront Liza, who was at the root of a whole host of his problems these days. Takashi and Brad barely registered with his consciousness.

"What's going on?" he demanded.

"Excuse me?"

The benign innocence in her big baby browns didn't fool him for a minute. Taking her arm, he steered her a few feet away, behind the divider that hid Mrs. Barnes's supplies from the rest of the room.

Liza snatched free, looking affronted. "What's the problem?"

"The problem is that that was a private moment between me and a little girl who's lost her frog, and I don't want it splashed all over the news tonight like I'm trying to win points for—"

"I know it was a private moment."

"Then why the hell were you film—"

"If you weren't so busy attacking me and gave me the chance to explain, *Senator,* I could tell you that Takashi wanted to film, but I asked him not to, so we didn't."

John blinked. "You…didn't?"

"No."

The wind whooshed right out of his sails. Didn't he feel like an idiot? Hanging his head, he rubbed the back of his neck and began his obligatory apology. "I'm, ah, sorry for—"

"Oh, don't apologize." Holding up a hand to stop him mid-speech, she backed up a step and flashed what was, quite possibly, the smuggest smirk he'd ever seen. "I'm going to enjoy having you under my thumb for a while. Your guilt should make you extra nice to me, don't you think?"

Damn, he wanted this woman. "Liza," he said with utmost sincerity, "I'd be thrilled to be under your thumb or anywhere else you'd like to put me."

Whoa. Had he said that out loud?

Yeah, apparently.

A pretty flush colored her face, and for just a fleeting second, he saw the flash of heat in her glittering eyes. She almost smiled. But then she caught herself and gave him a severe look instead.

The heat was still there, though. Banked, but still there.

"Let's go, Senator," she said. "Don't you have a schedule to keep?"

Pivoting on her heel, she swept out, leaving his pulse thundering at the base of his throat and his mouth dry.

John wrapped up a Sitchroo meeting at their Washington headquarters on the fourth floor of an office building and looked around for Liza. In a disheartening sign of how far gone he was for that woman, he was eager to submit to another interview or, come to think of it, any other activity that meant one-on-one contact with her.

Through God's grace and a whole lot of self-discipline, he'd managed to ignore his growing obsession with Liza for the last few weeks.

Glory hallelujah.

Just today he'd toured a factory, given a keynote address at a luncheon and spoken at the university, all without thinking of Liza much at all.

He was the man.

But…

Right now she was all he could think of, all he could see.

What was up with that?

Until she walked into his life, he never had a problem with distractions. He'd focused on his work because it was his calling, and that was the end of the story. Either he wanted to be president and worked toward that goal, or he didn't. Simple.

Seeing the world in black and white was a natural side effect of being a man with strong convictions, and he couldn't have come this far in his career without believing in a few core values.

Sure, he was happy to work with his colleagues on the other side of the aisle, and he had a well-earned reputation in the Senate as a consensus builder, but he never lost sight of the big picture, or of the things that were important to his agenda for the country.

He was always clear on where he stood, where he needed to be and how he needed to get there.

Until it came to Liza Wilson, the woman who made him feel like a junior varsity basketball player who'd accidentally wandered onto the court with the Celtics team during the finals: overmatched, outwitted and in serious danger of getting hurt. Until Liza Wilson planted the unwelcome thought in his brain that there could be more to life than work.

The situation was his damn fault. He should've ignored his attraction to the woman. Shouldn't've dreamt up the whole misguided *Inside Sitchroo* thing. Sure as hell shouldn't've selected Liza for the project. Shouldn't've talked to her alone that night, shouldn't seek her out, like he'd done at the pancake breakfast, and shouldn't be straining his brain, right this very second, to manufacture a reason and opportunity to spend time alone with her again as soon as possible.

Yeah, he shouldn't. But he would. He couldn't help himself.

There was something irresistible about the keen intelligence in her cool dark eyes, something about her unexpected flashes of warmth that lured him like a bear to an open jar of marshmallow fluff.

What would it take to make her warm up to him all the time? How could he get her to look at him the way she had that first night when they were alone?

Why was he even asking himself questions like this?

Because at some point during this interminable day he'd decided that they were going to be lovers.

Crazy? Yeah. Risky? You betcha. But that's what he was going to do.

The competitor in him couldn't resist a challenge or a puzzle. She was both. The strategist in him needed to tackle complex problems, and structuring an affair with a woman covering his campaign without blowing up both their careers was as tricky a situation as he was likely to get this side of a set of peace talks.

The man in him just wanted her.

Her smile, her warmth, her laughter. Her strength and intelligence.

Most of all he wanted her willing body in his arms.

With careful planning he could have it all. He was nothing if not a careful planner, and there was no time like the present to start.

John headed to the back corner of the conference room, where two chairs sat facing each other in front of a blue backdrop with the lighting umbrella overhead. As usual, Takashi looked around and acted as if he cared that John had arrived. Liza, who was now stooped over her open laptop on the conference table, didn't.

Liza's fierce insistence on ignoring him gave John a perverse satisfaction, and he had to stifle his Cheshire cat grin. He must really get to her if she had to work so hard to feign indifference whenever he showed up.

"We're starting at five-thirty tomorrow." John shook Takashi's hand. "Busy day."

"How nice." Liza snapped her computer closed. "We get to sleep almost as late as the roosters do."

John and Takashi both laughed, to her apparent irritation. At last she looked up at John, her brown eyes flinty.

"Are you ready, Senator? I've got some questions for you, and then I'd like to eat a whole yak because I'm starving."

"Liza's a people person, Senator." Takashi grinned. "Just so you know."

John gave her a grave look. "I'm sorry that covering my campaign is such an inconvenience for you, Liza."

"Oh, don't worry." She brightened a little and one corner of her mouth turned up in about a fourth of a smile. "I keep thinking about the Emmy I'll probably win for campaign coverage, and that keeps me going. Are we ready?"

John sat down and braced himself for a barrage of questions about his personal life, which the press had been hammering relentlessly. The interlude with the widow at the breakfast a while back had opened the whole can of worms and he hadn't managed to get the lid back on, but he was trying. Not everything should be trotted out and used as a campaign issue when convenient. Some things were personal and sacrosanct, such as his memories of his wife.

Even if the outlines of those precious recollections were growing vague.

Fearing the worst, John squared his shoulders, then realized he was doing it and forced himself to relax. The last thing he wanted was to look constipated during this interview, even if every on-camera encounter with Liza did shorten his life by a year.

Liza smiled her shrewd journalist's smile at him and opened

her mouth, and he felt as though he'd been caught squarely in the sights of a hunter's rifle. But then, once again, Liza surprised him.

"Senator, you come from a wealthy family and you had an Ivy League education. You've been dogged almost from the first moment you entered public life with complaints that you're out of touch with the working-class people who form your voting base and—"

John raised an eyebrow.

"—this morning, you played water polo with your staff, which is a sport a lot of folks are unfamiliar with. On the other hand, you've met with factory workers all over the country and worked the grill at a pancake breakfast. Senator Fitzgerald's chief of staff has already called the pancake breakfast a—and I'm quoting here, Senator—" Liza glanced down at her notes, then back up at him "—'stunt designed to show the voters that he was born with a plastic spoon in his mouth rather than a platinum spoon.'"

Plastic spoon? That was a new one. Pretty funny, actually.

"Senator, is there anything you can do to get past these ongoing claims that you're an elitist who's out of touch with the common voter?"

"Well, I don't think there's anything I can do to convince Senator Fitzgerald's chief of staff that I'm not an elitist, so I'm not going to try to win that battle." He shrugged. "But I don't think there's a kid anywhere who's ever been in a pool and not tossed around the ball with his or her friends and tried to score a goal. You can call it water polo or you can call it tossing around a ball in the pool. It's the same thing."

Liza, as usual, was not to be diverted. "True, but Senator, you had your own pool in your backyard when you grew up. Most people can't say that. Most people don't have servants or a prepaid higher education. Is there something to Senator Fitzgerald's claims that she can better understand the problems of the working class?"

"Liza, just because I had a pool growing up doesn't mean I can't look around and take an interest in working Americans. Going to a good college didn't make me deaf, dumb and blind. I want every American to have the same sorts of privileges—for themselves and for their children—that I had growing up. That's my bottom line."

Liza followed up by asking a couple of questions about his schedule for the week. John answered, still feeling tense, until he belatedly realized that Liza had no intention of asking him about his personal life or lack thereof.

Why? Did a woman's tender heart beat for him underneath all that journalistic armor? Was Liza respecting his zone of privacy?

"Thanks, Senator."

Liza stood and gave him that distant smile, the one that always said she was finished with him and hoped she wouldn't have to deal with him again anytime soon—the one that drove John out of his freaking mind. Turning away, she went back to her laptop.

Irritation prickled John's throat. Dismissed again. You'd think he'd be used to it by now, but no. Here he was, a United States Senator and presidential candidate, and it didn't mean jack to Liza. He wondered if the sitting president would receive better treatment from her and decided he probably wouldn't.

At least he was in good company, eh?

The enormous conference room was quieter now, with only Barbara off in a corner talking with Adena and Takashi making a phone call. Edging closer to Liza, John leaned a hip against the table and indulged his curiosity.

"Why haven't you asked me about my personal life?"

Chapter 8

Liza straightened. One side of her hair had slipped over her face, giving her that deliciously sexy, rumpled look, as though she'd just risen from bed after a long afternoon of making love. But her eyes were not the sultry, half-lowered eyes of a well-satisfied woman; they were the troubled eyes of a person who'd been asked a difficult question she preferred not to answer.

"I haven't seen the need." Fidgeting, she smoothed her hair behind her ear and then checked her watch and tried to look bored. John wasn't fooled for a minute. "I'm happy to ask you about it now, if you want. Since you seem so disappointed in my interviewing skills today."

So, she was sensitive to his feelings. A surge of satisfaction ran through him at the discovery that Liza Wilson did have a heart even if she kept it encased behind several layers of stone, barbed wire and cut glass.

"You've never asked me about my wife, either," he continued.

She looked up, exasperation etched in every line of her pursed lips. "Maybe you'd like to submit a list of questions for me to ask you next time, Senator?… Then you can be officially in charge. How would that be?"

"I think it's worth noting that you're not as prickly as you act."

Liza didn't like this. Shooting a death ray or two at him from her narrowed eyes, she squared her shoulders. "I'm prickly enough, Senator."

Maybe, but he could deal with a few jabs from her spiny barbs when the payoff promised to be so spectacular. It was time for him to start working on the wall between them, remove a brick or two.

If he opened up a little, maybe she would, too.

"Camille's been dead for a long time now," he said softly. "It's hard to picture her face sometimes." Because he didn't want to scare Liza, he left out the part about his memory of Camille receding faster the more time he spent with Liza.

"Oh," Liza said.

He waited and his patience was rewarded when something wonderful happened: *Liza* edged closer to *him,* a look of concern and understanding in her eyes. And he couldn't have been happier even if the party suddenly decided to forgo the nomination process and declare him the presumptive nominee right now.

"That's normal," she told him. "It doesn't mean that you're a terrible person or that you didn't love her."

"No?"

"No. She didn't want you to die with her, did she?"

Of course not. Camille was the soul of generosity and had encouraged him to find someone else after she died. He'd just never wanted to.

"I wasn't a perfect husband," he said, the understatement of the millennium.

"I'm sure you weren't, but imperfection from you is probably better than perfection from someone else."

They stared at each other while he struggled with the unruly urge to touch her, to announce his intentions outright. "I, ah," he said, his thought process trailing well behind the words coming out of his mouth because of the way she was looking at him, "I don't know what made me tell you that. You're probably going to ask to be switched to Senator Fitzgerald's campaign now. Then you'd only have to listen to her chatter about her cats."

Liza struggled for a minute. He could tell that she didn't want to relax and lower her barriers against him, even if it was only for this one brief second, but in the end she couldn't help it. Her grin, when it came, nearly knocked the breath out of him.

He'd never seen anything so beautiful.

"I'm not big on cats," she told him.

"No?"

"No."

"What about you?" he asked, deciding to push his luck a little. "You've been divorced for a long time, right?"

This topic stripped the smile right off her face. "Not long enough."

Careful, Warner. Don't scare her off. "What happened?"

Something bad judging by her scowl. Predictably, she tried to put the brakes on the whole conversation. "I'm sorry," she said sweetly, "but when did we start playing twenty questions?"

"I just told you something personal. This is only fair."

Worry lines creased her forehead as she gave him a wary once-over.

"What are all these personal details leading to, Senator?"

Oh, no. He wasn't about to show his hand. Yet.

"To a conversation, Liza. That's where two people talk, information is exchanged and fun is periodically had. Maybe you've heard of the concept?... So what happened with your husband?"

After another hesitation, she apparently decided the easiest thing to do was to answer his question and get it over with.

"He cheated on me while I was on assignment. He had several affairs."

She told him with a bare minimum of inflection, but the naked pain in her eyes said it all. John wanted to kill the SOB for hurting her and for making John's job in gaining her trust that much more difficult.

On the other hand, if the idiot had been a great husband, then John wouldn't be here with Liza now, so it was all good.

Well... No. He'd still like to hurt the man. Maybe if he won the election, he'd sic the IRS on the punk for a thorough audit. That could be fun.

"The last time with his boss's wife," Liza added.

John reined in his temper, hard. "Ouch."

"Oh, don't worry." She flashed a smile vindictive enough to shrink the testicles of the nearest male wrongdoer. "I hired a detective, who got all kinds of pictures for me. You'd be surprised how generous my husband was with the settlement after that."

John wasn't surprised; he'd expected this kind of painful fate for a man stupid enough to throw Liza away and foolish enough to underestimate her. He laughed.

"Good for you."

Liza's brow furrowed with open suspicion. "Don't you want to stick up for the Universal Brotherhood of Men?"

"I'd rather stick up for you. Tell me," he said quickly, changing the subject to keep her off guard and talking for as long as possible, "what're you doing during the break next week? It's our last chance to relax before Super Tuesday. I'll be spending time with my sister."

She blinked, looking unsettled by the sudden change of subject. "I, ah…I'll be cooking dinner with my father at my house. He doesn't get out much, and I've been traveling, so I want to spend some time with him."

"What'll you cook?"

"Chinese, probably. It's his favorite. He'll probably bake molasses cookies. They're my favorite."

A violent pang of longing caught John unawares, hitting him right in the chest, and it wasn't about the cookies. "Sounds like fun." He cleared his throat. "I'm sure he's looking forward to it."

"Yeah, well. If he remembers. I don't know how much longer he'll be able to leave the home to spend time with me, so I want to do it while we can."

John nodded and absorbed this information, filing it away for later. "All your travel must make that hard for you."

Liza gave him an accusatory scowl. "If only you presidential candidates would stay in Washington all the time and make my life easier."

"Don't worry." John laughed. "I plan to stay in Washington. You can look for me at 1600 Pennsylvania Avenue."

"There's that ego again."

The muttering didn't fool him—not with the smile playing around her lips. "But what about when you get the anchor's chair? Won't you have to move to New York? What'll you do with your father then?"

A shadow crossed her face. "I don't know. I haven't gotten that far yet."

"What about the travel? It won't let up much, will it?"

"No. I'll still be on the road way too much."

John filed all of this away for later too. "Hmm."

The conversation trailed off. Some distant corner of his mind warned that he might be staring and, worse, might have some sort of goofy heart-on-his-sleeve expression on his face, but those things were beyond his control with Liza around.

He could have stood like that forever, marveling at the thrill of having a plain-vanilla conversation with her without jockeying or bickering, when someone put a light hand on his arm, jarring him back to the real world.

Damn.

Why couldn't people just leave him alone?

Irritated, he looked around and saw his younger sister, Jillian, her brows quirked with bemusement. As always, her short black curls provided a pretty frame for her heart-shaped face, and her light brown eyes sparkled up at him.

John was glad to see her, this interruption notwithstanding. She'd met up with the group after campaigning for him out west and had been making calls down the hall in his office.

"John?" She spoke gently, as though waking a sleepwalker. "Should I come back later, or—?"

"You're fine."

Jillian turned to Liza, her eyes wide with speculation and interest. Extending a hand, she smiled. "Liza, it's so nice to finally meet you. I've watched you for years."

They shook hands and John belatedly remembered his manners. "Liza, this is my sister—"

"Jillian Warner Taylor." Liza shot him a tart look. "First lady of Virginia. Married to the governor, whom she met when they were both in law school. I've heard of her once or twice, Senator."

Jillian, who'd never met a person who didn't become an instant friend, laughed. "I like her, John."

"Great," John muttered.

Liza pursed her lips at him before turning to Jillian. "It's a pleasure to meet you. I'd better grab Takashi and get out of here. We start early tomorrow."

She left. Jillian stared after her, looking speculative. Finally, she turned to John and the knowing light in her eyes was so bright that he almost wanted to reach for sunglasses.

"She seems nice."

John shrugged. "She can be nice, on occasion. Usually by accident."

"You were staring at her when I walked up."

Uh-oh. He knew it. Here it came. "Really?"

"Yeah. Like you wanted to swallow her whole as soon as possible. You want her. Don't deny it."

"Wouldn't dream of it."

Jillian clapped and gave a little hop of excitement. "What are you going to do? Can I help?"

"I might enlist your help. Consider yourself on standby."

"Good."

John took a good look at her and didn't like what he saw. She had the sad eyes and drawn face that were becoming way too familiar. She and Beau were still having problems, then. He'd bet money on it.

"You feeling okay?" he asked.

"Fine."

John doubted it, but hope sprang eternal. "And…with you and Beau?"

"Fine," she said again. "But after the, ah…incident, things have been a little, ah, difficult. We're working on it, though."

Incident. So that was what they were calling it. The dark period a year and a half ago when the governor's criminally indiscreet e-mails had led to the press's revelation that the idiot had been having an affair with his personal assistant.

That had been a pleasant time.

As though it had been ten minutes ago, John could recall every detail of the resulting meltdown, both politically and personally. The frantic, middle-of-the-night phone calls. The endless consultations with the public relations heavy hitters. The excruciating meetings with party leaders, both local and national.

Worst of all, he remembered Jillian's behind-the-scenes devastation and her public bravery as she stood by her husband's side at the podium for the inevitable press conference apology. The governor had apologized to his wife and the public, sworn to mend his ways and retired into seclusion to "reevaluate and refocus his life."

How any of them made it through that whole apology without vomiting was something John would never know. The miraculous upshot was that Jillian had forgiven him; the governor had kept his job with a lot of skillful wrangling and crisis management by Adena, the party's chief strategist extraordinaire; and everyone's political life had proceeded normally.

There was no telling what Beau had told Jillian in private, but John figured it had been one hell of an apology followed by a lot of begging. John had warned her against trusting her husband again, but Jillian, as always, made her own choices, and John supposed he couldn't blame her. Beau did love Jillian. Even John could see it in the way the man looked at her. But he and Jillian had weathered several crises in their years together and Beau had self-destructive demons that made him do terrible things. John had never understood his brother-in-law, even a little.

Big deal, right? John wasn't married to him.

The bottom line was that Jillian and the governor had elected to stay together and try to heal their marriage. How much actual healing had gone on was up for debate.

Nevertheless, as Jillian's loving elder brother, it was John's solemn responsibility to support her choices. For now, anyway. For later he might have to pick up the pieces. They'd been picking up each other's pieces since Mom died when they were young, and that would never change.

"Working on it, huh?" John tried to smile. "Good for you."

"Back to you." Jillian leaned close, all earnest helpfulness and enthusiasm. John rolled his eyes. "What if you're elected—"

"I *will* be elected," John said sourly. "Have a little faith."

"You're not planning on four years—"

"Eight."

"—of celibacy, are you?"

Eight years of celibacy? With this kind of fire burning in his blood for Liza? Absolutely not. John shuddered at the thought of such unendurable torture.

"I don't plan to be celibate at all. The funny thing is," he confessed softly before thinking better of it, "I—forget it."

"What?"

Feeling like the worst kind of jerk, he told his sister one of his guiltiest secrets. "I'll always love Camille. But she's dead and I'm not. And I'm having a tough time remembering her face. I can't even hear her voice anymore."

Jillian squeezed his hand with infinite understanding. "You loved Camille, but she was a first love when you were still wet behind the ears. You've changed a lot since then. And she's been dead for a long time."

This was all true, as far as it went, but there was more going on.

Camille had been sweet and fragile. Liza was strong and fierce. Camille had been smart but uncomplicated. Liza was a brilliant and fascinating puzzle. John had become Camille's whole life. Liza had a big, interesting life in which John would be lucky to eke out a tiny space for himself.

Though it killed him to admit it, there were terrible moments when he thought that if Camille had lived, he would have outgrown her in a few more years. A woman like Liza, on the other hand, was endlessly fascinating.

Most of all, Camille had been sexy.

Liza stopped his breath whenever she walked into the room.

There was no telling how long he may have stared across the room, lost in thoughts of Liza, when Jillian's awed voice brought him back to reality.

"This is more about Liza than it is about Camille. Isn't it?"

Oh, no. John wasn't making any admissions. Not tonight.

"Don't even try—"

His automatic denial stopped dead in his throat when he saw Liza walk by the open conference room door. She had her briefcase in hand and her coat slung over her arm and was obviously heading home for the night.

And John was hit with a wave of yearning so fierce it almost flattened him to a smudge on the floor. He could no more let Liza go without reaching out to her again than he could sing backup for Aretha Franklin.

"Excuse me," he told Jillian.

Past caring what his sister would make of his behavior, he got up and dashed after Liza, who had, by now, left the office suite through the double glass doors and was stepping onto the elevator.

There was no time to think about it. Ignoring his security people calling after him with vague alarm, he followed Liza onto the elevator just as the doors slid shut.

Then they were alone.

Blessedly, absolutely and completely alone.

He leaned against the brass rail at the back of the car so that they stood side by side, both facing the front. His fingers itched to touch her, and the only way he could control his hands was to shove them deep into the pockets of his slacks with a stern warning to himself: *Don't do it, man.*

Staring straight ahead into the mirror, he could see her tense face, and he knew that if he touched her, she'd hit the alarm or something and it'd be all over for him.

So he worked on playing it cool.

"Hi."

"Hi," she said.

He looked up at the lighted numbers, trying not to sound as desperate as he was.

"Have dinner with me."

She hesitated, giving him courage, but then sent him straight to hell. "No."

"We can order pizza—"

"No."

"—or just have a drink."

"I can't."

"You could."

Another, longer hesitation had his hopes rising again, but not for long.

"I won't, Senator."

The car stopped and the bell dinged. John's stomach plummeted as though the elevator's cable had snapped and they'd fallen a hundred stories.

This was it, then. He had to let her go.

Screw that.

Throwing caution to the wind, he yanked his hands out of his pockets and punched the stop button before the doors could open.

She didn't like this at all. "Please."

For once there was no attitude or bravado in her voice or expression. She was just a woman now. A scared, vulnerable woman who wanted him as much as he wanted her and was too paralyzed to admit it.

Keep your distance man. Keep it quiet and gentle. Give her space.

Turning, he did his level best to keep the burning intensity he was feeling out of his eyes as he faced her.

"What can I do?" he asked.

"Nothing."

"How can I get you to think about the possibility—"

"You can't."

"—of a relationship with me?"

"It's not going to happen."

"It's happening, Liza."

They stared at each other, the tension ratcheting higher between them until John thought his entire body might shatter. Her eyes glittered and her harsh breath came in shallow puffs and he knew—he *knew*—that she was right there with him and only needed the tiniest little push to get past this hurdle.

"I think about you," he said helplessly. "If you had any idea—"

Like a miracle, she softened, right before his eyes.

"You have a couple other things you should be thinking about, don't you, Senator?"

Man, she'd hit that nail on the head. All his choked emotion converged in his throat and he shrugged, trying to laugh. "You wouldn't know it."

An almost-smile lit her face, telling him to take the chance. Touch her.

So he held out a hand and prayed she wouldn't leave him hanging.

She didn't. After a tiny pause, she reached for him and her soft, cool palm slid against his, the most perfect fit he could imagine. The contact zinged between them, and he saw the surprise in her wide eyes. When she tried to step away, he exerted enough gentle pressure to reel her in until she was right there.

Right *there*.

Because his retinas felt like they were burning, he couldn't stare at her incredible face. So he stared down at her palm instead. Traced circles in it with his thumb. Absorbed her shivering gasp up his arm and into his body. Then he raised that palm to his lips and kissed it.

Her breath caught and, man, he could swear his heart stopped.

Careful, Warner. Don't blow it now.

Taking all the time in the world, he lowered that precious hand back to her side and let it go. Only then, when he was no longer touching her and he thought he could handle it, did he look back in her gleaming eyes and try to speak.

He only prayed his voice still worked.

"Think about it," he told her. "Okay?"

"Okay."

Thank you, God.

The words were right on his lips, but he somehow kept his cool and didn't say them. Punching the door open button, he waited for the doors to slide open and strode off into the lobby, resisting the urge to shout and skip.

His night had been a complete success. If only Super Tuesday could go half that well.

Chapter 9

"What are you doing here?" Liza asked Takashi ungraciously when she opened her front door the next week on their campaign break to find him standing on the steps of her Georgetown brownstone.

Takashi scowled, his face shadowed by the porch light, and Liza felt a moment's guilt for being cranky, but then she thought better of it. If Takashi didn't want to deal with a cranky woman, he had no business showing up unannounced at her house at the end of a long day.

Especially when she was juggling both her growing feelings for the senator and her Alzheimer's-ridden rascal of a father, who was, even now, puttering around in her gourmet kitchen, baking cookies.

Part of her grouchiness was because she never got to spend enough time unwinding alone inside the three stories of her exquisitely decorated house. Even though she'd taken great care to pick out every earth-toned shade on her walls, every Indian rug on her hardwood floors and every pillow and cashmere throw on her overstuffed chairs and sofas, she could never enjoy her bounty because she was always leaving it to cover the latest story.

Lately she never even bothered to unpack her bags. Nothing felt permanent; everything was temporary.

She was getting too damn old and tired for this lifestyle.

"I'm sure I'm going to regret this," Takashi said, "but…can I come in?"

Liza put a hand on her hip, swung the heavy six-paneled door open wide and studied Takashi with narrowed eyes as he walked inside. He didn't look any too happy to be there—about like an unfortunate pirate walking the gangplank with his hands tied behind his back—and she had a bad feeling about his visit.

Shutting the door behind him, she turned and, without a word, led him into her high-ceilinged living room, where they sat on the sofa. "I wasn't expecting company," she warned, waving vaguely at her tank top, low-slung yoga pants and bare feet.

"I understand." He tossed his leather jacket on the nearest chair.

"I took my shower, washed my hair and wiped off all my makeup." Fixing him with a stern look, she ruffled a hand through her curly wet hair, which was not the sleek bob he no doubt expected. "I'm grumpier than usual. Just so you know."

"You smell good, though."

He picked up her plate from the coffee table and sniffed hopefully at the Kung Pao scallops. His wicked grin was, as usual, irresistible, and Liza couldn't help dimpling at him. Catching herself, she frowned and picked up her chopsticks.

"Don't expect me to share, either." She snatched the plate back.

"Why not?" Without missing a beat, he reclaimed the plate, relieved her of her chopsticks and took a large bite of her dinner. "What is this anyway?"

Liza glared. "It's *Asian* food. You should be somewhat familiar with it."

"Got any sushi?"

"I'm just looking for a person to kill, Nakamura," she said. "Don't let it be you."

Takashi laughed. Before she could demand to know what he was doing there, they heard a rattling sound in the kitchen and the Colonel came and stood in the huge arched doorway, a sheet of steaming molasses cookies in one mitt-clad hand and a spatula in the other.

Tall and wiry except for his paunch, slightly stooped and moving a little slower these days, the Colonel was as dapper as ever with his starched blue oxford shirt and khaki pants ironed to a razor-edged crease.

He stared uncomprehending at Takashi for a moment—Liza held her breath and prayed he'd recognize Takashi even though he hadn't seen him in a few months—but then his expression cleared and his eyes sharpened behind their Malcolm X glasses. He nodded curtly and grunted. This greeting from the Colonel was the rough equivalent of a bear hug from anyone else.

"Takashi." He held out the tray. "You want a cookie while they're hot?"

"He's not staying," Liza said.

Too late. Takashi was already on his feet and gingerly picking up several cookies. "How are you, Colonel? Keeping out of trouble?"

"Well, Liza's got me locked up in a home now." The Colonel frowned across at her, but Liza didn't rise to the bait. "Can't drive, can't leave, can't cook. Grown man treated like a child. Saddest thing you've ever seen, Takashi. Guess I'm lucky she doesn't try to wipe my ass for me."

Finished with his list of complaints, the Colonel turned and shuffled back into the kitchen while Takashi tried to stifle a startled snort of laughter and Liza rolled her eyes at the ceiling.

"You want some milk with those cookies?" the Colonel called over his shoulder as he disappeared.

"No, thanks," Takashi said.

"Good times," Liza muttered. "Good times."

They sat listening to the Colonel move around in the kitchen for a few minutes while Takashi wolfed down food as though he hadn't eaten in three years. Then Takashi spoke out of the side of his mouth.

"You're cruisin' for a bruisin', Za-Za. You know that, don't you?"

So that's what this unannounced visit was about. She'd figured as much, but that didn't make it easy to meet his troubled expression. Shrugging, she tried to sound unconcerned.

"I've got no idea what you're talking about."

"Oh, I think you do," he said easily, watching her as he reached for a spring roll and polished it off in a single bite. "We live in a bubble. I've seen you and the senator together, and there's talk—"

"What *talk?*"

"So far it's just been a couple of rude jokes about how the senator looks as if he'd like to warm you up a little."

"Oh, God." On top of everything else, people thought she was frigid. Wonderful. Could this whole situation get any worse?

"If this keeps up, there'll be more talk and it'll be worse than that."

Liza stared down at her coffee table, cheeks burning, effectively silenced for once in her life. She opened her mouth and floundered because what could she say without committing career suicide?

I'm attracted to the senator.

I'm losing all my objectivity.

I want to be a woman, not a journalist.

Yeah. That could work.

On the other hand, wasn't she headed for career suicide anyway? Takashi and Adena had already noticed the chemistry between her and the senator; despite all of Liza's best efforts, her poker face seemed to be failing—and failing *spectacularly*— when it came to John Warner.

How long until someone else noticed and commented on it?

Worse, how long until she did something stupid? It wasn't as if she had an iron grip on her feelings. Or any grip on her feelings, come to think of it. What would happen if they had another interlude on an elevator? Would she kiss him again? Probably. The thought made her shudder with dismay and shiver with anticipation.

Reminding herself that lots of women were attracted to the senator did nothing to cool her overheated blood. Much as she wanted to, she couldn't write off her situation as an attraction to a handsome and powerful man. Nor could she write it off as desperation caused by her pathetic lack of a sex life. She couldn't write it off at all, and that was what terrified her.

Any kind of a romantic relationship between her and the

senator—even the whisper of a romantic relationship—would end in disaster for both of them. The journalistic feeding frenzy would knock the latest debutant/celebrity-alcoholic/unwed mother/illicit affair controversy off the front pages, and there Liza would be, taped by every yahoo with a camera in his phone as she darted back and forth to the corner market with her head down.

There'd be endless speculation about how their romance developed, where they met for their horizontal shuffle—never mind that there had never been a horizontal shuffle—and how the affair had affected her coverage and his policymaking. Not to mention the pundits' outrage over the violation of the codes of ethics for both politicians and journalists.

Yeah. She could see it all now, and it wasn't pretty.

The senator's chances of earning the nomination would be jeopardized, and her reputation as an objective journalist would be destroyed. The chances of either of them emerging from an affair unscathed were zero.

In short, disaster was inevitable, as unavoidable as death and taxes.

And she wanted him anyway. How stupid was she?

"What's going on?" Takashi asked. "Maybe I can help."

Liza struggled, paralyzed with indecision. On the one hand, who else could she talk to and trust besides Takashi? On the other hand, she was terrified to acknowledge the depths of her problem, even to herself.

"I do have this…friend," she said carefully.

"Uh-huh," Takashi said, still chewing, eyes lowered.

"She's a journalist with the, ah, *Washington Post* covering the, ah, Warner campaign."

Takashi snorted. "Right?…"

"And nothing's happened, but…she's very attracted to the senator. Obviously it's a…risky situation. The senator is fighting for every vote, and the press—especially the tabloids—and Senator Fitzgerald's campaign would have a field day if his personal life became an issue. His campaign would become a joke, and he'd lose the nomination. We both know he would."

"And what about your reporter friend?" he asked. "What about *her* career?"

The warmth behind Takashi's brown eyes was too much, and Liza looked away. "Her credibility would be shot. She could forget about any, ah, promotions she'd had her eye on. All her years of hard work would be flushed down the toilet, and on her tombstone it would say Here Lies the Former Mistress of Senator Warner—"

Takashi grimaced.

"—and, of course, she'd be hated by millions of his supporters if she damaged his chances in any way. That's how it always works. The man comes up smelling like a rose, and the woman is labeled all kinds of dirty names."

Takashi scraped his plate, looking thoughtful. Having eaten everything in sight, he looked around for more and sighed when he didn't see it. "Well," he said slowly, "I can't predict the future or anything, but I have seen the sparks shooting off this, ah, couple. Other people are beginning to notice. The clock is running on this thing. And journalists are supposed to disclose conflicts. That's the ethical thing to do here."

"*No,*" Liza snapped, her voice rising with frustration. "Not when the conflict can be managed."

Takashi gave her a look of such astonished dismay—all dropped jaw and bulging eyes—that she wondered if he thought she was insane. He followed that up with so much cursing, muttering and head shaking that she fought the urge to duck and run.

"Those two aren't managing jack shit," he finally said, and his vehemence hit her harder than the cursing. "They need to get their heads out of the sand and come to a decision before this whole thing blows up in their faces."

Liza knew he was right, but that didn't mean she had a fix for this mess. Suddenly desperate for any help she could get, she decided to confide a little more to Takashi.

"The funny thing is…my friend isn't as, ah, gung ho about this promotion as she should be. The life is wearing her down. She's wondering if there might be…more."

"More *what?*"

Liza, who was a cynic down to the soles of her feet, hated owning up to a girlish thought or two, but she couldn't help it. "More to life. You know—a personal life. Maybe a—" she swallowed hard "—relationship or something."

Takashi stared at her. "This man isn't relationship material. No politician is. Look at Senator Gregory. Look at Governor Taylor. Look how great they handle their relationships."

Liza cringed, her cheeks glowing with helpless embarrassment. She couldn't believe she was thinking along these lines, much less talking about them.

"I know, I know."

"Tell your friend she needs to decide if she wants the promotion or not, and then she needs to decide if she wants Warner or not. She can't have both. If she keeps it up, she's going to ruin her reputation in the entire industry, not just lose this promotion she may or may not really want. You feel me?"

Feeling things wasn't her problem at the moment. She was feeling way too much lately, especially for the senator.

"I'll pass along the message, but I'm not sure she'll listen. I think she—she really likes this guy."

"That brings me back to where I started, Za-Za," Takashi muttered. "Your friend is cruisin' for a bruisin'."

The unexpected chirp of her cordless phone on the table spared her from having to think of any response to this dire assessment.

"Phone's ringing," the Colonel called from the kitchen.

Lunging for it with relief, Liza clicked it on with unsteady hands. "Hello?"

"It's John," the caller said.

In a sign of how frazzled she was, it actually took the neurons in her brain several beats to start firing and put the name to the voice she'd already recognized. *It's the Senator,* she thought, bewildered. *I don't know any John.* And then it hit her with the force of a nuclear strike. *The Senator. John. Oh, God.*

Stupidly wondering how he'd gotten her unlisted phone number—*he's a U.S. senator running for president, and he probably has a few resources at his fingertips,* she told herself, *duh!*—she schooled her features and hoped the expression on her face wasn't a screaming giveaway to Takashi.

"Yes," she said. "Hello."

"You're with someone besides your father," the senator said flatly.

"That would be correct."

"Who is it?" he demanded. "A man?"

Thrilled as she was to hear the jealousy in his tight voice, she couldn't go down this road with him, not even a few steps.

"That's irrelevant," she said pleasantly.

"I don't think so, but we can discuss it when I get there. I want to meet your father."

"Why?" she asked, immediately suspicious because nothing good could come out of such an event.

"I'm courting the elderly vote," he said after a pause. "Also the veterans' vote."

"This is not the veterans' hall," she cried, aghast.

"I'll bring my sister," he reassured her, "so it'll be completely innocent."

Innocent? *Innocent?*

Reaching behind to grip the sofa for support, she gave Takashi a weak smile and kept her tone casual. Takashi, who didn't look fooled for a moment, glared back.

"That's not the best idea you ever had," she said into the phone.

"Probably not," the senator agreed easily. "You're welcome to come here to my house if you want, but that might be trickier."

These were both such ridiculous suggestions that she couldn't answer.

"Liza?" The senator raised his voice, probably afraid she'd hung up. "Hello?"

"I—I'm sorry," she stammered, flabbergasted, "but I have to ask: are you insane?"

He laughed. *Laughed.* As though what he suggested was a perfectly normal proposition, like making an ice cream run after dinner. As though he didn't have her heart skittering and headed straight for cardiac arrest with his crazy talk.

"Will your *friend* be gone in five minutes, or should we make it seven?" The senator paused as if giving the matter careful consideration. "Or maybe we could all hang out together for a while, watch the DVD—"

"Five," she said quickly. "Five should do it."

"Great," the senator said and hung up.

Liza lowered the phone, thinking hard and not daring to look at Takashi. Feeling guilty and conspicuous, she gestured vaguely

over her shoulder, realized she wasn't pointing to anything in particular and cleared her throat.

"I need to…go." Lame, but the best she could manage. "Are
we finished?"

Takashi stood and frowned. "Who was that?"

"Salesman," she said, the first inane lie that popped into her head.

Takashi kept quiet even though he looked as if he wanted to
yell, "Bullshit." Snatching up his jacket, he walked back
through the living room and paused at the front door to issue a
final warning.

"You'll think about what I said, right?"

"Absolutely."

"Because your *friend* with the attraction to the senator is
putting a lot of people—including me—in a tough situation and
I don't like it."

Chastened, Liza hung her head and nodded. The last thing she
wanted to do was put Takashi in the position of choosing between
his loyalty to their friendship and his responsibility to the network.

Muttering something dark and unintelligible, he lobbied a
final glare in her direction and left. And Liza's sharp, clear-headed
brain left with him.

Panicked and manic with indecision, she shut the door behind
him and turned in a quick circle like a dog chasing her tail. What
should she do? Clean up the kitchen? Throw on some real clothes
and a little makeup? Leave?

Before she could make up her mind or even narrow down her
choices, there was a tap at her kitchen door. Spiked out on adrenaline, she jumped ten feet in the air. When her feet hit the floor
again, she glanced at the clock over the mantel; it hadn't even been
three minutes since the senator had called.

Losing her head for a minute, she flung herself onto the nearest
sofa, picked up a pillow, pressed her face into it, and screamed
until her vocal cords burned. Then she screamed again. When the
second scream did nothing to slow her racing pulse, she screamed
a third time, this time stamping her feet as well.

Better. That was better.

"What the hell's wrong with you, girl?" Liza threw the pillow
aside to see the Colonel frowning at her from the doorway, the

dishrag in his hands. "There's someone at your door back here. You want me to get it?"

"I'll get it."

Trying to reclaim some dignity, she walked sedately to the back door and peered through the curtain in time to see the senator, who was flanked by his sister and two giant bodyguards, knock again, harder this time. Sending up a vague but fervent prayer to heaven—*Help me, God, please*—Liza unlocked and opened the door.

Chapter 10

The unexpected guests streamed inside as if they paid the mortgage on the place, locking the door behind them and surveying the kitchen. The two bodyguards murmured a polite hello and fanned out. One went into the living room, the other up the back stairs, both presumably looking for any terrorists or assassins she kept hidden behind the furniture.

She gaped after them for a second—she had the hysterical urge to yell, "Make yourselves at home!"—and wondered nonsensically where the security company had found men that size. Had it crossbred NFL linebackers with NBA centers?

But then Jillian handed her a bottle of wine and a bouquet of beautiful yellow roses. "I hope you don't mind us barging in on you, Liza. We thought we might sit and visit awhile."

Before Liza could sputter an answer, Jillian turned to the Colonel, who was watching the proceedings with a suspicious frown, and took his hand.

"I'm Jillian Taylor. You must be Liza's father. Nice to meet you."

He glowered. "You can call me Colonel."

"Nice to meet you, Colonel." Jillian removed her scarf and coat and slung them across one of the bar stools. "Have you been baking cookies? These smell *wonderful.*"

The Colonel softened with this compliment, unable to remain gruff with a beautiful woman who appreciated his baking. "Molasses. Help yourself." Turning to the senator, he renewed his frown. "Who the hell are you?"

"John Warner," said the senator as they shook hands. "Great to meet you, Colonel."

The Colonel cocked his head and scrunched his face with concentration. "I know you, don't I? From the TV?"

"I'm running for president."

The Colonel shook his head. "That's not it. You're one of those house guys, aren't you?" He wagged his index finger. "I saw you fix up some old house last week. Laid the carpeting, didn't—"

"Ah, Colonel—" Liza interrupted and put her hand on the Colonel's arm before this whole scene degenerated into more of a farce than it already was "—why don't you let the senator have some cookies?"

But the Colonel wasn't to be diverted. Staring into the senator's face, he sized him up with the kind of universal once-over that suspicious fathers worldwide used on younger men.

"What are you doing here?"

"Visiting," said the senator.

"You sniffing after my daughter?" the Colonel demanded.

"Oh, my *God.*" Liza smacked her palm to her forehead and wished lightning would strike her dead on the spot.

The senator, on the other hand, seemed unfazed by the grilling, but of course he faced down hordes of ferocious reporters on a daily basis. "Liza's very special," he told the Colonel solemnly, a flush creeping over his cheeks. "I'm anxious to spend more time with her."

Liza's foolish heart fluttered.

The Colonel hitched up his chin and put a hand on one bony hip as he took the measure of the senator. "Liza's a lot of trouble. She's impulsive. Runs her mouth a lot. Lots of bluster and bravado, especially when she's scared."

"I know, sir," the senator said, his tone grave.

Liza spluttered, too outraged to manage anything coherent.

"She screws things up," the Colonel continued.

The senator's face darkened. "That hasn't been my experience with her," he said, and this quiet but firm defense of her claimed him a tiny corner of Liza's heart.

The Colonel nodded, his estimation of the senator apparently rising a couple of notches. "Don't let her walk all over you and spit you out."

The senator's lips twitched. "I don't plan to, sir. I'll take any advice you can give me, though."

"Well," said the Colonel with obvious satisfaction, the interview successfully concluded for now, "you'd better have a cookie. Keep your strength up."

"Thank you."

The senator took a cookie and smiled. Jillian, whose eyes were now bright with what looked like happy tears, took the Colonel's arm and steered him into the living room, cooing over the cookies.

Liza tried to breathe as the senator moved into her line of sight.

He looked less presidential at the moment in his Cleveland Indians baseball cap, puffy jacket, turtleneck sweater, baggy jeans and hiking boots, but he'd brought his aura of power and control with him and was somehow more dangerous than ever—even if she detected a new hint of vulnerability and uncertainty in his eyes.

He didn't look thrilled to be there all of the sudden, which was strange considering it'd been his brilliant idea to appear out of the blue at her house. Unsmiling, he let his glittering gaze slide over her and paid special attention to her breasts, hips and bare feet.

Her nipples hardened inside the thin satin cups of her bra; nothing she could do about that. Nor could she do anything about her mascara-less eyes or Little Orphan Annie hair. But when she found herself feeling grateful that she'd at least indulged in a pedicure and had bright red toenails, she gave herself a swift mental kick in the butt.

"I don't know how you do it," the senator said unhappily, "but you get more beautiful every time I look at you."

This threw her for a huge loop. It was no flowery compliment, the way he said it—it sounded more like a curse. As though he couldn't forgive her for tempting him like this and planned to hold it against her indefinitely.

Liza floundered. How could she make a sarcastic comment about him needing glasses when he had the exposed look of someone who'd just bared his soul?

"That was three minutes," she told him, deciding to back up and start at the beginning of his long list of transgressions. "Not five."

"Sorry," he said, but he didn't look sorry at all as he took off his jacket and cap and tossed them on the nearest chair. He looked grim but satisfied, as though he'd finally done something he'd wanted to do for very long time. "I was anxious."

"Yeah? Well, I'd be anxious too if I'd started doing crazy things."

Irritation flickered behind his eyes. "We're back to name-calling again?"

On firmer ground, she squared her shoulders and put her hands on her hips.

"What would you call a presidential candidate who engages in risky behavior like refusing secret service protection, sneaking around with two bodyguards who don't look smart enough to find their butts with an extra pair of hands and a flashlight, and showing up at the house of a journalist covering his campaign?" She broke off only long enough to draw a quick breath. "Is there some other word we should be using besides *crazy?*"

"Determined."

Her world did another crazy flip because the desire flaming off his body left no doubts about what he was determined to do.

He inched nearer, stopping when he was close enough for her to see the splintered shards of black in his brown eyes and smell the faint musk of the sophisticated cologne on his skin. His expression was somber, his jaw set. The hot energy of his passion for her shimmered around him, as powerful and visible as waves of heat rising in the Kalahari. Her answering want centered in a tight knot low in her belly, a torment of the worst possible kind.

The brighter the flame burned, the more she wanted to throw herself into it.

Reining in her growing self-destructive impulses, she worked up some renewed outrage and wielded it like a protective sword.

"Wait till one of my colleagues gets a picture of you slipping out of my house and it lands on the front page. You'll be wondering why you did something so risky."

"No one saw us."

"No?" She waved a hand toward her living room, from whence came the ominous sound of wobbling, as though bodyguard Number One had bumped her end table and almost knocked over one of her expensive lamps. "Those two saw you."

"Those two have signed a confidentiality agreement and are paid very well—by me personally—to keep their mouths shut."

"Really?" Lacing her voice with every ounce of sarcasm in her body, she raised one eyebrow. "What about if they get subpoenaed? Will they keep their mouths shut then?"

"Is there some investigation pending that I don't know about?" he drawled.

No, actually. There wasn't.

And all her colleagues no doubt thought he was safe at home, enjoying a rare night off from the campaign trail and relaxing with friends or some such. If so, he was lucky he'd gotten away with it this time, and she meant to let him know it. She opened her mouth to continue her rant—he could *never* do something this dangerous again—but something in his expression stopped her.

"What are you doing here?" she asked instead.

"I told you. Visiting. I thought we could watch a movie." Rummaging in the pocket of his jacket, he produced a DVD and held it up for her to see.

"Rocky?"

"It's my favorite."

"What are you doing, *Senator?"*

This subtle emphasis on his title had exactly the effect she'd hoped for, and he flashed a warning frown. "My name is *John.*"

"You are a *senator* and a candidate for president of the United States," she said, determined that at least one of them should acknowledge this crucial fact even if they both wished they could ignore it. "Have you forgotten?"

Before he could answer, they were interrupted by heavy footsteps. With a nasty start—how could she have forgotten they weren't alone?—Liza took a quick step backward and tried to look casual.

The two bodyguards emerged from the living room and headed for the back door. "It's all clear, Senator," one said as they left. "We'll wait outside."

"All clear," Liza echoed, acid dripping from her voice. "I feel so much safer now."

The senator let out a snort of laughter but didn't seem the least bit amused. "I spend a lot of time wanting to strangle you. I should be running as fast as I can in the other direction."

"Feel free."

"No, thanks."

Thoroughly baited, which was probably his point, she raised her chin. "Tell me something, *John*—how many other women have you snuck out to see on these nocturnal visits?"

His face twisted. Judging by the way his nostrils flared and his fists clenched, he really *did* want to strangle her. But beneath his obvious anger he looked affronted, as though he might demand an apology for this unforgivable slight to his honor.

"None."

None. Oh, how she wanted to believe it. Melting when she needed to be strong, she forced herself to smirk. *"None?"*

"Yeah," he said. *"None."*

There was a rough new note in his voice that was raw and primitive and much more dangerous than anything he'd said since arriving. Startled, she took an involuntary step away, but there was no hiding from him, no safe corner in her own kitchen. The counter hit her in the back, cutting across her kidneys, and she was trapped.

He crept closer, his eyes bright with purpose. "You're special to me, in case you hadn't noticed. Do you think I make a point of meeting the father of every woman I see?"

"We're not seeing each other and I—I don't do relationships," she stammered. "I've already told you. And I don't know what you think you're doing, but you're wasting your t—"

"You know what I think, Liza?"

"N-no."

He drifted closer and settled into place, hands braced on the counter on either side of her. He neither smiled nor touched her, but she found herself breathless and wet anyway, teetering on the edges of both hyperventilation and sexual meltdown. He leaned in and she looked up. Within half a second, she was drunk on his scent, heat, size and masculinity, intoxicated by the bottomless desire in his glittering eyes. He had the longest lashes, the smoothest skin. The keen intelligence and strength of will that were the biggest aphrodisiacs of all.

The images, never far from her mind these days, came, fast and hot. Him touching her. His big hands sliding over every inch of her body; his lips and tongue lingering on the pulse at the base of her throat, her nape, her belly button…and lower; his absolute possession, which would be ruthless, demanding and unforgettable.

Swallowing hard, unable to look away from his gleaming eyes, she tried to remember what was at stake here. Her career. The anchor chair. Prestige, permanence, history. She tried to recall how the set looked the last time she did the evening news, how it'd felt to interview the president a few months ago, the weight of one of her Emmy awards in her hands.

She couldn't remember any of it.

Only one thing was real in her world now: the phantom glide of his sweat-slicked body over hers and the need to make it a reality.

"I think," he said slowly, "that this is exactly the kind of bravado your father warned me about a minute ago. I think you're scared to death."

"I am NOT scared."

Outrage trumped her fear and gave her the courage to utter the ridiculous lie. She *was* scared—more scared than she'd ever been in her life—but he didn't need to know that.

To her amazement, he didn't call her on it. Instead, dropping his voice, he spoke to her in the soothing tones a man might use with a small child.

"Shh, darlin'." Slipping under his spell, she felt comforted and hopeful and terrified, all at the same time. "It'll be all right. You don't need to be afraid of me."

Liza gaped, disbelieving and yet wanting to believe.

They stared, unsmiling, at each other. A long time passed; it felt like hours to Liza, maybe an entire lifetime. The connection between them tightened and grew—Liza didn't want it to, but it did—and it had nothing to do with sex. At last the corners of his eyes crinkled, and he held up the movie again as he wheeled away.

"Let's go. Time's a-wasting, and there's a movie to watch." He disappeared into the living room, calling back over his shoulder. "Got any popcorn?"

They sprawled on various sofas and chairs, ate snacks, watched *Rocky* and had a grand old time. Actually, the senator, the Colonel and Jillian had a grand old time and Liza sat in shell-shocked silence. She couldn't have imagined a stranger collection of visitors to her house than the presidential candidate, the retired army colonel and the first lady of Virginia.

Maybe she should make up a joke: *So these three people walk into a bar...*

The senator talked with her father about politics, the military, football and every other topic under the sun. Liza couldn't think when she'd last seen the Colonel so animated about anything. The two men sat on a sofa across the room and largely ignored Liza, who lapsed into a full-fledged sulk. She was tempted to go do her laundry because she doubted either man would notice her disappearance. Glowering, she watched the men pump their fists and cheer during the fight scene and wanted to throw them all out of her house.

She didn't.

Weird thoughts crept through her mind the whole time the senator and Jillian were there.

How nice it was to hear laughter in her house, for one. She'd never noticed the lack of laughter in her house before, so why was she thinking about that now?

How great it was to see the Colonel having fun, for another. How the senator and Jillian had made themselves right at home and seemed to belong here. Only they didn't belong here and never would.

How the whole house felt more exciting when a man was here. Big whoop-de-do. She didn't need a man and didn't want a man—especially this one. The house would feel more exciting if she brought in a live crocodile, but that didn't mean she was going to go out and get one of those, either.

What did the senator think he was doing? What was he playing at? Why was he toying with her emotions and, worse, her father's?

Was this all a game to him? What did he think could possibly happen between him and Liza?

As though he knew he had her brain buzzing like a fly in a jar, he caught her gaze just then. By the flickering light of the screen, he shook his head at her, amusement bright in his eyes.

Liza, Liza, Liza, he seemed to say. *Stop thinking so much.*

She couldn't stop.

When the movie ended, they all got up and stretched, and Jillian, who Liza was beginning to suspect was on the senator's payroll, took the Colonel's arm again and lingered with him in the living room while Liza ushered the senator to the back door.

Boy, did she mean to let him have it. Fuming, she squared her shoulders and pointed a finger in his face, but he spoke first in a clear attempt to disarm her.

"You're a good daughter, Liza. The Colonel's lucky to have you taking care of him. There's a lot of love in this house."

This compliment was so unexpected that she floundered, taking a few beats to work up a response. Oh, he was good. He was very, very good—hitting her at one of her most vulnerable spots, telling her the thing she most wished was true.

She didn't deserve the compliment. The senator wouldn't say that if he knew how much she traveled and that she didn't spend nearly as much time with the Colonel as a good daughter should. He wouldn't say that if he knew how guilt ate at her for putting her father in a facility when he hadn't wanted to go, even if it was the best care arrangement for him. He wouldn't say that if he knew how she had to remind herself that the Colonel wasn't in his right mind, how she resented the Colonel's increasing memory lapses, neediness and occasional dementia-induced nastiness.

"I—I should do more," she stammered, flushing. "I'm not that great."

The senator stared at her with such understanding shining in his eyes that she felt another layer of the protective wall around her heart crumble to dust.

"We'll have to agree to disagree about how great you are."

Liza blinked and reminded herself that no matter how sweetly this man complimented her or how he touched the shriveled remains of her heart, he was still the enemy—still the man who represented the kind of emotional and career danger that she needed to avoid at all costs. Shoring up her defenses against him, she reclaimed her outrage and pointed that finger again.

"Don't try to get me off message here, okay? It's not going to work. You'd better not try a stunt like this again, mister."

"Stunt?"

There was that wicked amusement again, glittering in his eyes and curling his lip. "Showing up bearing gifts," she cried. "Cozying up to my father. Bringing your sister. Trying to show us all what a swell guy you are. Giving me compliments I don't deserve."

His raised eyebrow only fueled her outrage.

"I'm not going to have an affair with you and commit career suicide, so you can just knock it off, okay? Find some other object for your affections."

"Yeah," he said. "I don't think so."

"Why not?" she demanded.

In one of his presto-chango mood shifts, he lost all his amusement in a single blink and became, just like that, a predatory competitor determined to win his prize—Liza—through charm, attrition or whatever other means he deemed necessary. Restrained power and passion vibrated through his big body, and his eyes glinted with the keen intelligence of a hawk.

"Because *you* are the woman I can't get out of my head, and that makes *you* the object of my affections. No one else."

Chapter 11

Oh, God. The senator could stop her heart in a way no other man had ever done, but that was not the point. Why would he not listen to reason? Why was he doing this to her when he could have any woman in the entire world he wanted? For kicks?

Well, her heart was not in play here and never would be. Liza wasn't jeopardizing her career for sex, and she was done with relationships forever. Kent had cured her of that.

"If you can't get me out of your head, Senator, you should try harder."

"I don't want to try."

His face wore the same uncompromising expression she'd seen him wear while fighting for a bill on the Senate floor. Negotiating with a man who looked like that wasn't an option, and neither was diversion. A man with that kind of determination gleaming in his eyes was going to get what he wanted or die trying.

"Where do you think this is going?" she demanded, furious.

"You're not ready for that information, Liza." His implacable gaze never wavered. "And you should have thought about these issues before you kissed me. You created this situation. Not me."

A full-blown rant was right on the tip of her lips—how dare he blame her when he was the one who'd been flirting and whatnot that night, looking at her with hot eyes—but he cut her off with an impatient wave.

"I'm not going to waste precious time arguing with you, Liza. There's one more thing I came here to do."

Feeling mulish at being silenced in her own kitchen, she jammed her hands on her hips and jerked her chin up. "What?"

"This."

In a sudden flash of movement, he caught her around the waist and, ignoring her surprised gasp, brought her up against him until they were molded together, breasts to chest, belly to belly and straining erection to aching sex. For good measure he slid one of his hands over the low-riding elastic waistband of her yoga pants to her butt, which he kneaded, and the other up her torso to one throbbing breast, which he caressed.

The shock of this unexpected contact was so electrifying and complete that Liza's body gave an involuntary surge, an arch away from him that brought her hands up by her ears, but he held her tighter and ducked his head until his glittering brown eyes were all she could see.

"This time," he told her as his mouth claimed hers, "*I'm* going to kiss you."

Liza had never known that a person could kiss with his whole body, and there was no preparing for the senator's sensual assault. All she knew was that they were somehow all over each other and she had her arms wrapped around his neck in a death grip and her legs wrapped around one of his strong thighs. And he gave her an endless kiss that tasted of tart wine and earthy man and vibrated with his excitement and crooning passion.

For several precious seconds he gripped her butt and held her, unmoving, as he thrust against her, and growing ecstasy clouded her vision and fogged her brain. Then both his hands were skating over her arms and back, caressing her nape, angling her head and sinking into her hair.

A sound of some kind pierced her consciousness, a voice or a laugh, she couldn't tell which. The next thing she knew, the senator robbed her of his thrilling mouth and thrust her away from his supporting arms until she had to clutch the counter or risk falling to the floor in a haze of sensual dizziness.

Dazed and blinking, panting now, she registered his smooth and unhurried movements as he took his jacket, used it to casually cover what she personally knew to be a huge erection and turned to greet the Colonel and Jillian as they wandered, arm in arm, into the kitchen.

Forcing herself to recover, Liza took a deep breath, smoothed her hair and prayed her burning face wasn't as bright as it felt.

"Thank you for coming."

She aimed this stiff farewell at both the senator and Jillian, who was trying to repress what looked like a knowing smirk. Unfortunately, the senator wasn't paying the slightest attention to Liza and didn't seem to notice that she'd hurried to open the door to speed his departure. He shook hands with the Colonel, all business now and serious as a proposed tax hike.

"Pleasure to meet you, sir." Only two conspicuous patches of color on his cheeks gave any indication that they'd just engaged in ten seconds of foreplay that was more thrilling than any sex Liza had had in her life.

The Colonel squinted at him and cocked his head. "I know I've seen you on the TV. Are you one of those chefs on that cooking channel?"

Liza cringed but the senator smiled with utmost patience, as though he were prepared to have this same conversation a million more times if the Colonel needed it.

"I'm running for president."

The Colonel's expression cleared. "That's right," he said. "You're running for president. I saw you on the news. Don't let Senator Fitzgerald whip your ass now, you hear?"

"I'll try not to." One corner of the senator's mouth spasmed with repressed laughter. "And you try to remember who I am, okay? Hopefully you'll be seeing a lot more of me."

"On the TV?" asked the Colonel.

"No." The senator's penetrating gaze shifted to Liza and locked with hers long enough to send delicious shivers skittering up and down her spine. "Around here, with Liza."

* * *

Super Tuesday finally came, several nights later.

At the massive rally in New York City, Liza pressed the bud deeper into her ear, clutched her microphone and stared into Brad's camera, hoping all the while that she wasn't making a complete idiot of herself on live TV. It took a major effort to tamp down her exuberance, but she managed to restrain her grin until it was no more than the pleasant smile that the audience at home expected her to wear.

"I'm having a tough time hearing you, Kevin," she said to the anchor back at the studio. It was pretty hard to have an intelligent conversation and analyze the day's news when you couldn't hear the questions.

Behind her, on the convention center floor, roared a crowd of about 20,000 cheering, chanting, clapping, banner-waving people, none of whom showed any signs of going home any time soon. It didn't seem to matter that Senator Warner had already given his speech and left the building or that it was nearly ten o'clock on a school night. Adrenaline levels were running high, and the crowd apparently wanted to be a part of this historic moment for as long as possible.

Liza certainly understood the feeling.

She, Takashi and Brad stood in the press pen, the roped-off area where journalists were confined during the senator's rallies. They'd arrived four hours ago—two hours before the rally—to allow plenty of time for them to be wanded, searched and generally harassed by the senator's omnipresent security personnel. Then they'd stood around for what felt like days, waiting, chewing the fat and twiddling their thumbs.

And people thought she led a glamorous life because she was on TV.

Ha. If they only knew.

All around them shone the bright lights of other correspondents speaking to other anchors back in the studios of other networks. No doubt they were all reporting the same thing: Senator Warner excited a crowd like no one else—except maybe Bruce Springsteen or Prince, if they were lucky.

From deep in her ear came the faraway sound of Kevin's

amused voice. "Has anyone told those people that the senator *lost* the New York primary tonight? And several other states as well?"

Liza grinned. "Well, you can understand the confusion. The senator came in, very graciously congratulated Senator Fitzgerald on her wins, which were big ones, and then went on to pump up his crowd into the kind of frenzy you normally see at a playoff game of some sort. If he keeps up like this, I'm thinking Madonna will ask him to open for her when she goes on her next world tour."

Kevin laughed. "Tell us about his message because, obviously, this is a very serious loss for him. It's down to him and Senator Fitzgerald now and neither one of them can afford to lose any more delegates. So how did he manage to spin that into what had the look and feel of a victory rally? If I didn't know better and just wandered in from the street, I'd think this was the convention and he'd just given his acceptance speech."

Liza did the whole stare-into-the-camera-and-nod-while-listening thing, as though she were gazing deep into the invisible Kevin's eyes. "Well, as always, Senator Warner stayed on message and said that this was a setback but he was not going to give up because the future of the American people is at stake. He focused on public service, lowering taxes, health care and education, his four big points, and said that he was the underdog but that was okay because people often underestimate underdogs. And then this millionaire, Ivy League-educated politician—who has, by the way, spun himself into the underdog champion of the American worker—played some music, got the crowd started with his "Now Is the Time" chant and left the building to catch his flight back to Washington. But he can't go on losing like this, and I imagine we'll be hearing more in the next few days about some changes in his campaign staff."

"Yeah, because no matter how he spins it, Liza, the numbers aren't good."

"I think *horrendous* is the word you're looking for, Kevin," she said. "If the late, great Tim Russert were here, he'd pull out his white board, do a few calculations and show us just how bad the numbers are. But, again, the senator used his speech tonight to look ahead and warn people not to count him out just yet."

"Let's take a listen," Kevin said in her ear, "and I'll ask you some more questions on the other side."

Liza paused while they showed a thirty-second clip of the senator's speech from earlier. She didn't need to see it again at this moment—a video could never capture even a small portion of the synergistic energy between the man and the crowd—but she knew she'd see it again as soon as she had the chance. But she'd do it alone, in the privacy of her own home, where she could stare and grin and clap to her heart's delight and not have to wear the detached armor of an objective journalist.

Senator Warner had stood in his shirtsleeves with a Plexiglas TelePrompTer flanking him on each side and the crowd circling him in every direction. Speaking with the conviction of an idealistic true believer, he reassured the crowd that he still planned to fight for a better world.

"You know what they're saying," he'd told the roaring crowd, prowling to each far corner of the stage and giving everyone the chance to see him. His prepared speech scrolled by on the Tele-PrompTer but he ignored it, slipping into that hypnotic cadence that could convince the birds to come down from the trees. "You know who *they* are, right? *All* the pundits and *all* the naysayers over at Senator Fitzgerald's campaign—they're shaking their heads and muttering like Lurch from *The Addams Family*—" here he paused to mutter and shake his head in a pretty good impression of Lurch from that old black-and-white TV show, and the crowd screamed with laughter "'—Ohh,' they're saying, 'we can't curb our dependence on fossil fuels, and we can't do much about global warming, and we can't get health insurance for every family or a quality education for every child, and we can't lower taxes, and one person can't make a difference and it *just can't be done.*'"

A consummate master, he'd paused here to let the crowd grumble and boo. This, of course, built anticipation, and Liza had found herself holding her breath along with everyone else in the room.

"And here's what *I* say, '*Why not?*'"

He tried to continue but the crowd wouldn't let him go on. Waiting, suppressing his grin, he let the audience laugh and yell itself hoarse for the next several seconds. It showed signs of going on for longer than that, but he finally raised a hand and the noise settled down to an excited murmur over which his voice could barely be heard.

If there was a single person in the room—young or old, black or white, student, housewife, laborer or professional—whose feet were still touching the floor at that point, Liza couldn't see who it was.

"Why not?" Senator Warner asked again. "'Why can't each and every person listening to me go to the local park and pick up an empty can and put it in the recycling bin? Why can't we all turn off the lights when we leave the room and limit our showers to three minutes when we can? Why can't each and every person listening to me go down to the nearest elementary school and mentor a child? Why can't we all try to change our little corner of the world and see what a difference it makes?"

The clip ended and Liza pushed away the memories even if she could do nothing about the lingering adrenaline surge. She would not remember her heartbeat's frantic staccato as she listened to the senator's speech, her body's uniquely feminine response to seeing such an enthralling, powerful man in action or the fact that every other woman in the room was also mesmerized and half in love with him.

She was a journalist now, not a woman. And she had a job to do.

"There's one more thing I want to mention, Kevin." Liza called on every ounce of her self-control to appear objective for a few more seconds. "The senator talked about underdogs. He talked about fighting hard and not giving up, and then he ended with the ultimate never-say-die song: 'Gonna Fly Now,' the theme from *Rocky*."

"*Rocky?*" said Kevin.

Liza laughed. "I know what you're thinking, and you're right. It was hokey and it was over the top and it was blatant pandering. And guess what? It worked. It was perfect."

"Thanks for that report, Liza," Kevin said, wrapping up the segment. "I know you've probably had another eighteen-hour day and your feet are hurting. Where are you heading now?"

"Well, the day isn't over yet. I've got to get out of here and hop on Senator Warner's plane for the trip back to Washington and I'm hoping they haven't left without us. That's assuming that the weather issues out of the Midwest don't ground us anyway."

As she signed off, Liza felt the biggest surge of excitement she'd felt all night, and that was saying quite a bit. Senator Warner would sit for an interview with her tonight on the plane, and she couldn't wait. She'd been off the campaign trail for a few days, back in the studio substituting for the nightly news anchor, who'd been out with the flu, and she hadn't seen the senator.

It wasn't smart and it wasn't convenient, but God—she was so anxious to see him right now she'd happily sacrifice her right arm for the privilege.

The campaign went into full damage control mode starting the second the senator climbed on board the plane later that night. After standing in the aisle to address the initial barrage of questions, he went into the conference room for a more formal setting and was interviewed by each of the major networks.

Jillian, who'd been campaigning with him, hovered on the periphery with Adena and other staffers. Journalists waiting their turn stood around in the packed space, listening and taking notes. Off-camera they all yawned, grumbled about being tired—it was past two in the morning by then and weather kept delaying their takeoff—and wished for a hot pizza and a warm bed.

Not the senator. With the upbeat attitude and enthusiasm that Liza was beginning to realize was a deeply ingrained part of his personality, he explained, over and over again, why he hadn't quit the campaign.

One by one, all the other correspondents finished up and returned to the back of the plane until only Liza, Takashi and Brad were left. She'd just grabbed her notes and taken a step or two toward the now-vacant interviewer's chair, excitement burning in her cheeks and throat, when—oh, God.

The senator sat in his interview chair with his elbows resting on his knees and his face in his hands. His shoulders were stooped and his spirit seemed crushed. It was a posture of utter defeat and absolute exhaustion, as though he couldn't walk one more step or give one more speech if his life depended on it.

Liza had never seen him look so forlorn.

She had to do something.

Galvanized by the sudden and urgent need to comfort him, she took two quick steps in his direction—before Adena swooped in.

Get away from him, Liza wanted to yell, but she said nothing because she had no right. So she watched, seething, as Adena beat her to him, put her hand on his back and leaned down to whisper something in his ear.

The senator murmured something low in response and grinned at Adena.

They were lovers.

The horrifying certainty crept into Liza's mind on silent cat feet and the sudden and unexpected jealousy was a kick to the gut. All the old insecurities she'd felt when she discovered Kent was cheating on her roared to the surface like the snarling beasts they were, and she wanted to rage at both the senator and Adena.

But then common sense intervened.

Calm down, girl. Take a deep breath. *Think.*

The senator hadn't made her any promises, had he? No. He was a free agent, wasn't he? Yes. And not that it mattered one way or the other, but Adena was married.

Liza didn't do relationships anyway.

The jealousy still bubbled inside her, a cauldron of ugliness in her chest, and she couldn't stop herself from speculating.

Would the senator have an affair with a married woman? No. She didn't think he would. From everything she'd seen and read about him, he was a principled man guided by his strong inner compass. Moral men sometimes fell short, true, but Liza's gut told her this wasn't one of those times.

So…the senator and Adena were just colleagues. Very close colleagues.

Liza's jealous heart didn't care.

She was debating whether to approach the senator, when without a word, he got up and disappeared into his private cabin.

What the—?

Where'd he go?

Bewildered, she looked to Takashi, who gave her a don't-ask-me shrug.

After a few minutes, irritation set in. All the other journalists had gotten their interviews tonight—why not her? And why didn't someone bother to give her some explanation about his disappearance?

"What's going on?" Fuming now, she marched over to Adena, who was flipping through some papers at the table. "Where's the senator?"

Adena raised one sleek eyebrow and gave Liza exactly the kind of hateful look that made Liza want to smack her every time she saw her. "Liza. How nice to see you."

Liza was in no mood for Adena's nastiness. "Excuse me," she said, "but we've been standing over there for *two hours* waiting for our interview, and now that it's our turn, the senator just walks off. Would you please tell me—"

"Liza?" the senator said.

Liza wheeled around. He stood in the doorway with a sandwich of some kind in one hand, an open bottle of beer in the other and one brow raised at her rudeness.

"What's the problem?" he asked.

Chapter 12

"What about my interview?" Liza demanded.

The senator finished chewing, swallowed and raised his sandwich for her to see. "Well, you see," he drawled, taking another bite, "it's been kind of a long day. I missed dinner. I thought I'd get something to eat and then we'd do the interview in here." He indicated his private cabin. "I hope you don't mind."

"Fine."

Was that *her* voice? Snapping like that? *Wow.* She really needed to dial it back a few notches, didn't she? Turning over her shoulder to address Takashi and Brad, she stalked into the senator's cabin.

"Let's go."

The first thing she saw was the Senator's late supper on the side table: a gooey peanut butter and jelly sandwich—it looked like crunchy peanut butter and blackberry jam—spread on thick slices of whole grain bread, a handful of Cheetos, a Granny Smith apple and several enormous macadamia nut cookies.

Oh, man.

He ate Cheetos? How could she resist a man who ate *Cheetos?*

Tonight's music added to her ambivalence. The current selection was Al Jarreau's "Since I Fell for You," a breakup song of such beauty and misery that her soul ached for hours every time she heard it.

Swallowing hard, she tried to stay focused and aloof. Being sarcastic always made that easier, so she gave it her best shot.

"Is this the best they could do for you, Senator?" She caught his eye while Brad set up the camera for the interview and someone turned off the music. "Peanut butter and jelly? Did you make some heads roll in the galley tonight?"

He'd been taking a long pull on his beer, but now he lowered his arm and flashed that boyish grin at her, to devastating effect. "This is what I asked for. It's the best meal I've had all week."

"And people said the former president was a good old boy."

He laughed and quickly sobered. "It's good to see you, Liza," he said, low.

Liza's equilibrium did a cartwheel or two but she frowned and tried to ignore the swooping sensation in her belly. "Are we about ready? It's late."

A shadow fell over his face and she ignored that, too.

Once everything was set up and Brad was ready with the video camera, Liza and the senator settled into chairs facing each other. She fumbled with her pen, now as anxious to get away as she'd been to see him in the first place.

She opened her mouth to ask a question, but he spoke first.

"So you think my *Rocky* music is hokey, eh, Liza?"

How the heck did he know about that? "Have you watched the coverage tonight, Senator?"

Dumb question. Of course he hadn't had time to watch the coverage. One of his flunkies must've told him what she'd said.

"I try to watch here and there, whenever I can." He actually enjoyed catching her off guard. The turkey. "I like to stay in touch."

"The music *was* over the top, Senator."

"Ah, but it helps me make my point. And even you said it was perfect."

So much for hoping he hadn't heard that part. Flushing furiously, Liza fought to reclaim her journalistic detachment. "And what's the point?"

He answered in full presidential mode. "The point is that we are the underdog, but we knew that going in. Senator Fitzgerald is a fierce campaigner. I didn't expect her to make it easy for us, and she hasn't. But we've got a little fight left, so don't count us out."

"Tenacity is all well and good, Senator." Thank God they were back on firm interviewer/interviewee ground. "But this primary season has already dragged on and party leaders, meanwhile, are growing concerned—"

His brows sank low over his eyes, darkening his face.

"—and on the other side, Governor Grant will cinch his party's nomination by the end of the week."

"What's your question, Liza?"

"My question is this—when is enough enough? The numbers are not good and—"

"I understand the numbers."

"—people are wondering if you're damaging the party at a time when it should be coming together. What do you say to them?"

His expression turned to stone, as jagged and unforgiving as an Acapulco cliff. "Liza, I didn't know that democracy could be damaged by letting people vote. There is a process in place that needs to play out. I plan to travel the country and tell voters what makes this campaign different from Senator Fitzgerald's.

"After that, the voters need to vote and their votes need to be counted. People can decide when they have all the information. Not before. And I don't think this process should be shortened or circumvented because a few pundits and a few party leaders think it would be easier if we packed our bags and went home."

Man, he was fierce. Despite all her best efforts to see him as another sound bite-spewing politician, she never could. Especially when he was such a true believer. And all her pitiful efforts to keep him at arm's length were useless at best, ridiculous at worst.

Still, she was a professional with an interview to finish.

"Let's switch gears, Senator. Assuming we can ever get out of New York, the campaign is headed back to Washington for a couple of days of retooling and regrouping. What's on your agenda?"

"A nap."

They laughed together for one delicious moment, and Liza

prayed her growing feelings for him weren't shining like a light-house beacon on her face.

"What are your plans *after* your nap?"

"After my nap it's back to meeting voters."

She asked a couple more questions, nothing tough, and then it was over.

"Thanks, Senator." She stood and unclipped her mike. "I really—"

But he was already gone. Looking over her shoulder she discovered, with an unpleasant start, that he'd stalked off to his desk in the corner, kicking his soccer ball out of the way as he went. It ricocheted, hard, off the cabin door.

Vaguely alarmed, Liza exchanged raised-eyebrow looks with Takashi—she'd never seen the senator upset like this, *ever*—then followed him.

"*Liza,*" Takashi said.

She ignored his hissed warning. When he muttered a curse, she ignored that, too. She hoped he would continue to keep their secret, but at that moment she didn't really care one way or the other.

Only the senator mattered now. Reaching out, she touched his arm.

"What—" she began.

He cut her off and leaned down in her face, nothing but a snarl of heavy eyebrows and glittering eyes. "Is that what you think? That I should call it a day and go home?"

Whoa. Of all the things she might've expected him to say, this wasn't on the list. Startled, she blinked and tried to compose her thoughts.

"It doesn't matter what I think. I was asking on behalf of viewers—"

"But what do *you*—" for emphasis, he jabbed his index finger at her chest "—*think?*"

Liza, who was no dummy even if she had lost all objectivity where he was concerned, saw where this was going. With a vague but growing sense of panic, she shook her head and backed up a step.

"No one cares what I think."

"*I* care."

Everything crystallized for Liza in that one second—the euphoria of listening to his speech, the crowd's excitement, his absolute determination to earn the voters' trust and be an outstanding president.

More than that, she grappled with his intelligence, humor and *heart*. Remembered how he'd allowed himself just that one private moment of despair a few minutes ago and was now ready to climb back into the saddle and fight another day.

He was amazing.

"I asked you a question," he said. "What do *you* think?"

Though she would've liked to hide behind a scowl and a sarcastic comment, she could no more deny him in his moment of need than she could speak Farsi.

With a fortifying breath, Liza took a huge emotional risk. Expressing intense emotions had never been her thing, especially since her divorce, but maybe, just this once, it wouldn't hurt anything.

"I think that you have the heart of a lion, Senator. I think the country would be *lucky* to have you as president."

More frightening than saying the sentence aloud was his reaction to it.

After a sharp breath and an arrested moment during which he tilted his head as though he couldn't be sure he'd heard correctly, a change came over him and it wasn't subtle.

It was…oh, God, it was a blazing look of absolute adoration and worship.

They weren't alone, though. She had to remember that. Off in the corner Takashi was talking loud on his cell phone, and Liza knew he was reminding them of his presence without confronting them directly. Even so, she couldn't be bothered with Takashi now.

"I don't…deserve that kind of faith," the senator said.

His voice grew huskier and his breath harsher with each syllable, and she knew what it cost this proud, ambitious man to make such an admission. He was showing her a piece of his soul, and she was ridiculously honored and grateful.

"Things are bad," he continued. "I'm not sure I can win."

"I am."

Another smoldering look was her reward and her punishment.

He hesitated, apparently hovering between keeping his mouth shut, the smart thing to do, and telling her how he felt.

Liza wanted any confession he'd give her, even if it tormented her later.

"You're under my skin, Liza. I couldn't get you out now if I wanted to."

Having opened the door on her feelings, Liza let a few more creep through even though it was against both her nature and her better judgment.

"I know the feeling, Senator."

A faint smile lit his face.

Staring up at him now with the connection between them growing stronger by the second, Liza felt as if she had so much to tell him.

If only she knew where to start.

A movement out of the corner of her eye reminded her that now wasn't the time anyway. Reluctantly looking away, she saw Jillian standing across the cabin, watching them with such quiet understanding that Liza felt exposed and had to lower her gaze.

"Well," Liza told the senator, "I should get back to the peon section of the plane. I'll see you later."

"Okay."

Liza's whole body drooped with the pain of leaving his presence. Everything, including gathering up her notes and walking to her seat at the back of the plane, seemed as if it would require much more energy than she could ever generate. But then she caught a glimpse of Takashi, who was giving her the concerned, tragic look she'd seen him give starving orphans in Africa, and it helped. Automatically she straightened her spine and raised her chin because nothing strengthened her backbone like pity.

"Let's go." She headed toward the door to the conference room. "Time's 'a' wastin', and I'm starving."

Her renewed brusqueness actually seemed to relieve Takashi. With an approving wink, he fell in behind her, but then the captain's voice came over the intercom to announce that they'd been grounded for the night because of the weather and would be stuck in New York.

Everyone groaned.

The two of them were discussing their hotel arrangements for the night when a voice called after them.

They turned in time to see Jillian walk up and give Takashi an apologetic smile. "Can I borrow Liza for a minute?"

Uh-oh. What could Jillian want? Oh, but wait. Maybe she'd decided to grant Liza an interview.

Galvanized by this cheering thought, Liza put a hand on Takashi's arm, eager to get rid of him and glad for the commotion as people packed up their belongings and got ready to deplane. The dull roar would make it easier to speak with Jillian with a modicum of privacy.

"I'll catch up with you in a minute."

"Great." Takashi's curious gaze flickered between the women, and Liza braced for the worst, but he left without comment.

Jillian took Liza's elbow and navigated her back through the crowd to the conference room.

Always eager for the next great get—Jillian had never spoken to the press about the governor's betrayal, and the idea of a comprehensive interview with her got all of Liza's journalistic juices flowing—Liza plunged right in.

"I'd love to interview you, Mrs. Taylor. You know that, right? Is that what this is about?"

"Call me Jillian, Liza, okay? I'll never sit for an interview about my personal life with you or anyone. I'd rather have you as a friend."

"Friends." Liza couldn't keep her face from falling at the loss of the interview she'd thought was hers. *"Great."*

Jillian laughed. "You can socialize with friends, right?"

"Of course," Liza said dully, still trying to conquer her disappointment.

Satisfaction or something like it skated across Jillian's face. "Then I'd love to have you stay at my townhouse in the city tonight instead of at a hotel. Beau is home in Richmond, so you can keep me company."

Liza floundered. Stay…with her? What was up with that? Why would Jillian go to the trouble? It was great to have new friends and all, but they were barely acquaintances and Liza liked her privacy.

She was about to open her mouth and say so when the senator appeared in the doorway behind Jillian, distracting Liza. He'd had his head bent over some papers he was flipping through, but now he looked up and caught Liza's eye.

Suddenly she understood.

It was there in the banked intensity in his eyes and his air of expectant waiting. Most of all it was in her breasts, which now ached for him—and her sex, which wept for him.

Stay with me tonight, Liza. Come to me.

Liza's lungs hitched with sudden breathlessness.

Yes was her automatic answer, but she knew better than to give it just yet.

Slow down, Liza. Think.

There were a lot of implications to this invitation, this decision. Jillian was offering her home and discretion, but she'd know. The senator's security people would also know, of course, but they already had an inkling something was going on, didn't they?

Meanwhile, Liza could tell Takashi that she'd spend the night with a college roommate or some such who lived in the city. Maybe he'd believe her.

This could work. She could spend the night making love to the most intriguing man she'd ever met, and their secret affair could remain reasonably safe.

That covered the logistics.

What about the professional and emotional consequences?

If her secret affair with the senator came to light, she'd be fired because it was a gross breach of ethics for her not to disclose a personal relationship to her producers and the viewing public. Simple as that. If their affair became public, she could kiss the anchor chair goodbye along with her professional reputation and, basically, her entire career.

Put a huge check mark in the con column.

Another big check in the con column: she'd never had a successful relationship of any sort with a man. Kent had broken her heart and then, for good measure, stomped it and fed it through a meat grinder. Liza's emotions had lived in a state of suspended animation since then. So any kind of a long-term thing was out. Assuming, of course, that a politician was a good candidate for a relationship.

Yeah, right. Not in this lifetime.

But…if they were discreet and she went into it with her eyes open and her heart firmly out of the equation, as his surely was…a brief affair could work, couldn't it?

She would make it work because she wanted this man.

Violently, desperately, passionately wanted him.

She stared at the senator and a few more seconds passed—but he waited patiently, his paperwork in his hands, and let her reach her own decision.

"Liza?" Jillian interrupted her thoughts. "John will also be staying with me tonight. Why don't I give you a few minutes to decide what you—"

"I don't need a few minutes."

Still watching the senator, who was too far away to hear them, Liza let her lips curve into a private smile full of the meaning and feeling between them. Even across the distance she felt his new stillness, his excitement. And she knew that her gut instincts wouldn't lead her wrong. Not on this.

This one time, this one night, with this one man, she would take the risk.

He was worth it.

"I'd love to stay with you tonight, Jillian," Liza said. "Thank you."

Chapter 13

The moonlight filtering around the edges of the closed windows illuminated John's watch as he checked it for what felt like the billionth time in the last three minutes.

2:38 a.m. now.

He paced around his darkened bedroom inside Jillian's Manhattan townhouse, too excited to sit down. Back and forth between the massive platform bed and the seating area he went, each step making him more agitated and anxious. His face felt hot, his pulse alternately sketchy and thunderous. A fine sweat had broken out across his body, and he was pretty sure his hands were shaking although there was no real point in checking.

Damn, that woman made him a nervous wreck.

Contentious Senate votes didn't do this to him. Neither did town hall meetings with angry voters, televised debates or speeches before thousands of people. Only Liza Wilson did this to him.

Every particle of his being, every thought, every heartbeat and breath, had whittled down to one essential question, the one that was far more crucial than a mere presidential race: would Liza come to him tonight?

She was here. She'd arrived earlier, with Jillian, and been installed in her own room before he got there. Said room was upstairs, as far away from his as possible, and he'd practically made his eardrums bleed straining to hear sounds of her, but nothing.

Once or twice he'd had the disheartening thought that she'd misunderstood his unstated plans for this rendezvous, curled up in bed and gone to sleep. Without him.

But…no. He'd watched the conversation between Jillian and Liza and seen the sudden heat of understanding in Liza's eyes, the excitement and desire. Liza wanted this night as much as he did.

So where was she?

He wouldn't go to her; she had to come to him on her own. His pride required it. This wasn't a negotiation on a new bill, and he wasn't going for any hard sells here. Either she wanted him or she didn't. Either she was ready or she wasn't. Simple.

Except that his gut was tied in a thousand and one knots and nothing about this whole situation—or Liza herself, come to think of it—was *simple,* especially his feelings for her.

He was in love with her.

Yeah, love. Not just lust. It didn't matter that they hadn't known each other that long; he was a grown man and he knew what he felt, because he'd felt it only one other time—for his wife.

In an ironic twist, it was Liza's impulsive kiss that had made him realize how special she was to him. That brief lightning strike of contact between them had opened his eyes about her, and he wasn't quite sure why.

All he knew was that she was brash and hotheaded, intelligent and wounded, prickly and warm and, he was sure, a perfect match for him in every way.

Was she perfect? Hell, no. More often than not, she was a major pain in the ass and the kind of thorn in his side that he should ban from his life forever. But her strength and understanding made her perfect *for him.*

If only she knew it.

He couldn't tell her. Not yet. Slow and easy was the name of the game with Liza, thanks to the cheating ex-husband that had made John's job of gaining Liza's trust damn near impossible. But he would gain that precious trust and, more than that, her love.

Tonight's unexpected weather delay had given him the small dose of serendipity that he needed. If Liza would only cooperate, he'd spend what was left of the night showing her how he felt about her. If he couldn't tell her he loved her, he'd express it as thoroughly, passionately and tenderly as he knew how. And come morning she'd be his—forever—whether she was ready to acknowledge it aloud or not.

Slow and steady was the key with Liza.

First he'd make love to her.

Then he'd tell her he loved her.

Then he'd tell her he fully intended to make her both his wife and first lady.

Assuming he won, of course.

The last bit would require her giving up her career for him, and that would be a tremendous sacrifice, one he'd make sure she never regretted. If she married him and he won the presidency, she couldn't continue a journalism career; the network would never allow such a conflict of interest, because how could the network anchor ever cover any stories regarding his administration?

So, yeah, he felt terrible that she might have to quit her job for him.

A woman like Liza needed a fascinating career, and he would do his best to provide her with one. Maybe she could head a foundation for Alzheimer's research. Or maybe she could teach journalism or travel around the country on lecture tours. Whatever she wanted for the rest of her life, he would give to her. Whatever job she wanted, he would support. As long as she chose him.

If only she would come.

His relentless pacing led him to the window, where he settled. Leaning against the frame, he brushed the curtain aside and stared out, seeing nothing, until a tiny sound behind him broke the absolute silence.

He wheeled around, heart pounding, in time to see the knob turn and the door swing open. And then, in answer to his prayers, Liza slipped into his room. She wore short little shorts and a tank top or some such, had a hesitant smile on her face and was the most beautiful dream he'd ever had, sleeping or waking.

Reaching for her, nearly choked on his relief and emotion,

he knew that life would never grant him a greater blessing than this one impossible woman.

Liza's brain shut down the second she saw the senator open his arms to her. Limned by the faint moonlight filtering in around the edges of the windows, he was perfection in his silky boxers— all gleaming skin, sculpted shoulders, arms and legs, muscles and sinew. As best she could tell—and she meant to find out for sure at the earliest possible moment—there was no hair to dust the planes between his small dark nipples or to distract from the sharply defined ripples of his abdomen. Between his solid thighs was a jutting erection that tented his boxers, and the sight of it weakened Liza's knees and dried out her mouth because she couldn't believe it was for her. All for her.

Somehow she managed to take his warm hands and let him draw her deeper into the room. "I'm not sure I should be here, Senator."

"You belong here, darlin'." His smiling eyes gleamed at her in the darkness. "And let's work on you calling me John. Try it once or twice."

"John."

He liked that. His mouth dimpled as he pulled her closer, and then his extraordinary and unexpected tenderness made her cry. All it took was his gentle hands on her body, his smile and his velvety voice, and Liza, who suppressed her feelings whenever possible and didn't do relationships, couldn't stop wave after wave of emotion from crashing over her.

With slow and deliberate movements, as though he was afraid of either breaking her or making her disappear, he kissed her, but not on the lips. Not yet. First he took her cheeks between his palms, burrowed his fingers deep into her hair and rested his lips against her forehead.

"Oh, God," she murmured, her eyes rolling closed. "I'm not ready."

"Yes, you are. We've both been ready since that night on the plane."

His breath was hot and serrated, as uncontrolled as she felt, and they stayed like that for several beats, frozen with the thrill of being together and the freedom of touching each other. Then he trailed his slow mouth from one of her temples to the other in the kind of loving caress that women waited their entire lives to experience—the kind of caress that Liza hadn't known she'd needed.

Hot tears—ecstatic tears, wrecked tears—welled behind her closed lids, and there was no holding them back, not when his hands and lips on her body felt this excruciatingly perfect. When the tears overflowed and ran down her cheeks, he kissed those, too.

"Liza," he said in her ear, kneading her nape with fingers so strong and wonderful she almost came on the spot. *"Liza."*

"Don't stop." She slid her hands up his back, starved for the living silk of his bare skin, and thanked the stars for this moment, for him. If she'd just ended her career by crossing this line between them, so be it. Her career was a small price to pay for this moment. *"Don't stop."*

"Shh. I'm not stopping."

Stepping closer, she pressed her surging hips against his and felt like she'd come home. Tiny muscles spasmed high up between her thighs, preparing for him, and she writhed, unable to moderate her responses and desperate for so much more.

He crooned with unmistakable satisfaction. Those big hands left her head, dragged over her bare shoulders and back and clamped onto her butt, molding her soft sex to the rigid length of his erection. Liza cried out, jolted by the raw power of this connection between them, and so did he.

He shuddered convulsively, making a noise that was more laugh than sob, more joy than pain. Leaving one hand flattened against her butt, he stroked her hair with the other. Tightening his fingers, he tilted her head back and studied her face.

In the long seconds before he kissed her, she opened her heavy lids and caught a startling glimpse of his expression, which was tortured, astonished and adoring, all at the same time. Staring down at her, he tried to speak, failed, and tried again.

"I don't want anything as much as I want you."

"John." His name was all she could say, because the tears swelled in her throat and she wanted so badly to believe that she could mean this much to such a man when she knew in her heart she couldn't keep a man—had never kept a man. *"John."*

He trailed his searching mouth over her eyes and down her nose before finally zeroing in, and that was where the gentleness ended. As though a switch had been flipped or a page turned, John went wild.

Taking her lips in a bruising kiss, he made rough, joyous sounds from deep in his throat, rumbles of triumph and possession. After a minute he broke away to stare at her, panting, his eyes glittering and fierce. He shook his head once, looking as astonished and overwhelmed as she felt.

Then he kissed her again.

There was no attempt at finesse as they clutched at each other; they were both too far gone for that. Working his thumb into the corner of her mouth, he demanded that she open for him, apparently not wanting to take the chance that she'd refuse. She didn't. Nor could she imagine ever refusing him anything.

Sucking and biting—his lips, tongue or thumb, whatever he gave her—she took it all and searched for more, moaning and whimpering. She'd always been loud, but now she made a racket, not that she cared. He was loud, too—crying out when she nipped him, moaning when she sucked—and they drove each other higher, beyond pride or dignity until only their need for each other existed.

Then he pulled his hands free and went to work. Displaying a huge amount of strength—she was no flyweight, after all—he grabbed her by the hips, picked her up, plunked her on the chest of drawers, which was closer than the bed, and quickly reclaimed his spot between her thighs.

For one second he gazed at her, his expression rapt and absorbed, but then he was kissing her again, yanking her tank top off over her head, and there was no time for anything else.

"You're beautiful." A velvety murmur of approval—almost a purr—vibrated in his throat as he studied her breasts, her shoulders, her belly, skimming over them all with relentless hands. "It's killing me to look at you."

Lovely as this compliment was, it wasn't the swift, hard possession she needed and she reached between them to grip his hard length…to stroke…to squeeze. "I need this." Another squeeze. "I need you. Now, John. *Now.*"

This seemed to push him beyond some invisible limit. Groaning, he ran his tongue up the side of her neck, palmed a breast in each hand and circled her nipples with his thumbs, over and over, sending bolts of electric sensation straight through her belly to her pulsing sex.

"Don't stop." Shameless and greedy, not too proud to beg, Liza arched into him. "Don't ever stop."

"Don't worry."

Her body was in charge, not her mind, and her body needed more and needed it *now.* Obeying her body's overwhelming demands, she jerked his boxers down and out of their way. When they dropped low enough, he kicked them off and reached for her shorts and panties, which he slid off with much wriggling help from her. At last they were gone, and he tossed this last barrier between them to the floor. The second he did, she coiled around him, arms around his neck, and thighs around his narrow hips, guided by her blinding need.

As quickly as she touched his bare skin and cradled him between her legs, she flinched, scalded. This skin-to-skin contact of his penis to her throbbing wet sex, once she had it with *him,* was too much…too hot…too delicious.

Both gasping for air, they stared at each other, stunned.

She'd dreamt of this moment. Imagined it. Hoped for it. Blown her fantasies up into unimaginable heights of ecstasy, the kind that only existed in romance novels and romantic comedies. Or so she'd thought.

The reality with John was better. So unspeakably good it terrified her.

He held tight when she would have pulled away, chest heaving and eyes feverishly bright. "Let me make love to you."

It didn't sound like a request, but she knew he would stop if she asked. She wouldn't; that decision had been made long ago, certainly well before she came to his room.

"About damn time," she grumbled.

One edge of his mouth hitched up in a crooked grin of approval and relief, and then he swooped her off the chest of drawers and into his arms. She started to tell him that she could walk, but why would she do that when she could bury her face in his neck and press her tongue to the frantic beat of his pulse? When his unyielding strength made her feel this feminine and powerful?

Swinging her around, he lowered her to the bed, which was already turned down to reveal cool white sheets, and then stepped away to click on the lamp on the nightstand.

"I want to see you," he told her.

The husky urgency in his voice and unyielding gleam in his dark eyes cut through her sensual daze. Holding his gaze, savoring this moment to the darkest depths of her writhing belly, she scooted back and propped herself on her elbows.

Tracking her every movement and operating in excruciating slow motion, he took his erection in his hand and stroked himself.

Liza moaned because her body was open and ready for him—she could feel the honey flowing hot and thick between her legs—and she needed every thick inch of him inside her.

"Don't tease me, John. I can't take it."

Merciless now, he ignored the begging. "Touch your breasts, Liza. Squeeze them for me."

This man was trying to kill her.

Trembling, her gaze flickering between his unfathomable eyes and what he was doing to himself with his hands—every *up* and every *down* sent piercing streaks of pleasure to Liza's sex—she rested her head on the pillow and cupped her breasts in her hands, hefting their weight before she flattened her palms against her nipples and circled. Another moan rose up out of her, long and earthy.

He froze. Swallowed audibly. And resumed his stroking.

Liza drank in his reactions as the spasms started in her belly. It took every ounce of self-control she had not to come then and there. When she couldn't last another second, she reached for him, but he took one step back, stopping her.

"Are you wet for me?"

Wet? Was this a joke? Only the Pacific Ocean was wetter than she was.

"Yes."

"I don't believe you." He paused. "You'd better check."

Dying with embarrassment and excitement, Liza reached between her thighs and rubbed herself. Whimpering at this exquisite sensation, which provided only a small bit of the relief she needed, she lubricated the hard nub that was now the center of her existence.

His, too, judging from the look in his eyes. "Let me see."

Then he was there, stretched out over her, his fingers picking up where she'd left off.

With a groan, he ran his face and hands all over her torso…one breast…the other breast…belly…hips. There wasn't an unmarked inch of skin left when he was done with her, not one unkissed spot. And then he buried his face in the dark triangle of her curls and tasted her, his skillful tongue as tireless as it was relentless.

With a sharp cry, Liza opened her thighs to welcome him. The edges of her vision blurred with the intensity of the pleasure; only his fingers gripping her hips kept her from squirming off the bed and into oblivion.

"John. *Please.*"

Taking pity on her at last, he straightened and his face was dark with purpose. He never broke eye contact as he reached for the red package on the nightstand. In seconds he was ready, but he trailed his fingers in her juices and then sucked them into his mouth just to prolong her torment.

"I'm not going to always wear these." One of his hands gripped his length and ran it between her swollen wet lips in what could only be called torture. She arched her hips for him, but he didn't accept the invitation. Not yet. "I don't want anything between us."

The note of warning in his voice surprised and distracted her and, impossible though it was, she tried to focus. "Neither do I." She smiled to entice him. "Come here, John. I need you."

Levering himself up over her, he stared down with a mix of exasperation and frustration in his glittering eyes. "You have no idea what I'm talking about, do you?" he asked, and his voice was cool but his expression was wild and hot, almost primitive.

"No." When was he going to get this party started? Another second or two of waiting was going to send her into cardiac arrest. "All I know is that I want you."

"Let me spell it out."

That broad head stroked her again, and she writhed beneath

him and let her eyes roll closed. For a second or two he nuzzled her mouth, but then he tapped her chin to get her attention.

She lifted her heavy lids and stared at him with unfocused eyes.

"I want you to be the mother of my children, Liza."

Unsmiling, he entered her in one driving stroke that buried him to the hilt.

Chapter 14

Liza couldn't have heard what she'd thought she'd heard, but now was not the time to figure it out. They both cried out, loud and unabashed. Moving together, surging and flowing, they clutched at each other and tried to get closer, but it was no good. Liza crossed her ankles and clung to his hips with every ounce of strength she had, absorbing each punishing thrust and needing more, but it still wasn't enough. She almost wished she could die right now because a hundred more years of life on this earth could offer her nothing better than *this*.

He seemed to feel the same way and gasped. "Are you trying to kill me?"

"Yes." She almost laughed until another well-placed thrust ripped the smile off her face and trapped the air in her throat. "Ahhh...*John*."

The face-to-face intimacy of their position intensified every sensation and heightened their connection more than she would have liked. It was hard to pretend this was just sex when she was staring straight into his shining eyes and seeing his every reaction even as she felt her own.

As though he knew this, he held her gaze, refusing to look away or let his lowered lids fall closed.

"Don't you let another man touch you, Liza. Understand?"

She understood the primal possessiveness in his expression, all right, and she loved it—even if it set womankind back a thousand years.

"Yes."

"Is this what you need from me?" John's hips pivoted, every movement an act of ownership and a brand that made her his and no one else's. "Is this what you want?"

"Yes."

"Do you want it harder?"

"Yes."

Dark humor shone in his eyes. "I don't think so." The wicked man slowed down until he inched into and out of her body as though he was determined to take all night with this single stroke.

Liza's heart nearly gave out. Beside herself now, covered with her sweat and his, trembling and hovering at the precipice of an earth-shattering orgasm, she dug her nails into his nape, arched her breasts against slick slabs of his chest and begged.

"Do it harder," she panted against his lips. *"Harder."*

"No."

Taking her mouth, he kissed her long and deep, an unbearable counterpoint to the slow pace of his thrusts. After a few seconds of this torture, he resumed his interrogation.

"It's never been like this for you before." He said it with the kind of complete certainty that would have annoyed her if she'd been in her right mind. "Has it?"

Was this a joke? Did he seriously need to ask?

But still…she didn't want to admit it. She hesitated, and he knew.

"Don't you lie to me." The warning couldn't have been clearer. "Has anyone else ever loved you like this?"

Liza gave up. How could she resist him? Why did she even want to?

"No."

The lamp provided enough light for her to see the raw satisfaction in his eyes. He glowed with it, wallowed in it. "And no one ever will."

No, she silently agreed. *No one ever would.*

Catching her mouth again, he licked and nipped his way inside, and the sounds he made were helpless and broken. Thrilling. This time when he pulled back, there was a half smile on his swollen lips.

"You're never getting rid of me now, Liza. You know that, right?"

Wrung out as she was, she still managed a quick responding smile, a whispered tease. "Why would I ever want to get rid of you, Senator?"

His attention slipped away with a groan, and that was it for the talking.

Something about their position apparently dissatisfied him and, without warning, he gripped her butt, surged to his feet, swung her around and, still deep inside her, backed her against the wall.

Cursing, he buried his face between her neck and shoulder and increased his tempo until his hips moved with the force of a piston. His frenzied pumping nearly drove her through the plaster into the room on the other side.

It was the ride of her life. Frantic now, hanging on for all she was worth, Liza tightened her thighs around his hips, adjusted her body just *slightly* and angled herself so that he hit the exact right spot.

Ecstasy streaked through her. Ruined by the force of it, Liza threw her head back and came, the violent inner clenching of her muscles strong and endless enough to trigger an earthquake.

Her keening was so loud by then that she almost missed the hoarse shout that told her he was coming, too. But there was no way she could miss the way his shudders shook his big body and turned all that living marble to stone as his muscles tensed. Tightening his hold on her, he rode it out, crying her name over and over again.

They'd collapsed against the wall and were still trying to recover enough to catch their breath when a terrible noise destroyed the moment in the worst kind of surprise: his phone chirped from the nightstand.

Liza froze, and John swore. All their separate realities reared their ugly heads, reminding Liza that even if she wanted a relationship, she could never have one with *him* because his responsibilities took him in one direction and hers took her in another.

His fingers tightened reflexively on her hips, holding her to him, but then he raised his head and there was open regret in his eyes.

"I have to get that. I'm sorry."

Liza nodded, mortification already setting in.

Moving carefully and with all the reluctance in the world, he set her on her feet and snatched his phone up by the fourth ring. "Yeah?" he snarled, grabbing her when she would have stepped away and reeling her in until her back was to his front and he'd pressed a kiss to the top of her head. He kept her close and listened and did not let her go even when he heard something that made his entire body stiffen.

"Give me ten minutes." He hung up and let her go. When she turned to face him, his face was tight with worry. "There's been a string of tornadoes in Tennessee, Arkansas, Kentucky and Alabama. It's bad. We've got to go."

"Oh, God. That's part of the nasty storm system that grounded our flight."

"Yeah." Nodding, he took a deep breath. "We need to talk, Liza."

She knew he was right, but the enormity of what they had done was beginning to set in and she just couldn't deal with A Big Talk now. Not with his delicious musk on her skin, his taste in her mouth and her skin still hungry for his touch.

"It's a little late for talking, isn't it?" Pulling free, she turned her back on his grim face and found her clothes.

Despite the emergency, he seemed in no hurry to do the same and, after getting rid of the condom in the bathroom, came back and stood there in all his considerable glory. "How can we build a relationship?"

"We can't," she said flatly. "This was a one-time thing."

"Liza—"

"Do you know what's going to happen if we keep this up?"

He answered with unmistakable dread. "No."

"I'm going to end up like that woman in *The Godfather* novel—"

"*No,* Liza."

The sudden sharpness in his tone told her he knew exactly which woman she was talking about. She tried to laugh, but there was nothing amusing about any of this.

"Isn't this funny? I've seen the movie a million times, and I don't even know the woman's name. You know who I mean. Sonny's mistress? She waits in the shadows for him and has no life of her own. And then when he has time he rounds up ten body guards, and they all go over to her dark little apartment—"

"Don't—"

"—and he has sex with her up against the wall, like we just did, and the bodyguards always wait outside and snicker—they don't show that part in the movie, but you *know* that's what they're doing—"

This time, he grabbed her upper arms and shook her once. *"No."*

"—and then Sonny leaves with a smile on his face and the woman is left alone again in her dark little apartment, waiting for him to come back the next time, whenever he can squeeze her into his busy life."

They stared at each other and there was nothing but pain between them.

True to his reputation, the senator didn't go down without a fight. Those hands skimmed up into her nape again for a caress so tender she questioned everything she thought she knew about herself and what she wanted. Surely any sacrifice—her reputation, her career, her self-esteem—would be worth it if he continued to touch her like this.

"That's not what I want for us, Liza. That's not where we're headed."

She believed he meant it—maybe he wanted their affair to be more involved than what she'd just described—but that was irrelevant. "That's all you can offer me at this point in your life."

"The hell it is."

That light was back in his eyes, the one that was somehow quiet and wild at the same time and always scared her to death. His expression forcibly reminded her of what he'd said when he slid inside her—*I want you to be the mother of my children*—and panic stuttered in her chest. Had he really said that? *Why* had he said that? Why did those words touch such a deep chord within her?

Acting quickly, she held up her hands to stop him before he told her something else she didn't want to hear and couldn't handle.

"I don't do relationships anyway, Senator, so this whole discussion is moot."

He stilled, his features cold and icy-sharp now. "Why?"

"I can't make them work."

"Because your marriage failed?" He made her sound like the world's most yellow-bellied coward when he said it like that. "And that gives you…what? A lifelong exemption from trying?"

"Because I have a tendency to screw things up and have zero skills when it comes to picking men. I chose one who didn't see the need to stop dating just because he was married."

"I can go you one better," he told her. "I chose a woman who died on me."

Liza gaped at him. "It's not the same thing at all. There's a difference between selecting the worst possible person to be your life partner and selecting a person who gets a terrible disease and dies involuntarily. You went to law school—I'm sure you can see the distinction."

"I don't think you understand. I watched the woman I loved waste away to nothing, and I wished I could die with her. I prayed to die with her. For three—no, four—months after she died, I cried myself to sleep every night. If I can try again after that nightmare, why can't you? If I can take a risk, why can't you?"

"I don't do relationships." She reverted to her stubborn mantra because she was too drained to go head-to-head with any logical arguments.

"You've never been in one with the right man."

"The right man?" she muttered. "Talk about your oxymorons."

That was the wrong thing to say, judging from what she saw of his murderous expression before she had to glance away. Stalemated, they glared at opposite sides of the bedroom.

After a minute she heard a harsh sigh. "Liza."

She didn't answer.

"Look at me."

His infinite calm made her feel all the more strung out in comparison. Mutinous, she met his steady gaze and waited.

"This thing with us," he said, his measured voice full of warning, as though he needed to make her understand that she'd drown if she insisted on swimming in the undertow. "I'm not saying it's convenient. It's not. This isn't a good time for either one of us. But you and I are going to have to deal with our feelings for each other."

"We just dealt with them."

This lame attempt at defiance wavered before the absolute intransigence in his flashing eyes.

"Darlin'," he said, unsmiling, "we haven't even scratched the surface."

Another burst of overwrought emotions erupted from her, as uncontrollable as the last. "Don't try to guilt me for protecting myself. Do you know what kind of risk I just took by having sex with you? If people find out about us, you may lose the presidency, but you'll still be a senator. But my reputation as an ethical journalist will be ruined forever. *Forever.* Everything I've spent my entire life working for would be lost like *that.*" She snapped her fingers. "What would I do then? I support myself and my father—what would I do for money? Write a tell-all? Forgive me if I don't want to end up like one of those disgraced political mistresses, with offers to pose nude pouring in from *Playboy* and no one wanting to hire her—"

"That's the last thing I want for you. *Believe it.*"

Startled by his sudden urgency and vehemence, she stilled. He looked fierce, protective—as though he valued her well-being as much as his own. Sensing an opening, she tried to take advantage of it.

"Since we're on the same page, Senator—"

His low growl told her she was skating on splintered ice by using his title.

"—let's just agree that what happened here tonight will never happen again."

"I can't do that." he said. "I'll never do that."

"Why not?"

He swallowed hard, a flush creeping over his cheeks.

"Because I'm in love with you."

It was nearly dawn by the time the senator and his staffers and Liza, Takashi and the rest of the press corps converged on the plane. The only question was where the campaign was going.

Adena wanted to go back to Washington as planned, at least for now, but the senator wouldn't hear of it.

Liza and Takashi observed the debate inside Sitchroo while Brad filmed.

Liza watched, transfixed, as always, to see the transformation that came over the senator. He was passionate one moment, presidential the next—and always fascinating. For this crisis he'd switched to full warrior mode, concerned about the safety of his people and fighting to protect them.

"States of emergency?" the senator asked. "Red Cross?"

"It's all in the works," Adena told him.

"Good." Grim satisfaction bracketed the corners of his mouth. "How soon can we get there?"

Adena rubbed her chin and took a moment to think. "If we give it twenty-four to thirty-six hours—"

The senator looked uncomprehending, as though the subject on the table were an impromptu journey to the center of the earth by golf cart. "I'm not waiting twenty-four hours. We can do better than that."

"I'm not sure we can, John," Adena said. "We've got commitments for tonight."

"Nothing we can't cancel or reschedule," he said flatly.

"Well, maybe, but we've got no idea which runways are operable, what the roads are like or what kind of security we can arrange at this point, and we don't want to divert local resources to protect you—"

Adena trailed off, silenced by the obvious and growing irritation on the senator's face. The staffers shifted uncomfortably and exchanged worried glances. Apparently they all thought that someone needed to talk some sense into the senator, but no one wanted to be the talker.

Adena plowed ahead and much as Liza would have preferred to dislike the woman for the rest of her life, she felt grudging admiration for her. Squaring off against the strength of the senator's will, as Liza well knew, was no easy thing.

"John," said Adena, taking great care to keep her voice conciliatory, "I don't have a magic wand. I'm pretty sure the captain doesn't have a magic wand, either. If he can't land this plane—"

"Then you'd better find me someone who can," he said.

Liza and Takashi exchanged excited sidelong looks. No one spoke.

Taking a deep breath, Adena tried again. "John—"

To no one's surprise, the senator cut her off with an impatient wave. "We're wasting time. I don't care what you need to do. We can take this plane, or a smaller plane, or, hell, get me a blimp. I don't care. Once we get close enough, we can take a helicopter the rest of the way in, or you can just find me a parachute. We've got all the security we need and we'll cover our own costs. You got me?"

"Yeah," Adena said glumly. Liza actually felt sorry for her because the senator's demands were a huge logistical nightmare of the sort that was usually left to invading army generals. "I got you."

"Good."

The senator glanced over his shoulder at Liza and Takashi. Liza, who'd put all thoughts of their tryst firmly on the back burner for now, felt the force of that brief connection to the depths of her belly and in the lingering ache between her thighs, but then his unreadable gaze slid away.

"Tell the press what's going on," the senator continued, still speaking to Adena. "They probably know already, but give them the option of getting off here or coming with me. And make sure they understand that if they come with me, we're not going to be giving interviews. We're not going to politicize this. We're going to make sure those people get the help they need. That's all. Anyone who doesn't understand that needs to get off my plane right now."

His gaze flickered a last time to Liza, then away, and he did not look at her again. "Let's saddle up."

Chapter 15

"That's where the house was."

Liza's current interviewee was an unemployed former farm-worker named Vern Stubbs. Tall but dumpy, he looked to be in his early forties and had the craggy skin of a person who spent most of his time working under a hot sun. There were big muddy patches on the knees of his jeans, and his unbuttoned red plaid shirt hung limply on either side of a dingy white T-shirt.

"Right there." Vern pointed to a concrete driveway that ran twenty feet from the street and ended in a pile of bricks, wood and all the other debris that used to comprise a home, a life. A mangled black SUV peeked out from under the rubble, its back tires hovering a few feet off the ground. "That's all that's left."

Nothing was left.

Next door was the neighbor's untouched house, a Victorian that'd survived the onslaught without so much as a broken window or a lost shingle. Liza was about to contemplate the whims of Mother Nature but Vern spoke again and pointed.

"That was a hundred-year oak."

To the man's right, Brad caught the image with his video

camera as Takashi watched the proceedings. Liza tracked their movements and, gasping, stared at the remnants of something that in no way resembled a tree. It looked like a giant ice cream stick that had been splintered and stuck into the ground, jagged side up. The top of the tree, which had no doubt been leafy and green, was nowhere in sight.

Mother Nature had really outdone herself this time.

In the last eighteen hours Liza had seen the overworked coroner's refrigeration truck picking up body after body in a death toll that had passed thirty and was still climbing. She'd seen bewildered dogs wandering the streets with their heads hanging low and their tails between their legs. She'd seen mobile homes tossed and tumbled like a set of toy cars inside a child's pencil case.

Worst of all, she'd seen the walking dead—people like Vern who looked as if they wanted to burrow through the wreckage and join their loved ones in the afterlife.

Overhead, the morning sun blazed against the blue sky in the prettiest spring day Liza had seen in a while. A faint breeze ruffled her hair. Life, apparently, was still going on.

This man, in the meantime, would have to bury his parents tomorrow.

"Will you rebuild?" Liza asked.

"I don't know." His chin began to tremble. Blinking furiously, he pressed his lips together and tried to compose himself. "They rebuilt four years ago after the last one, but the damage wasn't so bad then. I don't...I don't know if I have the heart for it this time."

Pausing, Vern looked fifty feet across the debris-strewn grass to where the senator, flanked by his bodyguards and a couple of uniformed sheriff's deputies, was talking animatedly with several other men among the wreckage of another house.

Vern's lips thinned with simmering anger and a nasty new light ignited behind his eyes.

"Damn politicians don't help."

This guy wasn't playing with a full deck. Liza couldn't shake the gut feeling that his parents' deaths, tragic though they were, weren't the reasons for all of the controlled rage she was seeing today.

He'd seemed perfectly normal when she and Takashi approached him for this stand-up for tonight's news, yeah, but the more Liza talked to him, the more the fine hairs on her forearms bristled.

That prickly feeling was never a good sign.

"You don't believe the senator will help?" she asked. "Do you have more faith in Senator Fitzgerald or the president—"

Vern's derisive snort struck Liza as more of a warning growl. "One politician's as worthless as any other, if you ask me. They've all got an endless supply of empty promises—"

The senator doesn't.

The words were on the tip of her tongue, but she kept her mouth shut, listened and nodded like a good journalist should.

"—and the president didn't even come the last time. He sent the vice president." Another snort from Vern, this one revealing the uneven edge of the man's yellowed teeth. "And a fat lot of good he did us."

She'd heard this bitterness before, after Katrina. More and more people were angry at their government and felt abandoned. This man was just one example.

"What would you like to see the politicians do?" Liza asked.

Vern didn't hesitate. "Get the hell out. Every last one of them."

That was it.

Without saying goodbye, waiting for the few last words Liza had planned to say to him or even pausing to give her the finger, he wheeled around and stalked off, disappearing around the corner of a neighbor's house.

Relief hit Liza in a wave so strong she didn't even bother hurrying after him to get his contact information in case the network wanted to follow up in a few months. She swung around to give Takashi a raised-eyebrow look.

"We're going to want to give *him* a wide berth."

"You don't say. I've got several people lined up." Takashi pointed to a group loitering near the perimeter around the senator's fleet of black SUVs at the curb. They all looked hopeful and seemed anxious for their fifteen minutes of fame. "The woman from the day care center—"

"Let's check in with the senator," Liza said. Takashi shot her that look again, the one that made her cheeks burn with embarrassed heat. She ignored it. "Maybe he'll talk to the press now."

Takashi muttered darkly—he was always muttering darkly these days—but didn't argue. Which was good because Liza was so anxious to see how the senator was doing that she'd probably tackle Takashi and pummel him if he gave her a hard time.

Keeping their heads low to study the ground and avoid any sharp debris, they crept across the field toward where the senator was now dripping with sweat and shifting rubble to try to help a family find some valuables under that enormous pile of ruined dreams.

Liza stared at him. She couldn't help it. She never could.

Even in his jeans, polo shirt, hiking boots and leather work gloves, the senator was still a striking sight. He somehow grew more presidential by the second, as though this crisis helped him reach his full potential.

At his urging, they'd found an undamaged runway, landed safely and been among the first outside responders. Liza still wasn't quite sure how they'd done it, unless maybe the senator had magicked it out of thin air with the uncompromising force of his will.

Then he'd hit the ground running and hadn't stopped since.

The press—all seasoned, like Liza, all professionals who knew their way around a disaster—could barely keep up with him. He'd talked to the mayor, FEMA officials, and Red Cross workers, insisting they could do *more* and do it quicker. He had time for every survivor, an ear for every distraught person within his range of vision. If he'd sat down, eaten or rested—even once— Liza missed it.

The only thing he hadn't done the whole time was speak to the press.

True to his word, the senator hadn't mentioned slow response times, Senator Fitzgerald's belated appearance or—and this was a biggie for politicians—blame. He'd just helped and listened, like he was doing now. Picked through memories and debris, held hands and reassured.

As though he knew she was somewhere nearby thinking about him, the senator chose that moment to glance her way. Still flanked by bodyguards, he straightened, swiped his arm across his sweaty forehead and, in a gesture that seemed as natural as stretching first thing in the morning, turned his head to look at her.

Liza's heart fluttered.

God, she had it bad for him.

A good twenty feet still separated them, but she didn't need to be any closer to know how he was. The dark patches under his eyes meant he was exhausted. The slight droop in his shoulders signified the emotional toll this disaster was taking on him. The grim set to his mouth told her that he was determined to do whatever he could—and he could do a *lot*—to make life easier for the survivors.

Best of all, the faint smile that touched his eyes, if not his mouth, and the new warmth in his expression at the sight of her all announced that she'd just given him the strength to get through the rest of the day. That she helped him just by being there.

In that moment, she knew.

Just as the senator caught himself watching her with his heart on his sleeve, blinked and turned away, the unwelcome realization hit Liza, a missile strike right between the eyes.

She was in love with him.

Oh, God. *Oh, no.*

It couldn't be. She didn't do relationships, so it was impossible. More than that, it was inconceivable. Also irrational, ill conceived and incredibly self-destructive.

No good could come of it today, tomorrow or ever. She had a better chance of a successful romantic relationship with a baboon from the National Zoo.

But…she *was.*

She was in love with him.

The terrible revelation was just penetrating her brain when she caught a flash of movement out of the corner of her eye, a streak of red that was moving too fast for any innocent purpose.

What the—?

With dawning horror she saw Vern Stubbs lunging through the scattered crowd and toward the senator, but this wasn't Vern Stubbs, the pitiful but harmless loser who'd just lost both parents.

This was an assassin.

With a pistol in his raised hand and murder on his face.

"No."

Screaming, Liza ran to stop him.

If only she could get there in time.

"No, no, no!"

The bodyguards were already in motion, but they were several beats behind Stubbs, and Liza knew it was too late even if no one else did. The senator's head whipped around, and she had a glimpse of his bewildered alarm and his lips forming her name—*Liza,* he yelled, *LIZA,* as though *she* was the one in danger.

Then three shots rang out: crack-crack-crack—fast, just like that—and the senator's eyes widened in surprise.

And then, even though Liza had sounded the alarm and the sheriff's deputies were tackling a struggling Vern Stubbs to the muddy ground and wrenching the pistol out of his hand, it was too late and the senator was shouting with pain and falling to the ground in a crumpled heap.

Chapter 16

John's neck hurt like hell.

Worse than that, he couldn't get his hands to stop shaking. Almost getting killed could do that to a person, yeah, but he still didn't like it. Fingering the thick white bandage that was strapped to the side of his neck like a volume of the phone book, he caught himself fidgeting and shoved his hand back into his pocket, where it'd been for a good part of the day.

It'd be real nice to take another painkiller or three, but he needed to keep his mind clear, with *clear* being a relative term. He needed to keep his mind as clear as possible for a man who hadn't slept in several days, had nearly been assassinated a few hours ago and had felt a bullet graze the side of his neck.

In the last few hours, he'd been rescued, hospitalized, treated, cleaned, released and grilled by the authorities. Now he was being interviewed by a ring of ten or twenty of his closest friends from his press corps and the local press, all of whom had their arms reaching for him and their digital voice recorders shoved inches from his face. In the outermost ring stood the camera people, who shot the proceedings for tonight's news.

The only good thing about this whole scenario was the fact that he was almost done with the press for the day and would soon have several uninterrupted hours on the plane for the flight to Columbus. For the first time in his candidacy, he was putting a temporary but firm moratorium on the press's access to him.

Hallelujah.

He stood on the tarmac for this impromptu preflight press conference, the afternoon sun beating the tops of their heads so hard that they would probably all end the day with migraines. Adena and Jillian stood to his right, his bodyguards to the left. Jillian was plastered to his side and had one protective arm slung around his waist. Apparently she didn't want to let him go. Pretty soon, well…maybe in several hours or so, he'd tell his sister to give him a little space, but for now he enjoyed the human contact that told him he was still alive.

Behind them, serving as the backdrop for all this fun, was his plane, which was checked, fueled and ready to go. The blue heading, Jonathan Warner for President, stood out against the white fuselage and the stars and stripes logo on the tail.

Man, he really liked his plane.

If only he could get on it and fly away sometime soon.

"What now, Senator?" someone asked. "Are you keeping your schedule?"

"No reason not to. The doctors stitched me up, good as new, and gave me a little shot for the pain. I've got that fundraiser for Alzheimer's research tonight at Heather Hill." Thinking of his aunt Arnetta Warner's horror if he missed her yearly extravaganza in the memory of his uncle Reynolds Warner, who'd been felled by Alzheimer's, John shuddered. "Unless I turn up with an ax through my skull, my aunt's counting on me being there."

"What do you think should happen to Vern Stubbs, Senator?" asked the reporter from the *Washington Post*'s blog.

"It's not for me to decide," John said. "There's a legal process in place that needs to play out, but I do hope that he gets the psychiatric treatment he needs. They tell me he was able to hold a job for several years, while he was medicated, but obviously that fell by the wayside."

John's gaze flickered, as it always did between questions, to

Liza, who stood in the back of the clump of journalists and didn't look too good. Actually, she looked terrible. Her eyes were swollen and red, her makeup smudged and her hair ruffled. There'd even been a moment or two when he thought she was trembling.

Maybe she was in shock. That would explain her chalky complexion and vacant expression, as though her spirit had checked out of her body.

Was she worried about him? God knew he was sick about her.

"Senator?"

Blinking, John tried to focus on the person talking. Who was it? For the life of him, he couldn't remember the woman's name. "I didn't catch that."

This didn't seem to bother the woman at all. *Christie*—that was her name.

"I was just asking when your new secret service detail will be on board."

"Soon." John's lips curved up into a half smile, which was all he could manage with his neck screaming at him. "You know we don't discuss the details of our security arrangements, but let's just say I'll be very happy to see those agents show up for work."

This earned him a chuckle from everyone gathered except one.

"Are you second-guessing your decision not to have secret service agents in the first place, Senator?" asked a voice so cold it could have come from the heart of a glacier.

John's startled gaze flew to Liza, whose shoulders were squared in that fighting posture he knew so well.

She's back.

His jolt of relief was quickly followed by renewed uneasiness.

She was back and furious. Those dark eyes flashed torture and murder at him, and he had the disquieting feeling that if he wasn't careful, she'd grab the nearest digital voice recorder, jam it down his throat and twist it a time or two.

"I don't spend my time second-guessing things, Liza—"

"Maybe you should, Senator."

Everyone tittered except for John and Liza.

"—and all's well that ends well." John caught himself grinding his back teeth, and his temples and nape began to throb in the onset of that headache he'd feared. "My bodyguards saved my life, and

I saved the taxpayers a little money by not bringing in the secret service until it was absolutely necessary. So it's all good."

Glancing quickly away from Liza before things got any worse, John turned to one of the other news journalists. "Pete? Did you ask me something?"

Pete opened his mouth, but Liza interrupted.

"Of course, many security experts and a lot of your supporters felt that secret service protection was *absolutely necessary* the moment you declared your candidacy, Senator." Liza's derisive emphasis on those two words sent John's hackles rising up into the stratosphere. "They've already been saying that the secret service could have done a better job of securing the perimeter around you earlier. What do you say to people who were critical of your decision to delay that protection and feel it's a sign of recklessness?"

John couldn't believe his ears. Staring at Liza, he felt all of his extensive public relations training and experience fly right out the window.

"Recklessness?"

"Recklessness," she said flatly, nostrils flaring.

"I say that I made the best decision I could at the time with the information available—"

John heard the snarl in his voice just as Adena shifted next to him and murmured, for John's ears only, *"Careful."*

"—and when I received different information, I changed course. I'm not afraid to admit—" John broke off, realizing both what he was about to say and that it would be all over the Internet before he even landed in Columbus.

"That you were *wrong,* Senator?" Liza supplied helpfully, those delicate brows raised as if there was genuine confusion about the right word to use.

John swallowed his anger, too exhausted to keep his public mask from slipping and too drained to fight with Liza, of all people. Staring at her, seeing her turmoil and the fear that simmered just beneath it in her glinting eyes, John thought about how much he wished he could touch her to reassure her that he was fine. Then he thought about how the presidency, much as he wanted it, seemed like the worst punishment in the world if it kept him from the woman he loved.

Staring at her, he gave up the fight.

"Yeah, Liza," he said. "I'm not afraid to admit I was wrong."

Liza couldn't get her hands to stop shaking that night during the Alzheimer's fundraiser at Heather Hill.

The first martini helped slightly, but the second made it worse. So she'd better have a third martini and hope for the best.

Drifting through the bejeweled crowd, being careful not to step on the trains of any of the passing women, all of whom were wearing dresses that cost more than a couple of her mortgage payments, she wondered why she'd come and how soon she could leave. Was it wrong for one of the event patrons to show up, have two martinis within half an hour and then leave before dinner was served?

Yeah. She supposed it was.

Why had she come? Well, she knew why. She'd come because her father was demented with Alzheimer's and she was a newly minted board member of the association, as was Arnetta Warner, queen of Heather Hill, and she wanted to raise as much money for the cause as she could.

So, even though she'd had a pretty busy day today—what with realizing she was in love with the senator; seeing him shot, sprawled and bleeding in a pretty good impersonation of a man about to die; grilling him on the tarmac; receiving the unexpected news from her agent and then flying here to Columbus with barely enough time to shower and throw on her little black dress and heels—she was determined to be pleasant and schmooze with the guests.

Lingering in the doorway, she held the stem of her latest empty martini glass between her cold, trembling fingers and tried to get a grip before she had a full-blown panic attack. The unsteadiness seemed to be spreading through her body, and she could swear her knees were now also shaking and her teeth on the verge of chattering. With another deep breath, she blinked away the image of the senator's dazed, limp form being half carried, half shoved into his SUV, and tried to appreciate her surroundings.

Heather Hill was extraordinary. The rolling grounds, the mansion, the glittering crystal and china, the enormous bouquets of flowers, the priceless antiques—it was all unbelievably beautiful, elegant and over-the-top.

Liza's tax bracket was pretty good, and she could've bought her own Heather Hill if she'd wanted to. The thing was—she'd never want to. What would she do with all this space and stuff if she had it?

For that matter, what did she think she'd do with the fifteen million per year she'd been offered a little while ago? *More vacations?* As if. *A hobby?* Not in a hundred years. *A bigger house?* Why would she do that? She could barely manage her house as it was with the constant travel, and a spread like this was nothing more than an extra thirty rooms to be lonely in.

Why wasn't she happier now that her greatest ambition in life—the anchor's chair—was hers for the taking? Why hadn't she told her agent she'd accept the network's offer? Why had she said she needed to think about it?

Think about it? Where the hell had *that* come from?

What kind of home did the senator live in?

If he loved her and she loved him…could they work something out?

Rogue thoughts like these had been plaguing her all afternoon, as if the image of the senator shot and bleeding weren't enough to keep her overwrought brain occupied. Did he really love her? Today, when his life had surely passed before his eyes, had he thought of Liza at all?

He wasn't thinking of her now. She'd lay money on it.

While she'd been numbing her pain with martinis, he'd been networking, like he was now. Over near the fireplace of the enormous formal living room, chatting up some of his relatives, looking bright-eyed and unruffled. Laughing, even.

As though he sensed her looking in his direction, he glanced around, midsentence, and caught her eye. Stared at her for a second before turning back to his cousins, Andrew Warner, a corporate tycoon who'd recently bought his own company, and Eric Warner, a corporate tycoon who now ran the family's multibillion-dollar clothing company, WarnerBrands International.

Liza was left shaken, breathless and more conflicted than ever. He, on the other hand, continued his stupid little conversation like a happy social butterfly. She could have almost imagined he'd looked her way at all, but for the infinitesimal tightening of his jaw.

Jerk.

He had some nerve. For making her think maybe she could do a relationship. For planting crazy thoughts in her head about the two of them, a happily-ever-after and children. For making her agent's news tonight seem insignificant. For being so relaxed when she'd had two martinis and still couldn't get her hands to stop shaking.

For almost dying and taking her will to live with him.

"Liza?"

For looking so unspeakably amazing in his black tuxedo—tall and imposing, sexy and accessible, an irresistible combination of Will Smith and the Daniel Craig version of James Bond.

"Liza?"

The voice jolted Liza out of her bitter ruminations with an unpleasant start. What now? Why couldn't people just leave her alone? She wrenched her gaze away from the senator and looked around to see who was talking to her.

Ugh.

It was Arnetta Warner, which was fine, and her grandson Andrew's wife, Viveca Jackson Warner, which wasn't fine.

Arnetta was the eighty-ish matriarch of the Warner clan, and the word *formidable* had been invented for a woman like her. Impeccable, as always, in a beaded silver gown that perfectly complemented her sleek silver bob, Arnetta had been intimidating people with a single glance since before Liza was born. Liza knew from the research that Senator Warner regarded Arnetta Warner as the head of the family.

Intimidation factor aside—Liza hated being intimidated—Arnetta Warner was a lovely woman. Viveca Warner, on the other hand, was someone Liza disliked on principle.

A beautiful, brilliant investigative reporter for the *New York Times,* Viveca was too much like Liza for Liza to feel comfortable around her. Or maybe Liza's fiercely competitive nature wouldn't allow her to be friends with a woman who was nearly as accomplished as Liza.

Actually, Viveca was more accomplished now that she had the

gorgeous husband, three sons *and* the career. Whatever. The bottom line for Liza was that the night had just gotten a little worse and promised to be downright rotten before it was all over.

"Hello, Arnetta." Liza leaned in for Arnetta's air-kiss and felt the cool brush of Arnetta's cheek against her own. "Your house is spectacular. This is quite a night."

Arnetta nodded in a very fine imitation of a queen; the only things missing were the diamond tiara and the wave. And then came the obligatory modest comment: "I just hope we make a little money tonight."

Liza didn't snort, but she wanted to. If this event didn't make two to three million dollars for Alzheimer's research, Liza would eat one of the glittering designer stilettos that were, even now, pinching her toes.

Arnetta drew Viveca closer. "Liza, do you know—"

"Viveca Jackson Warner, of course. We've met." Liza held out her hand and the women shook while exchanging identical cool smiles. Liza decided to make nice. "I read your article about the problems with the public school system. That was—" Liza hitched up her smile, which felt as if it was slipping, and swallowed hard "—decent work."

Viveca's eyes glittered with amusement, as though she knew exactly how much it cost Liza to give her a compliment. "Thank you. And I saw your interview with the secretary of state after the last round of peace talks." She nodded with grudging respect. "That was a good get."

"Thank you," Liza murmured and then took a hasty step back as she was assaulted by a new woman who appeared out of nowhere.

The woman was one of those short, slightly plump, girl-next-door types, with wild black curls and the kind of sweet, wide eyes that made men melt every time. She wore a truly atrocious dress that was lavender and pink and so bright it made Liza wish she'd brought a deflector shield.

"Liza Wilson?"

Liza nodded and took the woman's proffered hand.

"I'm Isabella Warner. It's *such* a thrill to meet you. I watched you on the evening news the other night. I really hope you get the anchor job."

"Thank you." Liza wondered how soon she could politely extract her hand from Isabella, who seemed determined to pump it indefinitely. "That's very n—"

"I just want to give you a hug."

With no further warning, Isabella threw her arms around Liza and locked them tight. Liza, who didn't believe in public displays of affection as a firm rule, especially with perfect strangers, stiffened and tried to pull back, but it was no use. The hug just kept on coming.

"I feel like I know you already," said the exuberant Isabella. "I hope you don't mind that I—*uh-oh*."

Taking advantage of the woman's distraction, Liza freed herself. "What's wrong?"

"That girl," Isabella muttered, staring across the room at a young girl with a pretty orange dress and about a million tiny braids. While they all watched, the girl stooped behind a sofa and began to feed—Liza squinted to get a better look—stuffed mushrooms to a tiny Yorkie wearing a black bow tie and a mangy yellow Lab mix wearing a red bow tie.

"I told Thandy not to feed those dogs anything tonight," Isabella continued, sounding harassed. "She *knows* they don't need those treats. Excuse me, please."

Blinking and shell-shocked, Liza stared after Isabella, felt the beginnings of a migraine squeeze her temples and wondered how soon she could get that third martini.

Before she could make her excuses and lunge for the open bar in the corner, however, a new group joined them: the senator, Andrew Warner, Eric Warner and the senator's brother-in-law, Beau Taylor, the governor of Virginia, who'd been traveling around the country on his own and campaigning on the senator's behalf when his schedule allowed.

Liza gulped because she didn't think her hormone levels were ready to confront four of the sexiest men she'd ever seen all at the same time, nor was she ready for any interaction with the senator.

Unfortunately, it didn't look like she'd get a vote.

"Liza." The senator's gaze flickered over her dress and returned to her face. "Are you finished skewering me for the day, or will there be more?"

Liza glared. The sight of the thick bandage on his neck above his collar renewed her anger at him, and she made a show of checking her watch.

"It's only eight-thirty, Senator. I could never make a promise like that so early in the evening."

Dismissing him—from her thoughts and her line of sight—she turned to Beau Taylor, whom she'd met several times at political events over the years but never interviewed. Seeing him up close was always a jolt because he was one great-looking guy: fair-skinned with hazel eyes; a long, straight nose; sharp cheekbones and waves of sleek sable hair. He reminded her of a black JFK, Jr. both in looks and because he was all potent masculinity and disarming charm.

She held out her hand. "Governor. Nice to see you."

"Nice to see you, Liza," the governor said.

Liza looked away before she fell under his thrall. It was best not to stare vampires or Governor Taylor in the eye for too long—you just never knew what could happen.

She looked next to Andrew Warner, who also was not hard on the eyes.

"Liza Wilson," she told him. "A pleasure."

Andrew Warner, he of the slashing brows and lush, cruel mouth, turned away from Viveca long enough to shake Liza's hand. He'd gone straight to his wife, linked his hands low on her hips and nuzzled her cheek. Liza added this to the list of reasons she disliked Viveca: a handsome millionaire husband who openly worshipped her.

Andrew looked from the senator to Liza. One of his heavy brows arched toward his hairline, and his eyes gleamed with open amusement and speculation.

"I think it's *our* pleasure, Liza." His voice was velvety, deep and impressive but not as impressive as the senator's. "Welcome to Heather Hill."

"Thank you," Liza said. "You have three boys, I think?"

Andrew grinned and glowed, as thrilled a father as any she'd ever seen. "Nathan is eleven, Andy's almost two and Jackson is almost one."

Jillian, smiling and looking lovely in a red empire-waisted

gown, appeared just then and touched her husband on the arm. "I'm going to borrow Beau for a minute. I need to introduce him to someone. And then we've got a flight back to Richmond. Beau's got meetings in the morning."

After Jillian and the governor left, Andrew turned to Eric and introduced him to Liza. "This is my cousin—"

"Eric Warner—yes, I know." Liza shook Eric's hand and received a warm smile in return. "Your daughter was just feeding the dogs stuffed mushrooms."

"God help us," Eric muttered. "I'd better see what's up. Excuse me."

"And we'd better go tuck the boys in before dinner," Andrew told Viveca, although, judging by the way he was looking at his wife—all lowered lids and sultry eyes—he had no intention of letting her return to the party tonight.

Viveca seemed to know it; a pretty flush crept across her cheeks as she turned to Liza, and her eyes were a little too bright. "Come back and visit us again, Liza."

Something about being in her husband's arms seemed to soften Viveca and she looked sincere as they walked off. Unaccountably touched and feeling her frosty dislike for the woman melting, Liza nodded.

"Oh dear." Arnetta frowned after an elderly gentleman over by the door who looked as if he was having a problem with one of the caterers. "I'd better go help Bishop. You know I have to do everything around here. I'll see you at dinner, Liza."

With that she swept off, leaving Liza alone with the senator.

Liza prayed for composure.

A thousand feelings hit her at once, none of which she particularly wanted to experience with his intent gaze on her face. She felt hot and agitated. Fidgety. Vulnerable and, worst of all, weepy. She rarely cried. The fact that she felt like doing so now was further proof that she should never have come tonight, never have placed herself in the senator's orbit when work didn't require it. Looking off over his shoulder in the general direction of the governor, who was now talking to Adena, she waited because, much as she wanted to, she couldn't walk away.

"How are you, Liza?"

The rough, urgent note in his voice awakened something deep in her belly, something intense, dangerous and best left forever dormant.

"Fine." She didn't meet his gaze. "But I didn't get shot today."

Why couldn't she breathe? When she did manage to drag in a sporadic breath, why was the intoxicating scent of his musky cologne the only thing she could smell? How long until she could retreat into the guest cottage, where she was staying, and hide for the rest of the night?

Soon? Now?

"If you're so fine," he asked reasonably, "why are your hands shaking?"

An automatic denial rose to Liza's lips, but then she looked down to see that damn empty martini glass rolling back and forth between her fidgeting hands. Mortified, she lowered the glass and clasped her hands behind her back where they could shake in private.

"My hands *aren't* shaking, but I do need a drink, so—"

She trailed off, too flustered to even finish her sentence. Determined to get away before her knees gave out along with her voice, she took a couple of steps toward the bar but there was no escaping from him, not tonight. The senator put a warm hand on her arm, and she froze, trembling, deathly afraid to hear what he would say.

He waited.

She looked him in the face even though it was a bad idea. *Really bad.*

There was a blazing new ferocity in his expression, an urgency that told her that he still wanted her and meant to have her despite all her fears and protestations. This was the face of a determined man who would not allow her emotional brick wall to stand between them for another second.

"Please." Hearing the weakness in her own voice, the need, she swallowed hard and tried again. Tried to be strong. "Please don't do this to me."

His lips flattened, which was never a good sign. Right now she could see glimpses of the superhuman determination that had brought him this far in his career and would make him an effective world leader. What an unfair matchup this was between them—she was only a woman, and a weak one at that.

"I thought of you today." He eased closer, unblinking, merciless and unwilling to let her hang on to the precious detachment that was the only thing keeping her together. "When I saw that gun and felt that bullet and hit that ground and thought I might die—"

"Don't."

"—I thought of *you,* Liza. Just you."

"You need to *stop* thinking about me."

His thumb stroked over the tender flesh of her inner forearm and she almost swayed on the spot.

"I can't."

They stared at each other, a force field of misery, longing and electricity crackling between them. From a great distance, Liza felt the pinpricks of what felt like a thousand pairs of eyes watching her, and she knew that was an important detail, but she couldn't think why.

And then she remembered with a sickening jolt to her gut.

This was no ordinary man she was lusting over; this was the man who, she sincerely believed, would be the next president of the United States. And he couldn't scratch his chin without drawing an audience.

Peeling her gaze away from him, she glanced around the crowded room. Everyone seemed to be going about his or her own business, thank goodness.

Then the sudden flash of a camera made her flinch. *Oh, no.* Glancing wildly around, she saw a photographer capturing a couple twenty feet from her and felt a little relief, but not much.

How had she forgotten?

Grand events like this always had roaming photographers to capture every detail for the society pages. It wasn't the paparazzi or any of her colleagues this time, luckily, nor had the picture been of them—but one day, if they kept up like this, it would be. Did it really matter who took the picture that wound up splashed all over some newspaper or tabloid?

Speaking of that, had any of the guests already slipped their camera phones out of their beaded handbags and snapped a picture of Liza and the senator engaged in this intense discussion in the middle of a party?

She couldn't take that chance. Neither should he.

Get it together, Liza.

She took a step back and tugged her arm free. The senator was slow to let her go but eventually did. When the physical contact between them was broken, she saw the loss reflected in his dark eyes.

"People are watching, Senator. There are photographers here."

Clearing her dry throat, she worked up a smile for the benefit of anyone who may be staring. Out of the corner of her eye she had a glimpse of Adena and the governor standing together and gaping at them. The look of blind fury on Adena's face made Liza wonder if the woman would grab the nearest fireplace poker and bludgeon her to death with it.

"Adena is about to march over here and kill us both."

"Screw her."

Liza was so shocked that she let her false smile slip away.

"You don't mean that. She's just trying to protect you and the presiden—"

"Screw the presidency."

This was too much. In a day filled with mind-boggling events, this was the topper, no question. Aghast, she opened her mouth, floundered and had to try again.

"Y-you don't mean that," she stammered.

His smile was hard and flat and didn't come within a mile of his glittering eyes. It was so feral and possessive, so *hungry,* that her body went haywire. Goose bumps rose over her arms, thick honey flowed between her legs, hot and wet and only for him, and wicked jolts of sensation ran from her hard nipples directly to her aching sex.

He seemed to know it. His gleaming gaze skimmed over her body, lingering with interest on her breasts as though clothes couldn't shield her from his view.

When that gaze returned to her face, it was brighter than ever and there was something so determined—almost reckless—in his expression that she had the feeling he was capable of almost anything at that moment, at least as it pertained to her. His words, spoken in a low voice raspy with desire, confirmed this impression.

"You have no idea what I mean and don't mean, Liza."

"No? Well, I've had good news today. Maybe it'll make things easier."

"What is it?"

The wariness in his expression perfectly matched her own sick feeling, which was something along the lines of a patient receiving a grave diagnosis from her doctor.

Why couldn't she be happy? How had it come to this? This one man had rearranged her life until her body was no longer her own, but his. Until she wasn't sure what was up and what was down. Until lifelong dreams fulfilled felt more like dire punishments.

What had happened to her?

Opening her mouth, she almost couldn't bring herself to say it—that she'd be leaving him, that this was goodbye. "My phone's been ringing off the hook. My agent and the president of the network called."

During the pause while she cleared her hoarse throat and tried to swallow the baseball-sized lump lodged halfway down, his face turned to stone and then quickly lost any expression whatsoever. It was, in fact, a model of emptiness—white paint on white canvas against a snowy landscape. There was nothing behind his eyes. Less than nothing.

"You've reached a deal?"

Liza tried to dredge up some happiness about it, some enthusiasm, some *something,* but her face refused to smile again, and the effort produced only streaks of tension from her cheeks to her temples.

"I haven't given them my answer yet, but…yes. They've been so pleased with my coverage of your campaign and my ratings…they're giving me everything I want. The salary demands, performance incentives, it's all there. They've even green-lighted my special on Alzheimer's in America. It's…everything I've always wanted."

Everything she'd always wanted.

She would remember that. She was about to make history and fifteen million dollars a year while doing it. She was not going to stand here feeling sorry for herself. Trying to look upbeat, she waited for the senator's reaction.

It took a minute to come. He blinked…he swallowed…he tried to smile but couldn't. Finally he spoke.

"Congratulations, Liza." He paused as though he'd run out of steam and needed a minute to generate some more. "You deserve it. You're the best journalist in the business, no question. I'm so proud of you."

Despite his obvious unhappiness, he looked as though he was sincerely proud of her and meant every word. While she was grateful for his support, she was so upset to be leaving him that she felt as though a thousand more martinis would never be enough to dull the pain.

"Thank you."

No self-pity, she reminded herself. No self pity… No self—

"When do you go back to Washington?"

Too soon. "Tomorrow, I think."

"Then…this is our last night together. Isn't it?"

Lust was suddenly all over his face, flushing in his cheeks and blazing in his glittering dark eyes. His scorching gaze, all determination and desire, slid over her in one swift glance that was so hot she felt broiled alive. Broiled, unbearably aroused and almost ready to agree to whatever he demanded of her.

Those disturbing thoughts streaked through her mind again:

Maybe fifteen million a year was no victory if it kept her from him.

Maybe, this one time, she'd found a man she could trust.

Maybe, with him, she could do a relationship after all.

Liza started to smile, started to take a helpless step toward him, but Adena chose that moment to materialize at his elbow, looking upset, and the spell was broken.

"I need you, John." Adena flashed Liza a dark look. "Now."

John's face fell with disappointment and irritation. For a minute his gaze flickered between the two women, but then he gave Adena a curt nod and schooled his features.

"Excuse me," he told Liza in a polite voice that was neither troubled nor seductive, and Liza all but sagged with relief as they walked off.

Until he glanced back over his shoulder and hit her with a blazing look of such possessive purpose that Liza's heart skittered and stopped as she absorbed his silent message:

I'm coming for you tonight.

Chapter 17

John's hands were still shaking when he knocked on the cottage door.

It was 1:43 in the morning. Having endured the endless party and an ugly scene with Adena, he should now be on his way to bed in his well-appointed room at the main house for a much-needed night's sleep, but he needed Liza more than sleep.

Being here was dangerous. He knew that. Though there might be a bump in his popularity after the shooting and his work with the tornado survivors, his campaign remained on life support and a tabloid frenzy over his personal life could kill it outright. Not to mention the damage that would be done to Liza's journalistic reputation if the newest network anchor was caught in a secret affair with the presidential candidate she was covering.

So, yeah, he should be in his room back up at the main house. He should be enjoying a snack as he read through his briefing papers for tomorrow. He should not be sneaking down to the cottage to see Liza, but he knocked again anyway, harder this time.

He could've been killed today. Maybe he'd be killed tomorrow. Maybe his next assassination attempt would come from someone more skilled and detached than Vern Stubbs. Who could say?

All he knew for sure was that only this moment was guaranteed, and he planned to spend this moment making love with the woman he needed.

Still no answer. Frustrated and impatient, he pulled the screen door open and tried the knob. To his surprise, it turned, and John slipped inside, closing both doors behind him.

There she was. By the light of a lamp on the console, he saw Liza sitting in a tall-backed chair in the corner of the small entry, not six feet from him.

Her back was rigid, her shoulders squared. She hadn't undressed from the party, and deep slits in that super-sexy black dress revealed shapely long legs up to her thighs. Both her pretty feet, which were still encased in those strappy sandals, rested side by side on the floor, and her hands were clenched in her lap.

In her eyes he read equal parts fear and sensual knowledge.

So she'd heard him. Expected him. Knew why he'd come.

Good.

Maybe she still wasn't quite ready and would need a little more convincing, but she would give him everything tonight. With his urging, she would happily surrender, and surrender over and over again. Before the night was out, he fully intended to have her commitment to a relationship with him, and he wanted to hear her say that she loved him. He thought she did—he'd seen glimpses of it in her eyes—but he needed to hear the words.

Their wait was almost over—but not quite.

Liza unclasped her hands—they were still shaking—put them on the arms of the chair and stood looking none too steady. Then she took a small step toward him and hitched her chin up.

"Please leave, Senator."

While her courage was one of the many things John admired about her, she had no idea what she was up against tonight.

"No."

She blinked, her defiance wobbling and her voice fading. "What do you want? I told you I wouldn't have an affair with you. I warned you."

Maybe he should ease her into it, start with the easy things first. "I want you to tell me," he said nice and slow, "why your hands were shaking earlier."

Panic flared behind her eyes and she shook her head. Edging around him, looking as if she planned to run if given half a chance, Liza mustered her bravado, pivoted on those sky-high heels and marched past him to the front door, where she put her hand on the knob.

"Please leave."

John gaped after her—did she really think she was throwing him out?—until his brain came up to speed and he reacted.

Uh-uh, Liza. Not tonight.

Moving with sharp reflexes honed on the soccer field, he lunged and caught her from behind.

She cried out, struggling.

Too bad, darlin'. There wasn't a snowball's chance in the Bahamas that he'd let her go, especially when she felt so hot in his arms, so sweet, so unbelievably *perfect*.

Tightening his hold, he restrained his hands and kept them firmly around her middle, roaming neither higher nor lower even though he would have gladly sacrificed five years of his life to do so.

Shoving his nose deep into that shiny, fragrant black hair, he inhaled her, throwing caution to the wind and getting higher than a runaway kite.

"Shh," he told her.

She writhed against him, her body rigid and stronger than he'd remembered.

"Please let me go."

"John."

"What?"

"John." Maybe it was twisted to derive such immense satisfaction from ruffling the unflappable Liza Wilson with her cool eyes and nose-in-the-air haughtiness, but he did. "You should say, 'Please let me go, *John.*'"

After a last shudder she went so still he could no longer feel the rise and fall of her ribs beneath his fingers. Finally, she moved again, but her body was softer now, pliant. The obligatory struggle with still there, but it was more of an undulation—a feeble test of her will against his when the bottom line was that they both wanted the same thing.

With the obvious weakening of her resistance to encourage him, he let his lips slide down the sleek column of her neck and nearly died from the thrill.

Heaven.

"Please let me go...John."

"No."

She groaned. While there was some despair in it, there was much more excitement and need. Feeling the need himself, weak with it, he inched his hips forward until they just brushed the lush curve of her butt and he experienced more heaven with a healthy dose of torture.

Stifling his gasp, he waited.

Slowly, by degrees, her body loosened. The fight went out of her, bit by bit, and that was almost enough for John, but then she did something even better. Arcing against him, she turned her face toward his lips and rubbed that big butt against his erection.

The contact almost sent him over the top. His hard length jerked against the zipper of his trousers, well beyond his control. Sweat broke out across his brow and beaded at his temples. The trembling in his hands had long since spread to his entire body.

He wanted her. *Wanted...wanted...wanted.*

His desperation was so strong he felt as though he would kill for it or die from it, but it wasn't time. Not quite yet. First he had to bring her just a little bit further. Leaving behind the tender skin of her neck—he would come back to that later—he pressed his lips to her ear and whispered.

"Why were your hands shaking earlier, Liza? My hands have been shaking all day because I'm scared of dying without holding you like this again. Why were yours shaking?"

"For the same reason."

Good, but not good enough. "Tell me."

She turned her face toward him, strained to get closer.

"I was scared."

"Why?"

"Because it looked like...you were dying. There was so much blood—"

He nuzzled the delicate shell of her ear, determined to focus a little longer so they could get over this hurdle once and for all.

"Why does it matter to you whether I live or die?"

To his surprise, her ribs heaved beneath his fingers, and his hand slid against the slick silk of her dress. Was she...*crying?* God, she was. Liza Wilson, the strongest, fiercest woman he knew or ever would know, was crying *over him.*

And these were not the hot tears of a woman in a moment of passion but the emotional tears of a woman who felt something profound.

He felt a million times more humbled than he'd ever been while standing before a cheering crowd of supporters.

"Don't cry, baby," he murmured. "It doesn't have to be this hard. I love you and you love me. That's all."

That was it—the exact right thing to say.

She sagged and gave herself completely. He felt it in her body, which was now supple, fluid, and in her skin, which radiated new heat like the molten crater of a volcano.

"Yes," she said.

"Say it."

"I love you. I need you. Inside me. All over me. I just...I need *this.*"

Instead of leaving to shout his joy from the rooftops, which was a real temptation, he took a long moment to let it soak in, this amazing accomplishment of getting Liza Wilson to admit she loved him.

Pressing a kiss to her temple, he waited, not at all sure he wasn't about to start bawling like a baby.

"We're going to be together, darlin'."

"How, John?"

Man, he loved it when she said his name. *Loved it.* His heart thundering with enough energy to power a wind turbine, he loosened his grip a little, turned her in his arms and looked down into the bright brown eyes that would probably be both the death of him and the last image flashing through his mind on his dying day.

"I'm thinking…maybe it's time for me to concede the nomination to Senator Fitzgerald. Go back to being a plain old senator."

"What?" Wow. He hadn't expected her to look that horrified. "No. You can't. It's not over yet, and you can still win—"

"I don't know whether I can or not. The numbers—"

"You can," she said adamantly. "I know it."

It was beside the point at the moment, although he loved her all the more for her confidence in him. "You're the most important thing to me, Liza. By far."

"I don't want to be responsible for you quitting."

John became very still. The possibility that he could get the two things he wanted most was so glorious he had to creep up on it. This had been his hope, of course, but it suddenly seemed much closer to a reality.

"You could…help me."

Comprehension dawned and her mouth formed a surprised O. *"Help you?"*

"You could…do some work for Alzheimer's treatment and research or choose some other platform."

With that, he formally passed his future happiness into her hands.

"A president needs a first lady, and I need you as my wife."

It was too much to spring on her, the marriage idea more so than the first lady business. He knew it even before she went rigid and tried to jerk away.

Reacting quickly, he tightened his hold and kept her close until some of her tension eased. A fine tremble broke out over her body, and he hated it, hated the man who had done this to her.

Seething but trying to be gentle, he kissed her cheek. "Don't, baby."

"I'm never getting married again."

He kissed her again. "I'm not your ex-husband. Don't treat me like him."

"Men cheat. Politicians lie. It's what they do."

"Liza." Drawing back so she could see his face, he stared down at her. "I will never lie to you or cheat on you. *Never.*"

She wavered, looking as though she couldn't quite believe him. "It's more than that. I don't want to be a politician's wife or first lady. I don't want to campaign. This is your calling—not mine."

"You don't have to campaign or do anything else you don't want to do. Our calling is to love each other, and I just need you to be there when I come home at night. That's all."

Her jaw shut with a snap, and he decided to take advantage of the opening. Enough with the talking. They had more important things to do.

"We'll work on the logistics in the morning. Right now we're going to get to know each other a whole lot better." Palming her face, he tunneled his fingers through the black silk of her hair. "Aren't we?"

After a brief hesitation, she nodded.

Good girl. "I'm going to kiss you here." He stroked a thumb across her dewy bottom lip and she smiled. "And here." He let his hands slide lower and filled them with the delicious weight of her breasts. Just when her head fell back and she began arching into him, trying to get relief for her nipples, which he sincerely hoped were now hard and throbbing, he slipped his hands lower, to the center of his universe, and cupped the dark triangle he planned to explore tonight with the exhaustive thoroughness of Lewis and Clark.

"And here. Okay?"

"Yes." Her eyes were bright now, her face flushed and gorgeous.

Easing her closer, he palmed her butt and ground her against his straining erection. This nearly killed him, but it was worth it. He must have hit a sweet spot, because she whimpered and writhed against him, her body's needs making her shameless—just the way he liked her.

"And when it's time," he told her, "you're going to spread these thighs for me and let me in. You're going to relax and let me take care of you—let me do everything I want to do with you, everything I tell you to do. Aren't you?"

And Liza Wilson, the woman who'd traveled to war zones, interviewed dictators and made corrupt politicians sorry for the day they were born, shivered and said, "Yes."

"We'll deal with the rest of this tomorrow, baby, okay?"

"Okay."

John wanted tonight to be all about Liza.

Liza had other plans.

Maybe it was the martinis he'd seen her sipping tonight, in which case he planned to buy stock in Absolut and order vodka by the case, or maybe it was realizing he could have died today, in which case he planned to get shot more often. Whatever it was, it made Liza soft and easy, so sensual she stole his breath and scattered his thoughts.

That sleek hair had slid over one eye again, and she glowed with some secret inner light that put a tiny smile on her parted lips as she towed him down the hall to the bedroom, never breaking eye contact.

Her spring garden scent fogged his brain almost to the point of insanity. By the light of a single nightstand lamp he stared at her, unable to believe his enormous good fortune and ready to jump on her in a frenzied mating that would make a stallion with a mare in heat look like a G-rated peck on the cheek.

He'd never thought there was anything sexier than a woman's bare skin, but Liza in that black dress standing in front of that enormous bed gave him a whole new perspective as he shrugged out of his jacket and dropped it to the floor. The silk hugged her plump breasts and dipped low, flared over curvy hips and butt and fell away over juicy thighs.

Liza in that black dress was lethal.

As though she knew what she did to him, she beckoned him with the slightest tip of her head and widening of her smile.

"Come here."

But John hesitated, not entirely sure the dream had become a reality. "I pictured you like this. The first time I saw you—every time I saw you—I wanted you like this."

"What will you do with me, Senator?"

He had more than a few ideas.

They came together with his hands in her hair and hers gliding under his shirt, unhurried and gentle. Angling her head the way he needed it, he caught her mouth and drank slow and deep, trying to catch her elusive tongue, to hold it, to suck it.

But she slipped away, teasing him, a Mona Lisa smile curling her lips.

John wasn't sure he could play, not tonight. Running his hands up over her hips and butt, he cupped her heavy breasts, weighed them and enjoyed her shiver. A tremble rippled through him, and his aching erection leaped and strained for her. He pulled her close again, to bury his face in her neck, to breathe her in.

"You're so sexy." He barely recognized his own hoarse voice. *"So sexy."*

She didn't answer, and that inflamed him even more because she was just out of reach and still in control when he was already gone. Holding his gaze, she put her hands to her hips and gathered the skirt of her dress up, revealing inch by slow inch of legs and then a patch of black satin that covered what he needed, what he meant to have and keep.

Hurrying out of his clothes, getting rid of the heavy layers that kept his skin from hers, the pain in his neck all but forgotten, John watched that dress rise past skimpy panties…a taut brown belly with just a hint of softness…a slim waist…and then the generous curve of breasts tipped with nipples pointed like Hershey's Kisses.

John watched those breasts bounce back into place and his mouth went dry and his head felt light.

When she stared him in the face as she shimmied out of that scrap of satin, lounged across the edge of the bed, planted one foot on the duvet and spread herself like a banquet, inviting him to gorge until he was sick, he groaned, dropped to his knees before her and feasted.

She glistened with honey, intoxicated him with her delicious musky scent and tasted like ambrosia. He lapped her up, his crooning mingling with her cries as they both palmed her breasts. When her body went rigid and she spasmed against his mouth, he suckled, wrung every last drop of pleasure from her and felt like a king.

Sliding up over her body, he hurried out of his underwear, ran his tongue over her torso, dipped into her navel and latched onto each breast. Liza clung to his head and arched for him, offering everything.

He was just reaching between them, thinking that now was the time, *now,* when, with a surprising burst of strength and energy, she flipped over, straddling him.

John panted, his heart thundering.

Crouched on all fours over him, her breasts dangling like ripe fruit that needed plucking, she gave him that knowing, enigmatic smile, the one that was driving him right out of his freaking mind.

"Sit up," she murmured. "Watch me."

John broke out into a fine sweat and adjusted a pillow behind his head even as he shook his head, told her no. He could hardly speak.

"Not tonight. I can't—"

"I think you can," Liza said, and laughed.

He watched, mesmerized, as she closed her eyes and moved for him, stretched for him, reached sleek arms high overhead and displayed those round breasts for his hungry eyes. Then she ran her hands down through her hair, rolled her head back and showed him her neck, the arch of her spine.

Her hands slipped through the valley between her breasts, stopping to squeeze each one, to press them together from the sides, to let those dark nipples peek through her fingers and taunt him.

When her hands ended their journey buried between her thighs, stroking, he had to rein himself in and squeeze his penis, hard, just under the swollen head, to keep from shooting off like a Fourth of July rocket.

Her eyes opened, and they were bright with purpose.

"Don't, Liza," he gasped. "I'm already dying here. *Don't… don't…ahh.*"

She did.

Crept up over him like a cat, licking first one of his sensitive nipples, then the other, then eased lower, pressed her tongue into his navel, cupped his tight sac and took him deep into her mouth.

John's hips rose up and off the bed, and he nearly jackknifed at the hot suction. There was no way to hold back his astonished cries, to keep her name from pouring out of his mouth.

The last thing John saw before his eyes drifted shut was her round butt stuck high in the air, her shining hair in her face and her lush berry lips wrapped tight around his hard length. Then he clamped his hands on the sides of her head and let her bob at will, because she didn't need any guidance.

A few seconds of this torture was all he could take. When he was close to bursting, he gently pulled her hair and she let him slide out of her mouth with all the reluctance in the world.

Crawling back over him on all fours, her lips swollen now, she stared down at him and he stared up at her and neither one of them could speak.

Stunned, John struggled to find words, to tell her how she'd changed his life, what she meant to him. Nothing in his life had ever prepared him for this moment—not marriage to his first wife, dating other women or running for the presidency.

There was only Liza. His world began and ended with her and would until he died.

Turning her onto her back, he smoothed her hair away from her face with one hand, reached between them with the other and entered her with a long thrust that had them both moaning. She was tight, hot, wet and everything he needed.

"I love you, Liza," he told her as his hips began their slow circles. A big word but way too small for this moment. "Love you. Love you—"

"I love y—"

The rest of her sentence died on her lips as her eyes rolled closed, her beautiful face twisted with ecstasy, and she bowed and tensed beneath him.

Waiting only until she went limp, he flipped her to her belly and bit her on the shoulder hard enough to get her attention.

"Oh, God," she breathed.

"You didn't think we were finished, did you?"

He grabbed her hips, pulled her up on all fours and drove into her from behind. She was so slick his vision faded with the pleasure.

He could never get enough of this.

Not if he lived a million more years.

Increasing his tempo, he pumped his hips until their cries drowned out the slapping sounds and the small of his back began to ache.

More. He still needed more.

Sweat trickled down his forehead and into his eyes. It was all over both of them, his and hers, mingling together, as primal, earthy and sexy as sunbathing nude on the beach. Good. He wanted her marked because she was his and he was hers.

Reaching down, he squeezed her dangling breasts, one and

then the other, until her spasms began again and she nearly bucked him off onto the floor.

With her inner muscles clenching hard around him, sucking him even deeper inside her body, he came with a hoarse cry that went on forever.

Chapter 18

Liza woke facedown on the bed with the sheets tangled around her hips, weak sunlight filtering in through the blinds and John's lips pressed to the small of her back. Even though the clock flashed the ungodly time of five-forty, she smiled and stretched like a cat.

"Wake up, sleepyhead."

Oh, man. His husky morning voice was sexy beyond belief.

She looked up and was surprised to see him dressed in shorts and a T-shirt, a soccer ball anchored to his hip by one muscular arm.

"I've got to go."

"Go? You need to come back." Propping her head on one arm, she bent one leg into the sheets, rolled her shoulder back and gave him her best sex-kitten pose.

John blinked. Viewed. Swallowed hard and cursed.

"Don't do this to me, darlin'. I had to sneak back up to the house, change, and sneak back down here. Now I've got to sneak out for my soccer game. I'm already late."

Liza pouted even though she was deliciously sore and could use the reprieve.

"Why didn't you wake me up?"

"You needed to sleep." He stared down at her, a shadow dimming the bright happiness in his eyes. "We need to decide how we're going to work this."

"I know."

"Today."

"I know." She loved him all the more for his patience. "I need just a little more time."

He nodded. "Rumor is, my staffers are already sending out their résumés. I wouldn't be surprised if some of them try to get on board with Senator Fitzgerald—"

Liza scowled at this outrageous disloyalty.

"—so if I'm going to suspend my campaign, I need to do it."

"Okay."

"I'll see you on the plane?"

"Yeah," she said.

Satisfied now, he smiled and leaned in to kiss her goodbye. "I love you."

Liza, who'd never been one for flowery words when she could help it, especially in the cold light of day when there was no liquor involved, flushed and cleared her throat.

"Me, too."

"What was that?"

"Me, too."

"I can't hear you, Liza."

Burning with mortification and grinning like an idiot, Liza dove under the sheet. "I love you, too, okay? Happy?"

Judging from his chuckle as he left and shut the door behind him, he was.

Surfacing, Liza climbed out of bed. By the time she'd emerged from the shower, she could hear the whoops and yells of several male voices and, opening the blinds on the far wall, she saw John and his staffers charging across the green clearing at the bottom of the hill, the black-and-white ball flying between them and a huge smile on John's face.

Her heart contracted.

What should she do?

She thought about her career and the fifteen-million-dollar offer. She thought about the money she'd already earned and saved and the fact that she was burned out by the lifestyle and the travel and had been for a while. She thought about John's candidacy, her absolute belief in his chances of winning and the country's need for his leadership. She thought about using her platform as first lady to attack the terrible problem of Alzheimer's.

Most of all, she thought about how John was nothing like Kent and how she'd felt yesterday when she thought he was going to die. She thought about building a life with him and having children with him.

There was no decision to be made.

With one eye on the time and the other on John's exuberant face outside her window, she picked up her cell phone and dialed her agent in New York to tell him that she was turning down the network's offer for the anchor's job and would be resigning from her position as senior Washington correspondent.

Takashi met up with Liza on the tarmac a couple hours later. The expression on his face, which was some combination of anger and worry, jolted her even before he grabbed her by the elbow and steered her a few feet away from the other waiting journalists. Everyone was vibrating with an excited buzz that told her something big had happened, something bad.

"Where the hell have you been? Why haven't you answered your phone?"

Liza, who, following the difficult phone call with her agent, had all but floated through her morning and was still basking in the glow of John's love, felt the first prickling of alarm.

"I slept late," she lied, feeling a nasty twinge of guilt for having ignored the persistent chirp of her phone. "What is it?"

"Nothing good."

Her mouth dried out. She didn't like the warning in his voice or the way worry now seemed to edge out anger as his predominant emotion. This, whatever it was, was nothing she wanted to hear, but he'd never been a coward and she wasn't going to start now.

"Tell me."

"Well, the first thing's that we're going to Richmond, not Washington."

"Richmond? Why?"

"They haven't said, but I'm thinking that the good senator wants to nurse his wounds with his sister."

"What wounds?"

"He was caught on camera engaging in a little hanky-panky last night at Heather Hill—"

Oh, God. Did they have shots of her and John and their heated discussion in the middle of the crowd? She knew they should have been more careful.

"—when one of the caterers snapped these with her phone. They're grainy, but they're authentic—we've checked. Now she's shopping them around, trying to get the best price. We told her no, obviously, but she'll find someone who wants to buy them. Probably a tabloid."

He offered the pictures to Liza, whose reeling brain felt as if it was spinning in all directions at once. Swallowing hard, her arm leaden and slow, she took them and, with dread, looked down at the one on top.

It was a dark, grainy photo—the pictures had obviously been taken with a poor quality camera and without a flash—but there was no mistaking the people in it, and she had to stifle a cry of outrage and surprise.

It was John. With Adena. His senior adviser and a married woman.

They were all over each other.

No. It couldn't be.

Hands shaking again—would her hands *ever* stop shaking?—Liza flipped through one sickening image after the other, all of which seem to have been taken over Adena's shoulder.

John and Adena, in their formal clothes, sitting inches apart on a stone bench in a garden at Heather Hill, talking urgently; John, his face dark and intense and his arm around Adena's waist as she buried her face in his neck.

Those two were bad enough, but then it got exponentially worse:

John, standing now, holding Adena in his arms.

Exactly the way he'd held Liza later that very same night.

Last night.

And the most painful of all, the slash of a knife right through her heart:

Adena tenderly cupping John's face in her hands as she kissed him on one corner of his mouth.

No.

John could not have passionately held another woman in his arms on the very same night he made love to Liza. It just wasn't possible.

A thousand times *no.*

Yes, said a sly, cool voice in the back of her mind.

Why else did Adena dislike her so much?

These pictures sure explained *that* behavior, didn't they?

Here's the proof that John never loved you any more than Kent loved you, said the sly voice. *Believe it.*

It all came rushing back to Liza in that one horrifying moment: her husband's betrayals, magnified a million times. The stunned disbelief. The bottomless despair. The overwhelming rage.

Takashi was staring. She tried to speak, but the pain was so unbearable she could hardly even breathe.

"Photoshop?" Yeah, she was grasping at straws, but she had to.

"No."

The pictures were authentic. Of course.

Liza almost fell to her knees then, almost wished for death so she wouldn't have to endure this pain again. Not again.

All these years later and boy, she could still pick them, couldn't she? She was still as blind and foolish when it came to men as she'd ever been.

Worse, everything she'd experienced with John last night was a lie. Everything he'd told her, the loving whispers, the pleading for her to consider the possibility of them having a joint future— it had all been a fairy tale worthy of the Brothers Grimm.

Liza wasn't special, after all. And she was a fool for thinking she was.

No doubt the good senator, like countless politicians before him, had mistresses in every far-flung corner of the country. Because that's what Liza was, wasn't it? A mistress? One in what was probably a collection of many.

Bewilderment fueled her rage and added to her sense of betrayal. What about all his endless talk of their callings and being together? What about his offer to quit the race for her? What about his legendary moral code?

"Liza?"

"I turned down the anchor's job for him," she whispered.

Takashi's golden skin paled to chalky white. "Jesus, Liza."

"He offered to quit the campaign for me."

His jaw dropped. It was obvious he couldn't believe Liza had fallen for such a sorry line, and Liza felt so foolish now that her humiliation was complete.

You're the most important thing to me, Liza.

What's your sign, Liza?

She'd heard both pickup lines in her lifetime—which one was the smarmiest? What kind of colossally stupid woman fell for either one? Pressing a hand to her throbbing temple, she swayed on the spot and tried not to pass out.

After a minute, an unstoppable hysterical laugh bubbled up to her lips.

"I thought we were going to get married."

Takashi watched her with utmost pity and concern, especially when her ugly laughter continued and a couple of their colleagues looked around with open curiosity in their eyes.

Taking her arm, he pulled her a couple more steps to the side and passed her a handkerchief from his back pocket. "Pull it together, Za-Za. There's more."

"More. *Great.*" Choking back what was going to be a sob rather than a laugh, Liza dabbed her eyes.

"This isn't his first go-round with Adena, apparently."

What?

"I've made some calls to a couple of staffers from his first campaign. None of them were willing to speak on the record about the affair, but they were together then, too. This was before Adena was married."

The world swam out of focus, and Liza clutched Takashi's arm for support.

"But...*he* was married then."

Takashi said nothing.

It didn't matter. There was nothing he could say that would repair the mutilated remnants of her personal and professional lives or change what she was: a woman so criminally stupid that she'd given up her life's ambition and actually thought she'd marry a man who had another mistress and had cheated on his first wife. She'd actually thought John would be faithful to *her*.

She turned away, unwilling to let Takashi or anyone else see the bitter tears in her eyes. Inside her head, she heard her father's voice.

You always screw things up, don't you, girl?

Yeah. She always screwed things up.

"Have you seen the pictures, Senator?"

"Senator, do you have any comments about the cheating allegations?"

"When will you issue any additional statements, Senator?"

John paused at the end of the aisle, stepped aside so the flight attendant could shut the door behind him, stared into the blinding lights of what seemed like a thousand cameras and waited for the uproar to die down, which took quite a while.

He did his best to keep his face serene and unconcerned as the sharks circled around him, but it was no easy job. His press corps had never been quite this frenzied, not even yesterday after the botched assassination attempt.

One shark in particular held his attention. Liza was in her regular seat at the back of the plane with Takashi. Staring at him with shattered eyes that told him how hurt she was, how shaken.

He had to explain to Liza. Screw the rest of these vultures.

Resisting the urge to grab Liza, throw her over his shoulder and sprint with her into the restricted section of the plane, where it was safe, he raised a hand for silence.

"I'm not having an affair with Adena Brown, nor would I ever have an affair with a married woman. That's all I have to say right now. I'll issue a more detailed statement later."

This lack of information, naturally, pleased no one. Chaos erupted again as soon as he paused to catch his breath, and one detached voice rose over all the others.

"Where is Adena Brown today, Senator?" Liza stood, the better to address him over the heads of all the people in the rows in front of her. "We haven't seen her get on the plane. Is she still on your staff?"

John's gut contracted into a painful knot. Every inch of ground he'd gained with Liza last night was gone, every ounce of trust destroyed. His head spun with how quickly he'd lost his greatest prize—how easily she'd slipped away from him when he hadn't seen any danger coming.

But he would get her back. Oh, yes, he would get her back.

"She's home in St. Louis for a few days, spending time with her family."

Liza's flat eyes showed no expression. "What about the other part of my question, Senator? Is she still on your staff?"

"I've accepted her resignation," he said.

"Why?" Liza demanded. "Why should your chief strategist quit in the middle of a difficult primary battle if there's no affair?"

"We'll be issuing joint statements later."

A collective groan rose up from the journalists, and he counted himself lucky that there were no rotten tomatoes nearby or he'd have been nailed. Taking his time, he walked up the aisle and paused at the doorway to the restricted section, just like he always did.

"We'll have more information for you tonight."

As he left, keeping his shoulders squared and his chin up, he could have sworn he heard a couple of hisses along with the mutinous muttering, but Liza was his only thought.

Glancing over his shoulder, he caught her gaze one last time and it impaled him, accusing now, unforgiving.

No more and no less than he deserved.

Chapter 19

Liza's summons to the front came the second they hit their cruising altitude. She went and took the pictures with her.

Déjà vu overwhelmed her the second she walked into the senator's private cabin, and she remembered that first night she spoke with him alone. It seemed like a thousand years ago and yet a few things remained achingly familiar. The space was still cozy, the music sexy and evocative. Al Green sang his heart out on "Let's Stay Together," and Liza wished she had a baseball bat so she could smash the nearest speaker.

He stood in the middle of the cabin, waiting for her and doing a remarkable imitation of a man who cared—all tight jaw, thin lips and worried eyes. As though he was hurting as much as she was.

Man, he was good, she thought, watching him, her heart breaking again and again in an endless loop worthy of the movie *Groundhog Day.*

He was really, really good.

He opened his mouth once, shut it and opened it again. Floundered.

She waited, giving him time to get his lies in order.

"I'm sorry," he finally said.

This didn't deserve a response.

"I know how it looks, Liza, but I'm not Adena's lover."

"Oh?"

Having nothing better to do to pass the time during this short flight from Columbus to Richmond, she decided to play along for a minute and see what happened. Why not? Maybe compare outrageous falsehoods and see who was better at them, him or her ex-husband. Which of the men she'd loved was the best liar? They could run a contest.

"When did you stop being Adena's lover, pray tell?"

He paled but didn't deny the relationship entirely. "When we'd been married for about a year, Camille and I separated for about six months because we were both young and ambitious and were spending way more time on our careers than we were on our marriage. We talked about a divorce and I did something really stupid—I had an affair with Adena. She'd been working on my campaign way back when I had my unsuccessful run for office. And then Camille got sick."

Liza said nothing but remembered what he'd told her:

I wasn't a perfect husband.

"Camille's getting sick put things in perspective real fast." He did a great job with the whole misery and shame thing, hanging his head and looking sorry for the day he'd been born. "I realized how much I loved her and how much I had to lose. How immature and selfish I'd been. I told her about the affair and asked for another chance. She forgave me. We were together until she died. Closer than ever, if you can believe it."

Disillusioned and cynical as she was—she'd known he wasn't a saint, but hearing the proof was still a shock—Liza still found herself wavering because she wanted so much to believe in him and their chances for a successful relationship.

She tried to think. This story, if it was true, wasn't so bad, was it? Many marriages went through rough patches, didn't they?

Yes. Yes, they did.

But then her suspicious mind intruded, reminding her tha

what happened years ago had nothing to do with him being wrapped around Adena *last night*.

"How touching," she said sickened by her ongoing gullibility and foolishness, which seemed to have no beginning or end. "Irrelevant, but touching."

He stepped closer and held his hands out, palms up. "After Camille was gone, Adena and I worked together again. We've always been a good team professionally. But *that's all*. She was married by then, and I was never in love with her anyway. You're the only woman I've loved since Camille, Liza. *You*."

Staring into his earnest face, seeing the intensity, Liza softened for three hopeful seconds and then caught herself. Wasn't the hallmark of a good liar the fact that he preyed on your weaknesses? That he told you what you wanted to believe anyway?

Another rupture appeared in her ruined heart.

He had Kent beat by a mile in the liar department.

She would not believe this bullshit even though she wished she could. It was now inconceivable that all the whispers and glances she'd personally witnessed between the senator and Adena were platonic, or that Adena's obvious and instantaneous dislike of Liza was because of protectiveness of the campaign and not personal jealousy.

This man would not make a bigger fool of her than he already had, and Liza hated him for trying.

"This is all very interesting." An angry buzz started in her head, the way it would sound if a thousand agitated bees were trapped inside her skull, but she was determined to remain calm and keep her voice steady. "But what does it have to do with all these pictures—" she flapped the folder at him "—of you and Adena draped all over each other *last night*?"

With obvious frustration, he rubbed both hands over his head and then dropped them to his sides. His face looked splotchy now, his eyes wilder, almost feral, but when he spoke, it was in calm, rational tones.

"After you and I talked, she came to me—remember when she asked to talk to me?—made a big confession and offered her resignation. She's screwed up in a major way, done something that's going to hurt the campaign when it goes public—"

Liza gaped at him. "*She's* screwed up?"

"—and she wanted to tell me first. I was comforting her because she was distraught. That's all."

Comforting? The buzzing in Liza's ears got louder. *Comforting?*

"I have to get this mess straightened out, Liza, but I promise you that—"

"You...*promise?*" She felt her face twisting as she spoke, her mouth contorting into a snarl. "Promises from you are like gold in the bank, aren't they, Senator?"

"Liza—"

He reached for her arm but she jerked away. Raising his hands, he backed up a step or two to give her space but kept talking.

"You can't believe in your heart that I'd make love to her and you. You're the only woman I want, Liza. I love you. You *know* that—"

The buzzing in her ears erupted in a violent crescendo that had her crying out with rage. Destroyed in a way she'd never been before, even after she'd discovered Kent's third affair, she wondered if the agony would strike her dead on the spot and almost wished it would.

Because *she* had done this to herself. *She* had believed in love when she knew damn good and well that love didn't exist, at least not on the man's part. *She* had thought she was in line for a happy ending. *She* had chosen the wrong man—*again*—and given up everything she'd worked for to be with him.

Maybe this pain was no less than she deserved for being this stupid.

Undone, she lashed out, hurling the folder at him. He seemed to have been expecting something like this—had braced for it—because he didn't flinch or duck when the folder hit him in the center of his chest and the photos fluttered to the ground at his feet.

"I gave up the anchor chair for you," she screeched. "I quit my job for you. I thought you loved me—"

Without warning he lunged, grabbed her around the waist, trapping her arms at her sides, and swept her off her feet. Startled, she struggled against him, but there was no point.

It cost him zero effort to swing her around and sink into the nearest captain's chair with her on his lap. Holding tight so she couldn't smack him, he hooked his chin over her shoulder and spoke directly into her ear.

"I'm sorry." There was terrible control in his tone, an excruciating politeness that shredded her overwrought nerves. "I don't seem to be communicating very well right now. It must be because the woman I love thinks I'm cheating on her and my campaign is in the toilet. Let me try again."

She could never physically be afraid of him, but there was something so edgy, so determined and ruthless in his calm voice that she knew that, strong as she was, she was no match for him and never would be. The senator, when he got like this, could probably move mountains with his bare hands, hypnotize world leaders with the force of his will.

"Let me go."

"No. You're going to listen to me."

Liza roared with outrage. All the commotion finally attracted some attention and one of the new secret service agents opened the cabin door, poked his head in and surveyed the scene with an impassive face.

"Everything okay in—"

"Get the hell out," the senator roared.

The agent backed out and shut the door, and the senator continued as though there'd been no interruption.

"I haven't had sex with Adena in years, okay? That's number one."

The heat of his breath against her face made Liza's belly flutter, so she renewed her struggle, to no avail. His arms tightened, gentle iron bars from which she had no chance of escaping.

"Number two: I do love you. I haven't cheated on you and I won't cheat on you. I am not your ex-husband, and I'm not the same man who cheated on Camille all those years ago. I've grown and I've learned from my mistakes. You should understand that, right? I'm assuming you're not the same woman who married your ex all those years ago?…"

Fury all but blinded Liza—at him for doing this to her and at herself for being this weak and looking for loopholes in her vow not to believe him, for searching for ways his tortured explanations might possibly be true.

Squirming again, she inadvertently wedged her butt against his groin. She froze and choked off an involuntary whimper.

"Are you trying to make me lose control here, Liza?" he rasped in her ear, thrusting his hips for maximum effect. "Because that's what you're doing. You may want to keep still."

Liza kept still.

"Number three," he continued. "As soon as I have this all straightened out, which will be later on tonight, by the way, I'm going to come to you and we're going to negotiate a deal. Do you want to know what it is?"

"No," she said, terror in her heart.

"Too bad," he said easily. "We're getting married, you and I— as soon as we can manage it. I'm not letting your posttraumatic-divorce-stress nonsense, or whatever you want to call it, ruin our chances. Got that? The only question is whether I'm going to end this campaign. Whether I end it or not, I'm not letting my good name go down in flames like this. I need to straighten this mess out so I can at least stay in the Senate. Understand?"

She nodded, not daring to speak lest the sound of her voice prompt him to prolong this interlude on his lap.

"Good girl. I'm letting you go now. Don't hit me."

The second those arms loosened, she surged to her feet, wheeled around and glared at him. He rose, towering over her, and she wanted to rage at him for manhandling her and, worse, making her hope again when there should be no hope between them.

"You're insane," she spat.

His eyes glittered, although whether it was from irritation or amusement, she couldn't tell. "Maybe, but you see where I'm going with this, don't you, Liza? Let me spell it out for you: you're going to be my wife. The election isn't going to ruin that, your job isn't going to ruin that—not even *you* are going to ruin that. Now I've got some work to do to get my ass out of the fire. That's it for now. I'll see you later."

Liza's jaw dropped to the floor. "You're *dismissing* me?"

He looked around, his expression hard and wicked. "Not yet."

Lashing out, he grabbed her arms, hauled her up against him and molded her body to his. Liza jerked convulsively when their hips met, but his big hand clamped down on her butt, grinding her against him, weakening her knees and giving her no room for escape. With his free hand he grabbed a hank of her hair, pulled her head back and kissed her, hard and deep.

Furious and helpless to do otherwise, Liza kissed him back. His clawed fingers dug into her butt, hurting her with a glorious pain, and she stroked deeper into his mouth, nipping his bottom lip hard enough to draw blood as she withdrew. Their animalistic cries filled the air for a minute, and then they broke apart, panting.

Staring at her, he swiped the back of his hand across his mouth. "*Now* you're dismissed."

With a disbelieving cry—had she just *kissed* this liar?—Liza raised her hand to slap him, but he grabbed her wrist and wrenched it down between them.

"Don't do that."

Liza tore free and glared at him. She didn't know what to think, whether to believe or not. All she knew was that throughout her life the only person she'd truly been able to count on was *Liza*.

Patience was not one of her virtues; she couldn't wait.

"I'm going to do my own investigation, Senator. I'll get to the bottom of this with or without your help. I'm not going to sit around and wait for you to decide to come tell me the whole story."

He grimaced. "I know you will. That's not the issue. The issue is: how many innocent people are going to be hurt if you don't give me time to get this straightened out?"

On that incomprehensible note, he opened the door for her and she left. Huffing, she was just settling in her seat when her air phone rang.

It was the hospital.

The motorcade drove right up to the gated executive mansion in Richmond, as inconspicuous in the early afternoon hours as a runaway float from the Macy's Thanksgiving Day Parade. John didn't care. His only feeling, other than a blinding black rage, was gratitude that Jillian was, according to the housekeeper who'd answered the phone, not home to witness the ugly scene that was about to unfold.

Jumping out of his SUV almost before it came to a complete stop at the end of the circular driveway, John stormed up the front steps and pounded on the door. His secret service agents, assorted local police and his brother-in-law's own security detail, none of whom looked like his biggest fans at the moment, fanned out and scrambled to keep up with him.

There'd been some murmurings about John entering through the back, but screw that. The whole world would know what was going on soon enough.

Anyway, if ever there was a good time for a sniper to take him out, it was now. Before he had to do his grim duties as a brother and one of the party's top leaders.

They'd been expecting him, but that did not, of course, mean that his brother-in-law had the balls to come to the door himself. The harassed-looking housekeeper let him in and ushered him through the vaulted foyer and into the paneled library. John's footsteps echoed on the gleaming hardwood floors, an ominous sound in the otherwise oppressive silence of the house.

It was just like that punk to skulk like a coward.

"He's in here, Senator." The woman left, shutting the door behind her.

For a minute John didn't see anyone and he wondered where all the governor's advisers were. The cozy room was still full of sunlight, which glinted off the swimming pool visible through the floor-to-ceiling windows. There was no one at the desk, no one on the sofa or any of the chairs, no sign of human life.

Irritated, John was just about to call after the housekeeper when a movement on the other side of the entertainment armoire caught his attention.

Beau appeared, holding what was apparently a scotch on the rocks and looking a little gray under his light brown skin but otherwise calm. John wanted to kill him for his composure.

"You son of a bitch."

Temporary insanity caught John in an iron grip and wouldn't let go. Lunging across the room, he grabbed Beau by the collar and shoved him up against the wall, thunking his head and knocking his drink to the floor.

"I should shove your teeth down your throat."

Beau broke free and they faced off, snarling.

Why wasn't there some outward sign of this man's moral

decay—something that set him apart from everyone else and served as a warning to the unsuspecting? What had happened to this man to make his conscience more flexible than the average person's?

For God's sake, what destructive demons possessed Beau? After everything he and Jillian had already been through, how could he cause one more crisis?

"How could you do this *again?*" John roared, honestly trying to comprehend the man's thought processes. "Use small words so I can understand."

"Do what, John?" asked a female voice.

No. Oh, no. Not Jillian. Not now.

Shit.

It was her. She emerged through the library's side door, and John's nightmare was complete. If he'd thought he couldn't feel any worse for her, he was wrong. There was something about the combination of the bewildered look in her brown eyes and her squared shoulders—as though she knew something bad was about to happen but was determined to face it with courage—that just killed him.

John was forcibly reminded of the long-ago day their mother died and the look on Jillian's face right before their father broke the terrible news.

Lord, give me strength to get through this. Give Jillian strength.

"Jillian." John reached for her hand. "I didn't know you were home."

"I came back early. I was…on an errand."

She turned to Beau, who now seemed frozen except for the wild glitter in his too-bright eyes. Guilt was etched deeply in every line of his body, every hair on his head. That and desperation.

Swallowing hard, he glanced at John and then faced his wife.

"I need to talk to you, Jill."

There was an almost imperceptible shift in Jillian's expression, a slight hardening, but she didn't say anything and Beau wasn't in any rush to tell her.

Watching the excruciating scene, John tried to blend into the paneling.

Beau, to his credit, held his wife's gaze even when understanding began to dawn in her expression…even when she gasped…

even when the tears formed in her eyes and she hugged her arms to her belly as though she could protect herself.

"No," she whispered, shaking her head. "Not again."

"I'm sorry, baby." Beau's face crumpled but he didn't cry and didn't make excuses. Maybe he had none left, having used them all up the last time. His Adam's apple bobbed in a rough swallow. "I'm sorry."

John didn't snort, but it was a near thing. *Sorry.* Talk about your understatements. Beau was broken, the perfect specimen of a self-destructive personality, and beyond fixing. If only Jillian would write him off for good.

Then Liza's face intruded on John's thoughts. He thought of all the risks he'd taken and was still taking to be with her and decided maybe he wasn't the one to weigh in on crazy behavior where women were concerned. But when he caught a flash of Jillian's despair, he wanted to kill Beau all over again and any sympathetic impulse he'd felt crumbled to dust.

Jillian turned away from Beau and stared down at the rug's floral pattern, her expression vacant. Several tears fell, unchecked, and lingered on her cheeks. She looked utterly miserable, like an abandoned child, and John's throat burned with stifled emotion.

He ignored the impulse to touch her because he knew it would make things worse. Better to take his cues from her, wait to see what she needed.

She'd better not take the SOB back again, though. There was a limit to how many pep talks John could give and how many times he could pick up the pieces of her broken heart.

Never again.

Suddenly Jillian stared up at Beau, and there was nothing vague about her now, nothing weak. "Who?" Her voice shook with anger. "Tell me *who.*"

Beau hung his head in a pretty good impersonation of an ashamed man, but, hell, he'd had so much practice with his penitent act it was hard to tell. After several false starts, he finally got his mouth to work and said the name that would fan this flame into an inferno.

"Adena Brown."

John kept quiet; Jillian blinked.

"*Adena?*" Jillian tested the name to make sure she'd gotten it right.

Beau nodded, his nostrils flaring.

"But…"

Flustered, Jillian ran both hands through her hair as she struggled to get her mind around it. No doubt she was matching dates with deceptions, lies with opportunities. She turned to John, stammering in her confusion.

"They said that there are pictures of *you* and Adena, not Beau—"

"She came to me last night, Jill, and we talked in the garden. That's where the caterer shot the pictures. We never saw anyone." John scrubbed a hand over his face. "Anyway, she told me everything. The guilt was killing her, I guess, and it didn't help to see you and Beau together at the party. She said Beau broke things off a while back. She asked me to forgive her because she knew she'd let me down and was afraid of damaging the campaign if it came out." He trailed off and shrugged. "And then she quit so she could go home and tell her husband. Fix her family, if that's possible."

More blinking from Jillian, more staring at the ground. When she looked up at Beau again, she'd aged a thousand years and horror filled her face. "You had an affair with the woman we hired to get your butt out of the sling *from the last time you cheated on me?*"

Beau stood tall before his wife's rising hysteria and faced her like a man. The only sign of emotion was the sheen of moisture over his bright eyes. "Yes."

"*Are you going to defend yourself?*" Jillian screamed.

"We've had problems for a long time, Jill," Beau said. "We've never dealt with them. It's not about the other women—"

Jillian blanched. "So this is *my* fault?"

"Of course not," Beau told her. "But I don't know how to reach you anymore, Jill. You've shut yourself off ever since—"

"How dare you blame me?"

Beau stared at her. "I don't know how to get you back, Jill. I don't know where my wife has gone—and I need you."

"We can't get anything back."

Beau stilled and John could almost smell the man's fear. "What…what are you saying?"

Silence rang through the room for several long seconds, and then, with shaking hands, Jillian swiped at her tears, all business now.

"I want a divorce."

"*No,*" Beau said.

"You need to resign," Jillian told him. "Don't put the party—or the state—through any more scandals."

"Jill—"

"Do it now, so John can salvage the primary."

"I'll resign, but this marriage isn't over. It'll never be over."

"It's over now."

"We still love each other, Jill," Beau cried. "Even after everything we've been through. You *know* we still—"

"Our marriage is dead. You've killed it," she said simply. "You're so broken there's nothing left to love. I couldn't even if I wanted to."

Beau couldn't answer.

John watched the spouses stare at each other and witnessed the end of their marriage in those few seconds. He saw Jillian's quiet fury and bottomless despair and read Beau's desperation in the man's tortured face.

He remembered their wedding day, the joy they'd all felt and the hopes for their bright future together, and then he remembered the dark times, the pain. What had happened to them? Where had all that happiness gone?

The chords strained in Beau's neck as he struggled to hold his emotions in check; John wondered if Beau would survive a divorce. Jillian would, but Beau might well harm himself. Whether it was purposeful or not, Beau Taylor was his own worst enemy and always had been.

"I never want to see you again," Jillian told her husband, tears spilling down her cheeks. "You're dead to me."

Beau's lips twisted and he blinked furiously. Even John could see the valiant effort he put into not crying. He stared at his distraught wife, his gaze hungry and ruined.

"I'll always love you, Jill. You'll be the last thing I think about on my dying day. And it'll never be over between us."

He turned and, shoulders squared, left the library, leaving a hysterical Jillian to collapse, sobbing, in John's arms.

"I'm pregnant. Jesus, God—I just came from the doctor."

John gathered her tighter. As he had the day their mother died, John held her and told her a lie: that everything would be okay.

Chapter 20

Liza sat at her sleeping father's bedside and inventoried the indignities that had befallen this proud man in his old age. Alzheimer's and the disappearance of a lifetime's memories. The loss of his ability to care for himself. Now, pneumonia and the attendant oxygen cannula stuck up his nose and IV lines stuck in his frail arm. Restraints lashing his arms to the bed so he wouldn't pull the needle out. A powder-blue gown that gaped open in the back and a hospital door that provided no privacy from the endless stream of medical personnel in and out of his room.

She wanted to bury her head in his blankets and weep for him—and for herself, for that matter—but crying was a waste of time and the Colonel needed her to be strong now.

After leaving the senator and the campaign in Richmond and taking the shuttle back to Washington, she'd come directly here, where she'd sat for most of the day rather than follow up on leads concerning the senator's evolving scandal. She had no idea what was happening now and couldn't bring herself to care.

Much.

Just then, the Colonel's lids fluttered and opened and he

stared at her with watery eyes sunken in his gray face. Dredging up a reassuring smile, she took his hand, which was a little too warm from the fever, and prayed for the oxygen to get some air into the man's sick lungs and do it soon so his color would return to normal.

"Hello, Colonel."

He blinked and focused his gaze. "What the hell happened, girl?"

"They brought you to the hospital. You have pneumonia, but you'll be fine. You're getting antibiotics and some oxygen."

"Where's Mama?"

Liza's smile slipped. Some days it was harder than others to maintain the lie, and this was one of those days. But she was not going to tell her father over and over again, every time his memory failed, that his wife was dead and had been for decades. Wasn't a kind lie better than that brand of pointlessly cruel honesty?

"Mama's resting." Resting in peace.

The Colonel grunted, looking dissatisfied with this answer, but he let the issue drop. "What the hell's wrong with you? You look terrible."

"I'm worried about you," she tried.

"What else is wrong with you?"

Liza felt her chin quiver and firmed it. Blinking furiously—there was always something so unnerving about her father's insight, even now—she tried to stay upbeat.

"Well, Colonel, I've gotten myself in a real mess this time." She decided to tell him what had really happened because, hey, what were the chances that he'd remember later? "I fell in love with someone and I think he's cheating on me."

The Colonel, who'd been testing his restraints and trying to break free, stilled and stared at her with eyes that were suddenly as sharp and focused as they'd ever been.

"That guy who's running for president? The senator?"

Surprised, Liza drew back. "Well…yes."

The Colonel snorted and gave one hand as much of a dismissive wave as he could manage with the restraints and the IV. "That man's not cheating on you, girl. Trust me. I'm a good judge of character and he's a gentleman. Not like that jackass you married. You've got that senator's nose so wide open he can't see straight. Stop your worrying."

Liza gaped at him, too stunned to reply.

Could it be true? It wasn't a good idea to rely too much on an Alzheimer's patient's perceptions of reality, but the Colonel had always been a shrewd judge of character, and he had warned her in no uncertain terms not to marry Kent in the first place. Goodness knew he'd been right about that.

Could he be right about the senator?

"Where's Mama?" he demanded again. "I've got to pee and someone needs to help me get these straps off."

So much for his moment of lucidity.

If there was one good thing about her quitting her job, Liza decided, it was having more time for her father, who needed her now more than ever. How did she think she'd've managed his care if she'd had to move to New York to anchor the evening news? People managed their parents' care long distance all the time, sure, but the guilt would've eaten her alive. Thank goodness she wouldn't have to go down that road now.

Getting to her feet, she rang for the nurse. "Mama can't come," she told him, "but I'll get someone in here to help you."

Following a fair amount of fussing and commotion, Liza grabbed her purse and left the room while someone came in to assist her father. She was just loitering in the hall by the waiting area, wondering how long things would take, when Takashi, who was at the station, called on her cell phone.

"You're not going to believe this," he said by way of greeting.

All Liza's earlier turmoil came rushing back in a crashing wave. All kinds of terrible scenarios ran through her head as she headed for the waiting area, each more horrifying than the last:

Adena had confirmed her affair with the senator.

Three other married women had also admitted affairs with the senator.

The senator routinely had affairs with staffers.

The fact that none of these scenarios jibed with her observations about him did not keep her stomach from churning or her heart from skipping every other beat.

"First things first," Takashi said. "How's the Colonel?"

"Better. What've you got?"

"Well, I talked to Adena's assistant, who wouldn't say a thing, even off the record, and Adena's spokesperson hasn't returned any of my one thousand calls."

"Oh."

"I talked to my source with the senator's private security firm, who, obviously, is speaking on condition of anonymity—"

Would this man please get to the point while they were still young? "Yeah, yeah, I know. He signed a confidentiality agreement and doesn't want to be fired. So what?"

"I'll tell you *so what*. It might interest you to know that even though it's a poorly kept secret that the senator spent last night with you in the cottage at Heather Hill—"

Oh, God. Her face burned to cinders.

"—he swears that that's the first time since they began working with the campaign back in October that he's been with a woman. Except for the night he snuck out to your house, that is."

Liza tried to process this information. "So...you're telling me...*what?*"

"I'm telling you," Takashi said, "that unless the senator is significantly better at sneaking around with Adena than he is at sneaking around with you, those pictures do not show a man with his mistress."

"But...what do they show?"

But Liza already knew. Her gut was telling her, and so was the senator's voice in her head: *I was comforting her.* Had he...actually told her the *truth?* Stunned at this inconceivable possibility, Liza collapsed in a chair and stared at the nearest coffee table with unfocused eyes.

John—funny how she thought of him as the *senator* when she wanted to keep him at a distance and *John* when her heart wouldn't let her—hadn't lied to her.

Relief washed over her, so blessed and powerful it would've knocked her on her butt if she'd been standing. Pressing a hand to her heart, she tried to keep it inside her chest, where it belonged.

"So what's going on?" she wondered. "What's the big scandal?"

"Aren't you watching TV?"

"No."

This seemed to be too much for Takashi, and she heard the exasperation in his voice. "Have you not been watching the news this afternoon while you've been sitting by your father's bedside?"

"Of course not. Why would I do that? So I can drive myself crazy?"

"Crazier," he muttered. "Turn on the TV."

Liza punched a button on the wall-mounted TV, and an unbelievable scene came into vivid color focus. It was the governor—*jerk*—standing on the driveway of the governor's mansion—flanked by several members of his staff. A bunch of reporters were shoving their microphones and digital voice recorders in his face.

Liza checked the red *Breaking News* crawl at the bottom of the screen, blinked and checked it again:

Governor of Virginia resigns amid cheating scandal.

Liza gasped. "Oh, my God."

The governor had that Hall-of-Shame hangdog expression all over his guilt-ridden face, but his voice was strong. "—inexcusable behavior. I would like to apologize to the other family, which has been greatly affected by my selfish actions; to my wife, who did not deserve this betrayal; and to people of the great state of Virginia, who put their faith in me."

He paused to take a deep breath and swipe at his nose. "Because I do not want my behavior to serve as a distraction to my state or to the party in this election year, I've tendered my resignation, effective as soon as Lieutenant Governor Bradshaw can be sworn in tomorrow morning. I'll have no further statements."

With that, the disgraced governor ignored the reporters' shouted questions, turned and walked back up the driveway toward the mansion in the background. The coverage switched to the anchor back at the studio.

"Oh, my God," Liza said. "Adena and the *governor?* Is this for real?"

"He hired her to dig him out of his hole the last time he cheated on his wife. Guess they made the most of all that quality time they spent together, eh?"

"I hope that was some good sex," Liza said. "Because it's cost him his career. Idiot."

Takashi snorted. "I don't get how another guy this smart could do something this stupid. I thought he'd run for president one day."

"Where was Jillian? I didn't see her waiting in the background and doing the dutiful, stand-by-your-man thing."

"She did that the last time," Takashi reminded her. "I'm betting this is it for her."

"Oh, my God." Liza knew exactly the sort of ugly scene that had to be going on inside the governor's mansion right now. She'd lived it herself. "Poor Jillian. I don't think she's—*wait.* What's this?"

She stared at the TV again, where the scene had changed and now showed an unsmiling Senator Warner striding across the tarmac with an overnight bag slung over one shoulder and something gripped in his hand. He impatiently paused for the reporters' shouted questions and submitted to their microphones, lights and cameras being shoved in his face.

"We need to make this quick, guys," he said. "I need to get back to Washington."

"Senator, what's your reaction to your brother-in-law's resignation?"

The senator's frown deepened. "I think he did the right thing, and I commend him on doing it so quickly. Obviously my thoughts are with my family now, my sister."

"What about your senior adviser, Senator?" asked another reporter.

"As I've said before," the senator said, his jaw tightening, "I've accepted Adena Brown's resignation, and I wish her and her family the best. I don't have any more comments about that."

He edged toward the plane, but the reporters had one more question for him.

"Senator, we've been hearing rumors that a special relationship has sprung up between you and Liza Wilson. Would you care to comment about that?"

Liza's jaw dropped. She watched a smile soften the corners of the senator's eyes as he tried to control the beginnings of a grin. The many lights on his face illuminated the flush that crept up from his neck, and Liza knew that the whole world could see it.

Oh, God. The cat was out of the bag now, wasn't it?

"Liza Wilson is a fine journalist," the senator said, "and she's had my butt in the fire for most of this campaign—"

The gathered reporters and Takashi laughed; Liza couldn't breathe.

"—and you folks need to excuse me because I've got a call to make and a plane to catch."

Then the senator waved goodbye and Liza saw the flash of his iPhone in his hand. A wider shot showed him striding across the tarmac and up the steps of the plane while simultaneously punching a couple of numbers and putting the phone to his ear.

The coverage was just switching back to the anchor in the studio when something happened that stopped Liza's heart:

Her phone beeped, indicating she had another call.

She and Takashi both gasped. Neither of them spoke.

The phone beeped again.

Takashi recovered first and she heard the wry amusement in his voice. "I think that's for you. You may want to answer it."

"Bye," she said quickly and clicked over. "Y-yes?" She cleared her throat and tried again. "Hello?"

"It's John."

"Hi," she breathed.

"How are you, darlin'?" he asked, and she heard the smile in his voice, the huskiness just for her.

"Shaky."

"How's the Colonel?"

"How did—" she began.

"I know everything. How is he?"

"Better. But he'll be in the hospital for several days while they give him intravenous antibiotics."

"Good. Will you be home when I get there?"

"Get here?"

"I told you I was coming for you tonight." There was a slight pause, during which she felt him silently dare her to deny or contradict him, but neither of those thoughts crossed her mind. "I'll be in the motorcade. You don't have any problems with that, do you?"

Liza's pulse skittered.

This was not, she knew, a throwaway question. Her answer to this one query held both their futures. If she said *yes,* that she had a problem with it, then he'd probably sneak to her house as he'd done before. If she said *no,* no problem, and his motorcade pulled up in front of her house for the whole world to see, it was tantamount to a declaration of intent, an announcement that they were together and didn't care who knew it.

Liza hesitated because this was a monumental turning point in her life and she wanted to give it the weight it deserved. But the answer was in her heart and had been almost since the second she first laid eyes on him.

She belonged with Jonathan Warner whether he lived in a van down by the river or the White House. He was hers and she was his. Period. The whole world needed to know, the sooner the better.

"Liza?"

"No," she said. "No problem."

"I'll be there as soon as I can."

Chapter 21

Liza stayed at the hospital until the Colonel went to sleep for the night, and then she drove home. She'd barely showered and changed into another tank top-yoga pants combination when a commotion outside her front door announced the arrival of the senator's motorcade.

Breathless and all but levitating with excitement, she at least had the good sense to click off the lamp nearest the window before she peered out through the blinds.

The sight on her quiet street, which was normally dark and sleepy at this time of night, nearly knocked her on her freshly washed butt: six or seven huge black SUVs with blacked-out windows trailed a couple of motorcycle cops with flashing lights.

Gaping, she watched as all the vehicles stopped at her curb and various doors began to open. Secret service agents emerged, one after the other, and fanned out around her house. The scene reminded her of clowns emerging from a Volkswagen Beetle at the circus, and she had to stifle a hysterical giggle.

But then the senator appeared in his shirtsleeves with his jacket slung over his shoulder, and there was nothing funny about anything, especially when she saw the hard determination in his jaw as he jogged up her front steps from the sidewalk.

Goose bumps broke out over her entire body and, manic now with jitters, she turned in a tight circle, wondering what was happening to her life tonight. They'd wanted to go public with their relationship and, by God, *that* was public; only the sitting president rolled quite like *that*. And now the whole world knew—it'd be in the papers by the morning and on the Internet tonight—and John was coming for her like he'd said he would, and she had no idea what she would do now.

That hysteria rose again in her chest, and she had to let it out. Flopping onto the sofa, she buried her face in a pillow and screamed until her throat burned. Then she screamed again. On the third scream she also kicked her feet, and that helped. By the time the senator knocked, she was calm again and ready to face him.

Standing, she tossed the pillow aside, walked to the door and let him in.

He came inside and bolted the lock. Then he turned to face her, their gazes connected and Liza felt that familiar surge of electricity between them. He seemed to feel it, too, because he was as breathless as she was and didn't speak, or maybe it was just that in this moment words were unnecessary.

Several seconds passed, marked by the relentless beat of Liza's heart.

Those unsmiling eyes held hers with a possessive glitter that left nothing to her imagination. *Oh, God. Oh—*

Without warning, he flung his jacket to the floor and reached for her, his big hands claiming her hips and butt while his mouth claimed hers. Liza cried out, already frantic with need and mindless in her desire to make this man a part of her body. She clutched his head and neck and opened for him as they nipped, licked and stroked their way deep into each other's mouths.

His taste was the same—a familiar intoxicating combination of mints and man that almost had her sobbing in remembrance. She sucked his tongue and gave him her own because she would die if she didn't have everything, and he crooned with approval. The primitive sound resonated in her aching breasts and tightened in her belly, and she teetered on the edge of a cataclysm even before he tightened his grip on her butt and rubbed her against a heart-stopping erection.

They grappled with each other for a minute, their eager hands everywhere at once and yet nowhere in particular. In rising desperation, she searched for skin and got none—only the starchy cotton of a dress shirt that made her wonder why in God's name this man would come to her with so many unyielding clothes on. He, meanwhile, sank his fingers in her hair and angled her head, taking her mouth as though he'd never kissed before and never would again.

It was all too much. By some silent but mutual understanding, they broke apart long enough to stare at each other and pant their way to a deep breath, but then the dance began again.

John reached for her and, stooping, pressed his face to her breasts and dragged his open mouth over her nipples. Clothing did not slow him down. Suckling hard, he used his tongue to rub a nipple against the roof of his mouth, and the unspeakable abrasion of the soft cotton against her sensitive flesh made her come in a blinding wave of pleasure that radiated from her pulsing sex to her contracting belly and up out of her mouth in an astonished cry.

Groaning, John stooped lower, pressed his lips to the curve of her stomach and slid his hands under the waistband of her pants and panties. In a flash, he had them down her legs and off and she kicked them away.

She froze, agonized, as he buried his face in her nest of curls and nuzzled, rooting for her scent. She was soaking wet and now he knew it. Running two fingers between her legs, he spread her hot honey around, lubricating the swollen flesh and making her more ready for him than she already was. And then he straightened, stared her in the face and sucked his fingers into his mouth. His eyes rolled closed in unmistakable ecstasy.

Liza almost swooned, but he didn't give her time.

In a surge of movement, he gripped her butt and hefted her until she wrapped her thighs around his hips and her arms around his neck. Staring down into his gleaming eyes as he carried her through the foyer and into the living room, she saw the sheen of sweat on his brow, the glisten of her juices on his swollen lips and the warmth of his expression. She opened her mouth to tell him how she felt about him but couldn't find the words.

And then he lowered her to her back on the sofa, and she spread her legs wide and waited as he unzipped his pants and freed himself. When she saw that heavy dark length straining for her, throbbing for her, she hissed out a breathless "yesss" and reached for him.

He didn't need the encouragement. With a quick thrust he was inside and she was coming all over again, arching back into the pillows and undone by the tight friction of his body's slide into hers.

John levered himself up on his elbows and watched her, catching her endless cries in his mouth as though he meant to keep each one forever.

When she'd recovered and settled a little, he drew back and spoke to her, with only the slight tremble in his arms telling her how much it cost him to keep himself in check at this moment.

"I'm not going to lose you, Liza," he whispered. "Not to stupid rumors or your doubts or your fears. Do you understand?"

"Yes." She writhed against him because the tension was building inside her again, demanding release, but there was no point.

"You have to trust me." Locking his hips, he resisted all her efforts to drive the pace. "I've never given you a reason not to trust me. Have I?"

"No." She stroked his face and palmed his cheeks. "I'm sorry I didn't believe you."

The reward for this apology was a nice long stroke. He pulled slowly out…out…out…and then eased in again, inching back inside as though he had a millennium to rub against her sweet spot and bring her to the edge of insanity.

"Oh, God." She arched away from him again because she just couldn't take it, not one more second of this torture.

The trembling in his arms increased, but he did not succumb to it. "You're mine, Liza. You know that, right? You'll always be mine."

Gasping in a breath, she demanded her due.

"And you'll always be mine, won't you?"

"Darlin.'" The ghost of a smile flickered across his face and disappeared. "I've been yours since I laid eyes on you. You just didn't know it."

She smiled her joy up at him and watched him fly apart in response.

Calling her name in a hoarse voice, he let himself go in a frenzy of pumping that rasped the tender insides of her thighs with the fine wool of his suit. Liza held on, angling her hips to take him deeper…deeper. Dropping his head into the hollow between her neck and shoulder, he came in one convulsive shudder that stiffened his body to stone.

Liza held him, absorbing his body and his love and everything he gave her.

They quieted and remained like that for a long time, stroking each other and part of each other. The thrilling heavy weight of him encompassed and protected her, and she rejoiced in it.

Finally he lifted his head. "So…we're getting married, right?"

"Right."

Her easy agreement seemed to bewilder him. Quirking his brows, he stared down at her. "I hate to press my luck, but…am I going to be a presidential candidate or a plain-old-vanilla senator? There are a few people I should tell one way or the other."

"Yeah," Liza said. "I've been thinking about that."

He waited.

"Have I ever told you that *Rocky II* is one of my favorite movies?"

His eyes lit with interest. "Is that right?"

"Have you seen it?"

"Once or twice," he said dryly. "What's this got to do with us?"

"Remember that part where they're in the hospital after Rocky Jr. is born and Rocky volunteers to withdraw from the rematch with Apollo Creed if Adrian wants him to?"

He went very still as he studied her face, hardly seemed to breathe. "Yes."

"And Adrian says there's one thing she wants Rocky to do for her?"

He didn't move, was incapable of answering as far as she could tell, but it didn't matter. Pulling his head lower, she brushed his mouth with hers and loved him just a little bit more.

"Well, Senator," she said, "There's one thing I want you to do for me."

It took a very long time for him to speak. "What's that?"

"Win," she told him. *"Win."*

Epilogue

The walk down Pennsylvania Avenue was longer than John had
expected, but he floated most of the way anyway. The bright blue
sky was icy, but once he registered that it was cold and catalogued
the weather for his memory, he didn't care at all. He had Liza to
keep him warm.

Two things—and only two things—held his attention: his
wife's hand in his and the cheering crowds of people. They lined
the streets, waving and cheering for them, at least a hundred deep.
He and Liza had ridden part of the way in the limousine, of
course, and they'd get back in it in a minute so they'd get to the
Capitol in time. The secret service had grumbled about the
security issues, of course. Plus, several of his advisers had mentioned that the president normally walked *after* the swearing in,
not *before*.

To which John said: who cared?

So he'd prevailed and he wouldn't have missed a moment of this walk for anything. What was a little cold compared with the chance to meet some of their well-wishers and receive their blessings for their new marriage and the presidency?

Every now and then, when they'd stop to shake a few hands—the secret service really *loved* that—the people seemed more interested in Liza. *What was she wearing? What would she say next? Was she really as beautiful in person?*

"*Liza, Liza, Liza,*" the people chanted.

He couldn't blame them.

What had President Kennedy said? Presidential history was very much on John's mind this morning, but he didn't think anyone would blame him for that. JFK had said something about being the man that accompanied Jackie Kennedy to Paris. John felt exactly like that—proud and fortunate. Other men might not like being overshadowed by their wives, but not him. He wouldn't be here now without her support and faith, her relentless campaigning for him despite what she'd said about not wanting to. God had truly favored him with the presidency, yes, but the greater blessing was Liza, and he wanted the world to know it.

"You're beautiful." He leaned in to brush her face with his lips as he spoke, to make sure she was really there, really his, to smell the flowers on her skin.

She'd been waving to the crowds on her side of the road, her hand high overhead, but now she turned to face him, a pretty flush staining her cheeks that had nothing to do with the cold.

"The purple's okay, then?"

She was referring to her long wool coat and sexy-as-hell black high-heeled boots. The selections had been the subject of intense press interest for the last few weeks. Before that, the press had been obsessed about the gown for their simple Christmas Eve wedding, an ivory satin number that had almost made him drool onto his suit and tie.

Anyway, he hoped Liza never had the heart to tell anyone that she'd chosen the purple for today because it had the deepest pockets for carrying tissues and lipstick.

"The purple's pretty, Mrs. Warner," he told her. "*You're beautiful.*"

And Liza, who'd been doing less and less scowling lately, grinned like a thirteen-year-old with her first boyfriend. "Are you flirting with me, Senator?" she asked, raising her voice above a gaggle of particularly loud teens waving Warner banners.

Squeezing her fingers in his gloved hand, he pulled her a little closer to his side. "You're not going to be able to call me *Senator* anymore in a few minutes. You know that, right? Although…I did love hearing you say it over and over again last night, I must admit."

Now she was simpering, her face nearly as bright as her dress, and she squeezed his hand back in warning. "Stop it, John. You know they've probably got analysts trying to read our lips right now and tell people at home what we're saying to each other."

"Hmm." At the edge of the crowd he saw a father with his young daughter—she looked about threeish—riding on his shoulders. John waved and smiled. "Maybe I should enunciate more clearly so everyone will know that tonight, after all the balls, I'm going to strip you out of your slinky back panties and kiss your—"

"John!"

Laughing and delighted, he decided that was enough teasing for now. He tried to remember the topic at hand as they neared the Capitol.

"So your days of calling me *Senator* are about over, Mrs. Warner."

"That's fine," she said sweetly. "Mr. President."

Decorum was one thing, but they were honeymooners and he was in love with his wife. Startling her, he pulled her in for a quick brush of his lips across hers—a reminder of last night and a promise for tonight—and enjoyed her peep of surprise.

Then they got back into the warm limo and rode the rest of the way.

"See you soon."

Inside the rotunda, Liza kissed him as she left to take her seat and he mingled with the former presidents, waiting for their formal introductions to the crowd outside.

It all happened so fast.

All the other officials were introduced, while he, the guest o honor, was saved for last. And then he was walking through the dark waiting area and out into the blinding sunlight on the balcony, where the ceremonies were held.

A deafening cheer rose up the moment he came into view, and it humbled him as nothing in his life ever had before.

Waving, he made his way through the members of Congress, to the seats up front, where his family and Liza's dad were standing and applauding with everyone else.

There was the Colonel with his attendant. He thankfully seemed to be having a good day and was beaming at everyone he saw. Aunt Arnetta was pretty in pink, with Bishop looking sharp in a fedora tilted low over one eye. Andrew and Viveca were there, and so were Eric and Isabella, all smiling at him, all clapping, and...

There was Jillian.

She was divorced now, thank God. And a mother. A child was always a blessing, especially to Jillian, and especially after all she'd been through, and baby Allegra had saved her from complete despair these past few months.

Jillian's ecstatic grin couldn't've been wider. John hoped some of her excitement was due to the bed-and-breakfast she would soon own outside Atlanta. That would keep her challenged and busy.

One of his biggest wishes, now that he had Liza and the presidency, was that Jillian could find happiness with a man who appreciated her for the jewel she was. God knew she deserved it.

Catching John's eye, Jillian winked at him, and he winked back.

Then it was time for songs, poems and the vice-president's swearing-in. John enjoyed the songs the most. He'd chosen "America the Beautiful," among others—Liza had expressly forbidden the theme song from *Rocky*—and he listened to them with tears in his eyes and his heart in his throat.

He just wanted to be worthy of all *this*.

There was nothing more sobering than knowing so many people had put their faith in him. Trusted him.

He would give this country his very best effort or die trying. With Liza by his side, he could be a great president.

And then it was time.

Was it time—already?

The chief justice of the Supreme Court, Marva Jones, signaled to him, and Liza held the massive Warner family Bible that had been in Aunt Arnetta's library for the last thousand years or so.

John's heart thundered with sudden nerves—*Jesus, Lord, what had he gotten himself into?*—and he faltered for a millisecond.

But then Liza squeezed his hand, winked and mouthed all the encouragement he needed: *You can do it.*

Yeah.

With Liza's love and faith shining so brightly in her eyes, he could do it.

Turning to the chief justice, he smiled. "I'm ready, ma'am."

The chief justice supervised while he put his left hand on the Bible and raised his right, and then she gave him a crisp nod.

"I, Jonathan Matheson Warner," she began.

"I, Jonathan Matheson Warner," he echoed and then, because he knew the oath by heart, continued without prompting. "Do solemnly swear that I will faithfully execute the office of President of the United States, and will, to the best of my ability, protect and defend the Constitution of the United States."

Chief Justice Jones, looking startled, added the end—"So help me, God."

"So help me, God."

That was it. It was done.

He was president. Of the United States. The greatest country in the world.

A deafening roar erupted around him on all sides while the band played "Hail to the Chief" and happy chaos reigned for a minute.

He had eyes only for his wife.

For that one joyous second, he even forgot about the speech he was about to give, the one he'd written and reworked and prayed would inspire Americans for years to come.

Turning to Liza, he leaned in to kiss her over the huge Bible.

"I love you, Mrs. Warner."

"I love you, Mr. President."

REQUEST YOUR FREE BOOKS!

2 FREE NOVELS
PLUS 2 **FREE GIFTS!**

KIMANI™
ROMANCE

Love's ultimate destination!

KROM09

HELP CELEBRATE
ARABESQUE'S
15TH ANNIVERSARY!

ARABESQUE®

2009 marks Arabesque's
15th anniversary!

Help us celebrate by telling us about your
most special memories and moments with
Arabesque books. Entries will be judged by
the Arabesque Anniversary Committee
based on which are the most touching and
well written. Fifteen lucky winners will
receive as a prize a full-grain leather duffel
bag with the Arabesque anniversary logo.